# THE KING AND VI

### Misfortune's Favorites
### Book One

## Shana Galen

## ARE YOU SIGNED UP FOR DRAGONBLADE'S BLOG?

You'll get the latest news and information on exclusive giveaways, exclusive excerpts, coming releases, sales, free books, cover reveals and more.

Check out our complete list of authors, too!

No spam, no junk. That's a promise!

### Sign Up Here

www.dragonbladepublishing.com

*Dearest Reader;*

*Thank you for your support of a small press. At Dragonblade Publishing, we strive to bring you the highest quality Historical Romance from some of the best authors in the business. Without your support, there is no 'us', so we sincerely hope you adore these stories and find some new favorite authors along the way.*

*Happy Reading!*

CEO, Dragonblade Publishing

# CHAPTER ONE

*Scotland, 1797*

W ITCHES SCARED HIM.
Even at thirteen, King wasn't afraid of much. Not the dark, not rats or spiders, not even dead bodies. He couldn't think of anything he feared save poverty and the aforementioned witches. He could think of many things he disliked—the cold, the rain, the food at school, and Scotland in general. That entire list figured into the reason that he, George Oxley, the Marquess of Kingston, the eldest son and heir to the sixth Duke of Avebury, and one of the wealthiest persons in England, if not the world, was spending his night lying in the mud, rain sluicing over his damp and dirty cloak, and staring at the hovel just down the hill. The hovel was dark at this hour.

But that didn't mean the witch slept. Oh, no. King wasn't about to let his guard down.

Henry elbowed him in the side, causing King to let out a small *oof*. "This will be easier than we thought, King."

King (everyone called him King because of his title) grunted and blew out a breath, watching the puff of heat flow from his mouth out on the night air. On his left, Rory, a younger son of the Duke of Tralee, practically vibrated with energy. He was always tense as a violin string, but at a time like this, he all but hummed with anticipation. "Let's go," he said, his tone barely concealing his eagerness.

King didn't move. He was the unofficial strategist tonight. Usually their pranks had no strategy, but if they had to cross a witch, King wanted to make sure he was in charge. So it was he who'd suggested they circle around to the back of the witch's hovel, rather than come up the main road. He was the one who had pointed out that the cask of whiskey, half hidden under a burlap tarp, was located under the rear eaves of the abode. A rear attack made the most sense...and would hopefully keep them from being spotted by the old crone.

In the yard, two clotheslines, bare of garments, whipped in the wind and rain, and leaves tumbled down from the limbs of skeletal trees. Behind him, he heard several of the underlings who had accompanied them snigger. Their schoolmates wanted to watch the prank from far enough away to run if anything went wrong. Cowards, King thought, and lifted into a crouch. He gave a nod, and the three of them—King, Henry, and Rory—started down the slope toward the witch's yard.

Henry and Rory elbowed each other and snickered. King glanced over his shoulder and threw them a cocky grin. It wouldn't do to show any fear. He was King. He pummeled boys who showed fear, looking down his long, aristocratic nose at the sniveling cowards as they groveled for mercy. There was a hierarchy in school as in life, and King, Rory, and Henry were at the top. The problem, King thought now, as his boot sank into a mud puddle and cold, slimy water seeped inside, was that it took a lot of effort to stay at the top. He didn't want to be out in the rain, darting into shadows, watching those clotheslines swing like ghostly jump ropes. He would have liked to be back in the dormitory, asleep under his thin covers. Who the holy hell had even thought up the idea to steal the witch's whiskey?

It hadn't been him. Had it?

He thought back to the whispered conversation at dinner.

Someone had complained about the food. The food at St. Andrew's Preparatory for Boys was abhorrent. Someone was always complaining about it. They'd had better food at Eton, and decent food at Harrow. King hadn't even minded the food at Tonbridge. But he'd been expelled from Eton, Harrow, and Tonbridge, as well as half a dozen more boys' preparatory schools. He'd met Henry at Harrow and Rory at Tonbridge. Together, the three of them had been tossed out of every respectable school in England.

Which was why they had been sent to the wilds of Scotland and a school whose headmaster had promised to keep them in line if only he was given free rein. King still bore the bruises on his arse from the headmaster's last beating.

But the headmaster hadn't been in the dining room that evening. That was unusual. He had given the boys the sobriquet of Misfortune's Favorites. He said it was because anyone who met the boys suffered misfortune. Perhaps the man had some personal misfortune, because he'd been absent all through dinner. If the headmaster had been present, he might have sniffed out the plan before it had taken shape and snuffed it out. Then King could have done something like put a dead mouse in one of the teacher's beds rather than go out in a rainstorm.

Now, he slipped under one of the trees whose scrawny limbs, all but bare of foliage this late in the fall, offered no protection from the rain. Was it his imagination, or had it started raining even harder? He wiped the water from his eyes and thought back to dinner.

"This is worse than pig swill," one of the other boys had said. King didn't know their names. He didn't need to. The only boys who mattered were himself, Rory, and Henry. They were the sons of dukes and the highest-ranking lads at the school. And they didn't let the underlings forget it.

"It's worse than piss," one of the underlings had said, shooting a look at Rory to see if he approved.

Rory hadn't even noticed. He'd looked up from his bowl and

narrowed his eyes. "Might be better if we had something to wash it down with."

"Maybe some wine," one of the underlings said.

"Not wine," Henry said. "Whiskey."

"I know where we can get whiskey," King had said. "The witch up the road makes her own and sells it for a pretty profit."

"She needs the coin to buy her potions and broomsticks."

The rest of the underlings spoke up, each with a suggestion more ridiculous than the last. The witch and her sister were popular topics of conversation. Rory said they weren't witches, just two old hags who lived near the school. Publicly, King agreed. Privately, he had his fears. And he should have kept his knowledge of the cask of whiskey to himself as well. As soon as he'd mentioned it, all the boys had made elaborate plans for how to steal it, and then King had dared one of the underlings to do it, and that boy had said no one was brave enough to steal from a witch, and King had said, "I am."

"No, you're not." This from one of the underlings.

King had crossed his arms and narrowed his eyes. "Is that a dare?"

The underlings had all oohed in unison and started banging on the table. "Dare! Dare! Dare!" they'd chanted. After one of the teachers had admonished them and slapped a few hands with rulers, King had said, voice low, "I'll steal the witch's whiskey tonight. Who's with me?"

Of course, Henry and Rory had volunteered immediately.

Under the tree, King swore. This *had* been his idea. He looked at Rory and Henry then back at the half-dozen heads peering down from the slight rise in the road. Well, they couldn't turn back now. King would rather be cursed by a witch than lose face in front of the others. Once you showed weakness, you were done for.

"That cask will be heavy," Henry said.

"We'll take turns," Rory said. "Two at a time. The other watches our backs."

"Let's go," King said, wanting to get it over with.

The three moved out from under the tree. King had barely stepped into the open when a crash of thunder rent the relative quiet of the night. He jumped involuntarily, catching the looks of surprise on the other boys' faces in the flash of lightning that followed. It had been quietly raining all day. It seemed like it was always raining in Scotland, but he didn't remember any thunder and lightning earlier in the evening.

Rory gestured for King to move forward, and King dragged his feet out of the sucking mud and forced his legs to carry him closer to the hovel. Now that he was close enough, he saw the hovel was a little more than a rickety collection of boards amassed into a wobbly structure. He could practically see the low light from the hearth through the cracks in the wooden beams. He moved closer, keeping an eye out for movement. This time when the thunder rumbled, he ignored it. He ignored the crackle of lightning too, though it was so close he could smell it and all but taste the acrid smoke of it.

Suddenly, something smacked him hard across the face. He raised a hand to ward off the blow and caught the clothesline. It had come lose from its mooring and whipped about in the wind. King's cheek stung from the slap, and he thought he could feel the heat of blood running down his cheek. If he'd been alone, he would have turned back now. But he'd never backed down on a dare before, and he wouldn't do it now. Instead, he kicked out at the nearest pole anchoring the line and kicked it over. The ropes went down, landing in the mud.

Thunder boomed again, startling King, but also urging him into action. He and the other two reached the eaves and leaned against the boards of the hovel. In the next burst of lightning, they had a clear picture of the whiskey cask. Rory moved to the other side and gestured to Henry. The two of them hoisted the cask, and King moved forward to help steady it on their shoulders. A grown man might have been able to carry the cask on his own, but at only thirteen, none of the boys could manage it alone.

King led the escape, picking his route to avoid puddles and fallen tree limbs. Rory followed, grunting with the effort of it. Thunder boomed, and King turned to make certain his friends hadn't jumped at the sound, but they were trudging along. Lightning flashed, and King turned back to the yard before him then yelped as he saw the figure illuminated by the flash of light.

It was the witch.

"Holy hell," he said as he took her in. She was dressed in rags, her tattered dress reaching only to her calves. The ends of it were lifted by the wind, showing pale legs and bare feet. She had one bony arm outstretched, her thin finger pointed at him. Around her head, white hair flew about, seemingly dry and impervious to the driving rain. King's gaze met hers. Her face was thin and her cheekbones prominent. Her nose was long and crooked, and her eyes—her eyes were as black as a moonless night.

The lightning receded, and she was cast into darkness. King took a step back, colliding with Rory, who swore. Then he looked up, saw the witch, and dropped his end of the cask. Henry called out, "Hey!" but it was cut off by the sound of the wood splintering as it hit the ground. Dimly, King was aware that whiskey splashed over his legs.

Thunder boomed again. How the devil could it thunder so often? Lightning lit the sky again, and now Rory and Henry swore at the sight of the witch. Her face was twisted in what King could only describe as rage. He knew why. The whiskey flowed like a small stream over the dirt yard. He could smell the sweet tang of it. A cask that size was worth a great deal, and since whiskey had to age for months, if not years, it would not be easy to replace. Belatedly, he realized that the loss of the whiskey would probably mean the loss of many pounds, dooming the witch to worse poverty.

Not that he cared if she starved to death. But he could see the anger on her face and hear it in her voice as she screamed, *"You!"*

Her voice seemed to open the heavens. Rain poured harder,

the drops painful as they hammered at his head and shoulders. Thunder boomed and rumbled incessantly. Lightning lit up the sky in jagged zigzags, and King swallowed hard when he saw the sky had turned a sickly greenish color. His gaze flicked to where the underlings were hidden, but he didn't see them any longer.

They'd fled, leaving Rory, Henry, and himself to the witch's mercy. "Ye will pay for this!" the witch screeched.

Rory, the bravest—or perhaps the stupidest—of the three of them, stepped forward. "Send the bill to my father." And then he pushed past the old hag. King and Henry did the same. King tried to hold his head up and show no fear, but his skin crawled as he passed the old crone. In front of them, lightning crashed down from above, striking the upthrust branches of one of the bare trees. The sound was so loud, and the burst of flame so hot, the three boys jumped back. King threw his arm up as the branch hit the ground, spraying tree bark and charred wood over him in a wave. The dead limb blocked their path, slowing them.

Dread filling him, King looked over his shoulder. The witch was right behind him. How had she moved so quickly? She reached out and swiped at him with a long, bony finger. He jerked back, but it was too late. The crimson splash of his own blood marred the paleness of her skin. King trembled, and it was no good to lie to himself that his shaking was only from the cold and wet.

He was scared witless.

The old crone raised her hands, the trickle of his blood running down her arm in a sickly pink ribbon. Above her arms, the green sky was lit with blinding bolts of lightning.

King felt Rory's hands on his elbow, pulling him away, and he stumbled back. The three boys stood in a line, retreating. King didn't know about the other two, but he wasn't about to turn his back on the crazy woman flinging her arms to the sky. Just as she opened her mouth to speak, another figure burst from the hovel.

"No!" the other figure screamed.

"The witch's sister," Henry said, his voice filled with awe.

The sister might have been older or younger. Who could tell? They both looked ancient to King. But the sister had long black hair streaked with white, and she wasn't quite so bony, though she was still thin as a stray cat. She took in the broken cask of whiskey and let out a small cry. Lifting her gaze, she looked at the boys, accusation in her eyes.

A strange sensation tugged at King's chest. Was this guilt? He could barely remember ever feeling remorse for any of his actions. In the beginning, they had the benefit of catching his father's attention. And now his misdeeds kept him at the top of the school hierarchy.

"Oh, boys," the sister said, sounding sad and disappointed. "How could you?" This seemed a rhetorical question, because she turned to the witch, whose hands were still raised, even though the thunder and lightning had ceased momentarily. "Sister, nae. They are but weans."

"Evil weans," the witch answered, her black eyes meeting King's. He felt cold pierce him under her gaze and was relieved when she slid it to Henry and then Rory.

Thunder crackled and hissed. The sister attempted to pull the witch away, but she was wiry and strong. She shook her sister off. Then she lowered her arms and began to move her hands as though turning a large, invisible ball between them. There was nothing between her hands, save air, but King might have sworn he saw smoke and the glow of...something else emanating from that dead air. The smoke seemed to form into the shape of a cup with a thin neck, almost like a wide bottle.

Then the witch opened her mouth, and the sound that came out was otherworldly. It wasn't a voice, and yet he could understand the words.

> *"Take tooth of giant; seize nail of dragon.*
> *Unite with holy water in this flagon.*
> *Hear me now, oh great lords of night.*
> *Give me my revenge; ease my plight.*

> *These three lads have taken what's mine.*
> *At the age of thirty, repay them in kind.*
> *Pilfer, purloin, and pinch what it is they love best.*
> *And then and only then will I find my eternal rest."*

King didn't know what happened next. Later he would chalk it up to a particularly close strike of lightning, but when he dreamed of the experience—and he would have nightmares for years to come—he experienced it as a push of air so strong that it sent the three boys reeling. He landed hard on his bottom, his head hitting the hard ground and rendering him momentarily stunned.

He lay in the mud, staring up at that strange greenish sky. From far away, he thought he heard the sister speaking and the witch arguing. Thunder boomed again, and he closed his eyes. The sound hurt his head. When he opened his eyes again, the rain had ceased and the night was quiet. He rose on his elbows and peered about the yard. The remains of the broken cask were there, as well as the fallen clothesline. The tree limb still lay smoking a few feet away. Near him, Rory and Henry were stirring, pushing up from the ground.

"What happened?" Rory asked.

"Lightning strike," Henry said matter-of-factly.

"Where did they go?" King asked, staring at the empty yard and the dark witch's hovel just beyond.

"Who cares?" Rory said, climbing to his knees. "Crazy old bat."

"Did you see her?" Henry said with a smirk on his face. "She was waving her hands in the air and muttering curses. She really does think she's a witch." He laughed. Then Rory laughed too.

King didn't think it was such a good idea to laugh. He glanced at the dark building in front of him and just wanted to get away. Rory offered him a hand, and King took it, allowing the other boy to pull him to his feet. "We'd better get back," he said.

"Too bad you dropped the whiskey." Henry gave Rory a

pointed look.

"*I* dropped the whiskey? *You* dropped it!"

"No, I didn't."

"You both dropped it," King said. "Too scared of the witch to hold on."

"I wasn't scared," Henry said. "I slipped in the mud."

"I'm not scared of that mad old crone," Rory said. He struck a pose, arms lifted in the air, face screwed up in rage. It was a poor imitation of the witch, but it was still funny. King laughed, and so did Henry. And then Rory doubled over laughing too. The three of them clapped each other on the shoulders and pushed and shoved all the way back to the school, one of them pausing every few feet to imitate the witch with her hands in the sky or muttering curses.

King laughed until his sides hurt, and he only looked back over his shoulder once. What he saw made him catch his breath. The witch stood in the middle of the road, watching them.

He stumbled then ran to catch up with his friends. Henry elbowed him, and King joined their laughter.

King and the others crept into the dormitory without being detected, and he was relieved when he finally lay under his bedclothes, dry and safe. And yet he couldn't seem to fall asleep, couldn't shake the idea that his actions tonight would have dire consequences. King wasn't afraid of a thrashing or even expulsion. So what was keeping him awake? Why was he trembling with fear like some sort of stupid baby?

*Witches aren't real,* he told himself, pinching his arm to drive the point home. *Curses aren't real.* Another pinch. He looked over at Henry and Rory, both still and obviously sleeping. They were unharmed. The three of them hadn't managed to bring the whiskey back, but they'd had one hell of an adventure.

And now he was safe. They'd gotten away with the prank.

And for many years, he actually believed that.

# CHAPTER TWO

*London, 1814*

K ING WAS DRUNK. This was nothing new. He was often drunk and stumbling up the walk to the Town house he'd leased for the Season. He was alone, having lost his compatriots somewhere between Covent Garden and Mayfair. He vaguely remembered someone throwing a jug at them as they stood in the middle of the road singing at the top of their lungs. So what if it was four in the morning? A man could sing if he had a notion to.

He made it to his stoop and sat down for a moment, willing the world to stop spinning so quickly. His ears rang. Had he been hit with the jug? Perhaps not, but he had been hit in the jaw. He touched the sore spot gingerly.

Behind him the door opened, and his valet stepped out. "My lord, will you come inside?"

"I will, Danby," King said. "I most certainly will. Just waiting for this ringing in my ears to cease." A moment later, he was vaguely aware of Danby bending over him.

"You seem to have a lump on your head, my lord."

"The jug," King muttered, allowing Danby to help him to his feet. Then it came to him, and he snapped his fingers. "No, not the jug. The brawl."

"My lord?" Danby said, guiding King toward the steps to the second floor, where his bedchamber was located.

"There was a brawl, Danby. A very big, very loud, very violent brawl."

"There always is, my lord," Danby said.

That was true. It did seem like everywhere King went, chaos followed. Tonight two of Misfortune's Favorites had been together. No wonder there had been a brawl. "Blame it on Henry," he said.

"Henry, my lord?" Danby asked as he led King into the bedchamber.

"Oh, right. He's Carlisle now. The Duke of Carlisle was slumming it with us in Seven Dials." King sat obediently while Danby yanked off his boots.

"I do worry about you, my lord. Some parts of the city are not safe."

"That's what makes them entertaining, Danby," King said. He stood so the valet could peel off his coat. "And don't go reporting this to my father. I know he pays you to spy."

Danby looked shocked. "My lord, I would never!" He was quite good at feigning shock, and it didn't fool King in the least.

"The hell you wouldn't."

"About your father, my lord."

"Don't want to talk about him."

Danby looked like he might proceed anyway, but then closed his mouth and seemed to reconsider. Instead of speaking, Danby reached for King's neckcloth, but King batted his hands away. "You know what, Danby? Go to bed. I can undress myself. After all, I'm a man of thirty now. I don't need a nursemaid."

"Yes, my lord." Danby retreated, closing the door behind him and leaving King in the large chamber with only the sound of the fire crackling.

He loosened his cravat and undid the buttons at his throat, leaving the neckcloth to spill across the open V of his shirt.

"Happy birthday to me," King said as he crossed to a decanter of wine near the fire. He poured a quantity on the carpet before managing to slosh some in his glass. Then he raised a toast. "To thirty triumphant years." He drank. "And thirty more," he said, voice hoarse as the wine tickled his throat.

He thought about lying down in bed, but the room would spin too much if he lay flat. Instead, he slumped in a chair and stared at the fire. Sparks flew up the chimney and the flames danced, seeming to coalesce into the shape of...a barrel? No, a cask, like one might store wine or spirits.

King blinked and shook his head, and the fire was just a fire again. He closed his eyes and began to drift off into sleep. Then, quite suddenly, his chair was pulled from under him. At the same time, a blast of cold air whipped through the room, slammed the dressing room door closed, and extinguished the fire and all the candles. King blinked, looking up from the floor and about the dark room.

"Danby!" he called.

"He cannae hear ye," said a low voice.

King started at the sound. It was a sound he could only describe as evil, not male or female, but filled with menace. As he stared, a shape began to materialize in the hearth. The figure of an old woman.

King scrambled back. He recognized that woman. She ducked her head and stepped out of the hearth and into the chamber.

"What the holy hell?" he muttered. He hadn't thought of the witch from Scotland in years. A decade. What was she doing in his chamber?

"Hell isnae holy," the witch said. "Nae, not at all. I ken that from experience."

King shook his head. He must be drunker than he thought if he was imagining a witch in his chamber. Or perhaps he was dreaming. He shook his head, trying to rouse himself.

"I see ye remember me, George Oxley, Marquess of Kingston," the witch said, looking down at him.

"Get out."

"Gladly. I wanted a wee look at ye now that it's begun." She peered down at him, her black eyes boring into his face. King closed his eyes tightly. When he opened his eyes, she wouldn't be there. This would be nothing more than a dream stoked by bad rum, his penance for drinking too much in Seven Dials. He wouldn't be surprised if that blue-eyed taverness from the pub had poisoned him.

"Wake up," he muttered to himself. "You're only dreaming."

But when he opened one eye, the witch was still there. And she was smiling, showing gaps in her mouth where yellowed teeth had rotted away. She leaned close, her fetid breath causing his belly to roil. He gritted his teeth together to keep the bile down and pinched his leg to attempt to wake himself. He felt the pinch, but the witch didn't disappear.

Instead, she extended a long hand and poked him in the chest. King looked down at her dirty finger, grime under her long nails, with distaste.

"Remember the curse," she whispered, her hot breath making his nose wrinkle. "I shall enjoy watching ye suffer." And then she threw back her head and laughed. She laughed and laughed and laughed. King closed his eyes again and covered his ears.

"Danby!" he yelled. "Danby, get in here!"

A moment later, he felt a hand on his shoulder. King shoved it off and jumped to his feet. But when he opened his eyes, it wasn't the witch who cowered before him, but his valet.

"Where is she?" King turned and surveyed the room. It was empty save himself and the valet.

"Who, my lord?" Danby asked.

King stared at the hearth then moved closer to peer inside it. He felt quite sober now, though he could still feel the rum sloshing about in his belly. The kindling in the hearth was undisturbed, the fire crackling as usual. There was no trace of soot-stained footprints on his carpet. The chair he had been sitting in was right where he'd placed it. "You didn't see her?" he asked, walking about the room and checking behind curtains and doors.

"No, my lord. You didn't—er—"

King returned to stand before his valet, noting the man's cheeks had gone quite pink.

"There was no companion with you tonight, my lord," Danby said, ducking his head.

"Not a woman," King said, exasperated. "Well, yes, a woman, but not..." Not a courtesan or a pretty widow. Those were the women he usually took to bed. "This was an old hag, a—" He almost said *witch* but stopped himself just in time. Danby might call the doctor if King started going on about witches. King half believed he *needed* a doctor, except the witch was gone. It had been a nightmare. That was all. A very real, very hellish nightmare, but a nightmare all the same.

He sat in the chair again. Tested it carefully and, finding it solid, looked up at Danby. "I'll need more wine, Danby."

"More, my lord?"

"Yes." If he was to sleep deeply and not dream—and God knew he didn't want to dream of that witch again—he would need a great deal more wine. "Pour it, Danby." Then he had another idea. "And pour one for yourself."

Danby started as though pinched. "A glass for me, my lord?"

"Drink with me," King said, indicating another chair with his toe. "Sit with me." That would show the witch—er, the nightmare. Danby would be here if he started having that dream again.

"Yes, my lord." Danby did as he was told and sat on the edge of the offered chair, back ramrod straight. He held his wine glass as though it would explode if jostled. King sipped his wine, slouched back in the chair, and settled in for a long night.

VIOLET BAKER STOOD with hands on her hips and surveyed the damage in the public house. Somehow it looked worse than it had last night, even though she'd spent two hours cleaning up after the brawl. Broken glass glittered in patches of sunlight, stacks of broken chairs took up one corner, and five of her eight tables listed to one side or another. One was broken clean in half. She remembered when that had happened. One of the young bucks had tossed a man on the table, and the weight of him had caved it in.

She wiped her hands on her apron and turned her attention to the bar itself. That was the bread and butter of a public house, but it too was in shambles. The mirror behind the bar had been shattered, and the sight of it caused her heart to clench. It had cost a pretty penny to purchase and have the mirror installed. She'd justified the cost because it made the pub look a bit larger and brighter. *How can we attract superior clientele if we don't have a superior environment?* That's what she'd said to Joshua and little Georgie. At thirteen, Joshua had been skeptical, but Georgie was only six, and he had thought the mirror a wonder. He'd loved to climb up on the bar and peer at it for hours, making silly faces at his own reflection.

But if it had just been the mirror, that would be bad enough. Below the mirror had been bottles of gin, rum, brandy, beer, and wine. Those were smashed all to pieces. The sickly scent of the various types of spirits mixed together in the air, making her head ache. She'd tried to mop some of it up last night, but there was so much broken glass and other debris, she hadn't had much success. The floor behind the bar would be sticky and slick.

At least the casks of wine and spirits had been untouched. All but two were in the back, and those in the front of the pub had been underneath the bar and thus safe from flying objects and persons.

"Vi?"

She turned to see Georgie step inside the tavern, his brown eyes wide and his blond hair tousled from sleep. He'd been roused from bed the night before when the fighting had begun, but he knew better than to come downstairs. When she'd finally gone up, he had fallen asleep in her bed, where he had obviously been waiting for her. Now he was seeing the damage for the first time.

"What happened?" he asked.

Violet reached up and smoothed her dark hair, squaring her shoulders as she did so. She forced a smile on her lips. "Oh, just a small disagreement between some of the men last night. Nothing for you to worry about, love."

"But-but—" Georgie gestured to the mirror, tears glittering in his eyes. "Our beautiful mirror, Vi."

Violet could have cheerfully murdered the men from last night. She didn't care what they did to the public house or even to her, but how dare they cause her little brother to cry? She'd known as soon as the party of well-dressed men had sauntered through her door that there would be trouble. There had been four of them, and that was not so many, but they did not belong. It wasn't that her regular patrons were unfriendly. Men, and the occasional woman, came in all the time, and many of them did not belong in Seven Dials. Some were obviously from the countryside, their accents and clothes rustic. Some were from other places, like Scotland or Ireland or even France. Once a man from China had come in. His English had been perfect, and he'd ordered tea.

But all of those outsiders had kept to themselves. They'd sat in a corner or at a table to one side and kept their heads down and their mouths closed. The nobs who had come in last night had taken the middle table and behaved as though they owned the place. Violet had been wiping glasses dry in the back when they'd come in, but she had heard the hush settle over the place and stepped out to see what the matter was. Archibald, her publican, had given her a look and slid the crowbar he kept behind the bar in case of trouble closer to hand.

A feeling of helplessness had swept over Violet, making her fist her hands in her apron. She hated feeling helpless. But what to do? She knew men from the upper classes liked to frequent

SHANA GALEN

establishments in the rookeries. They even had a name for it—
*slumming it.* But the Silver Unicorn was not a slum to her. It was
her family's home, and their only means of support. She could tell
there would be trouble by the way the other men, many of
whom she knew as regulars, eyed the newcomers. The nobs were
preening and talking loudly, laughing uproariously, and making
themselves hard to ignore. They'd already been drinking. That
much was clear. Their faces were pink from over-imbibing, their
eyes bright and slightly glossy from intoxication.

They were just drunk enough to be dangerous.

But what was she supposed to do? Ask them to leave? Refuse
to serve them? That would only invite trouble. Men like that
expected service, and if they didn't receive it, there were
consequences. They'd call the magistrate or some lord secretary
or other, and soon she and Georgie and Joshua would be out on
the street, to say nothing of Archie or Peggy, the girl who helped
with the cleaning and cooking.

One of the men had stood and looked about. He had green
eyes and brown hair that was a bit long and swept back off his
forehead. His cheekbones were high and his nose straight, and he
would have been very attractive if his mouth wasn't twisted in a
sneer. "A bottle of your best champagne!" he'd shouted to Archie,
who had rolled his eyes.

"Don't have any champagne," Archie had answered.

The men seemed to think this was the funniest thing they'd
ever heard. They laughed and laughed until one of them finally
ordered rum. Violet had brought the mugs herself, and after a few
minutes of hovering anxiously near the bar, her hands tightly
fisted in her apron, the men seemed to settle down to drinking.
She slipped behind the bar, and Archie leaned an ear toward her.
"Keep serving them," she murmured. "If we're lucky, they'll
drink themselves into oblivion."

Archie grunted. "If we're lucky, they'll go somewhere else."

Violet had hoped luck was with them tonight, and returned
to the back to finish drying glasses and mugs. When that was

18

done, she took a new tray of glasses and placed them in the soapy water to start a new batch of washing. But she hadn't even finished with those dishes when she heard the thump and crash. A moment later, the sound of raised voices. By the time she had run for the door to the front, the fight was in full bloom. She considered trying to quell it for a half-second, but then a bottle had crashed against the wall beside her face, and she slammed the door and barred it. If Archie couldn't stop the brawl, then what hope did she have?

That helpless feeling she so hated stole over her again, and she pressed her hand against her lungs, which felt tight and pained. She blinked back the sting of tears. She had to do something.

She could run for the Watch or the constables, but by the time she reached them, the fight would be over. No guarantee they would come, either. The Watch didn't like to be caught in Seven Dials at night. She could step into the fray, but she would more than likely be injured. She couldn't be hurt. Joshua and Georgie needed her. She was all they had.

And so she'd stood on the other side of the door, listening to the destruction until finally Archie's voice rose above the din. Then there was more crashing, most likely Archie bringing his crowbar down on something solid, and then she'd heard the sounds of the melee moving away. She waited a moment longer, thinking Archie might knock and tell her to come out, but when no knock came, she straightened and unbarred the door. She'd stepped out into the wreck that she surveyed now.

The fight had moved into the streets, and her tavern was almost completely empty. Except for Archie, who leaned heavily against the bar, his crowbar dangling from one hand. He turned to look at her, and Violet gasped at the stream of blood running down his cheek. "Archie!"

"I'm fine," he'd all but croaked. "Go bar the door so they can't come back in."

But Violet hadn't been able to move. There was so much

blood. Archie's shirt was splattered with it, and his hair was matted and soaked on one side with crimson.

"Vi?"

She'd whirled at Joshua's voice. He stood in the doorway to the back, his eyes wide as he surveyed the damage. Joshua might be thirteen, but he looked more like he was ten. His voice hadn't lowered, and he hadn't begun to grow into his adult size. Tonight that worked to her advantage, as he was small and fast enough to dart about the rookeries undetected.

"Bolt the door," Archie said again. Violet nodded, and Joshua raced to the door of the pub, closed the heavy wooden piece, and bolted it. He then went a step further, closing the wooden shutters and bolting those as well. With the windows closed, the sounds of the riot—for it had turned into a riot now—dimmed. The smell of alcohol and blood became more pungent, though.

Joshua turned, his eyes widened, and shouted, "Vi!"

She followed his outstretched hand and ducked under Archie just in time to keep him from falling over. He was a big man, and she was rather petite, so she was only able to see that he slid down to the floor slowly rather than crashing down. She tore off her apron and pressed the clean linen to his temple, which seemed to be the source of the injury. Joshua was beside her in a moment. "Should I fetch a doctor?"

"No doctor will come here and into that"—she lifted her head and inclined it toward the sounds of the riot—"tonight. Fetch me clean water from the back."

Joshua turned to do her bidding, but she grabbed his hand. "Is Georgie upstairs?"

"Yes. He's in bed. I told him to stay there."

"Are the doors and windows bolted?"

"Yes."

She nodded and released him. Violet turned her attention back to Archie, but her thoughts were still on Georgie, and she had one ear trained on the sounds of violence outside. They were safe for the moment. The building was made of stone and could withstand most types of assault. Her main fear was, as always, fire. Thankfully, it had rained this morning, and the fog tonight was damp and low. Everything would be wet, making it difficult to light a fire, much less allow it to spread.

In the daylight, with Georgie safe beside her, Violet glanced at the area beside the bar where she had knelt with Archie for hours. She'd been able to stanch the blood by pressing her apron hard against the wound, but he'd lost consciousness and not opened his eyes again. When the sounds of the commotion outside had subsided, she was able to have Joshua find two men to carry Archie home. He had a wife and two small children, and Violet could only imagine their terror when Archie had been carried inside, pale and unconscious. She would stop by later today and see if he had opened his eyes. She didn't have much money, but she would give what she could to Archie's young wife and children.

Of course, she had two children to support as well, and without Archie, she wasn't sure how that might be accomplished. She still had those casks of spirits in the back, but so much of her stock had been destroyed last night. The smashed bottles and the sticky liquid on the floor were lost profits. She had to pay for the wine and spirits in advance, and she counted on the money she made from selling cups of the stuff to pay for food, rent, and other expenses. Most weeks she barely had enough to pay Archie and Peggy and feed herself and the boys. She was already late on her rent and her taxes—the legal and illegal ones. She worried about the legal taxes, but the threat of debtor's prison or being hauled into court was nothing to what Ferryman and his gang would do to her if she did not pay him in time.

Still, she couldn't give up. If she gave up, she'd certainly be dead. Instead, she hugged Georgie in a hard embrace. "We'll get a new mirror," she said, wiping his tears away. "An even larger and better one."

"But we don't have enough coin for that," he said.

Violet hated that at the tender age of six, Georgie worried as much about blunt as she did. "We will," she said. "Everything will be all right. You'll see."

He gave her a hopeful look, but behind his big brown eyes she could see the doubts forming. Soon he wouldn't believe her pretty lies. He'd be as jaded and downtrodden as she and Joshua.

As though summoned by the thought, Joshua himself stepped through the doorway and into the Silver Unicorn. Before he shut the door, Violet saw what looked like patches of sunlight on the dirt street outside the tavern. The streets were too narrow and the buildings too crowded to ever allow much sunlight into Seven Dials, but on a sunny day, a few rays could be counted on to fight their way through the poverty and gloom.

"How is he?" Violet asked without preamble. When she'd wakened after a restless few hours of sleep, Joshua had been gone, and she'd known where he was.

"The same," he said. "Mrs. Archie said he hasn't opened his eyes."

Her name wasn't Mrs. Archie, of course, but she'd told the boys to call her that, since all of them except Violet called the publican Mr. Archie. "Did she send for the doctor?"

He shook his head. "Said she will if he becomes worse."

Violet nodded. Mrs. Archie was young but practical. Most of the time it was a waste of money to call for a doctor. Those who would come to this area of Town were incompetent at best and dangerous at worst. They'd take your coin and give you some miracle potion that would turn out to be water mixed with lamp oil. A doctor was as likely to kill a man as save him.

Violet did worry about the wound on Archie's head, though. It had seemed like it would need stitches, but then, that was the province of the surgeon. And it was even harder to get a surgeon to Seven Dials. If one would come, his instruments were usually crusted with blood, and the infection from the surgery killed the man quicker than the initial injury. Mrs. Archie would most likely sew up the wound better than any surgeon.

Joshua took a chair from the top of one of the remaining

tables and set it on the floor. "Come and sit, Vi. You were up for hours cleaning."

Violet took the chair while Joshua pulled down two more—one for Georgie and one for himself. Georgie climbed onto his chair and put his arms on the table, looking like a little statesman. "What will we do now?" His eyes traveled over the wreckage with concern. Violet was glad he hadn't seen the place before she cleaned some of it up. It looked bad enough now.

"Peggy will help me clean when she comes in," Violet said. "I'll need you two to help as well."

"I can sweep!" Georgie volunteered.

"And when we open again, I'll act as publican."

"Oh, no you won't." Violet pointed a finger at Joshua. "It's not safe. I'll do it."

He snorted. "As though it's safe for you."

Violet felt her head throb harder and pressed her fingers against her temples. Joshua was right. It wasn't safe for a young boy or a woman to work alone at a public house, but she had to do something. That panicky, powerless feeling rose in her, and she stubbornly pushed it down.

"Why did this have to happen?" Georgie asked forlornly. "Why do bad things always happen to us?"

It was the sort of question Violet asked herself, but one she couldn't afford to entertain now.

"Because life isn't fair," Joshua said. "If it were fair, them nobs who started the trouble last night would have to pay for all this." He waved toward the wreckage.

"Can't we *make* them pay?" Georgie asked.

"They're rich. They don't have to do anything they don't want to," Joshua said.

"I wish I were rich," Georgie said, plopping his small chin on his hands.

A quiet tapping sounded, and Joshua and Violet exchanged looks. Violet nodded, and Joshua went to open the door. "It's just Peggy," he said as he pulled it open.

"Just Peggy! I never." The girl stepped inside, and her mouth dropped open. She was eighteen, three years younger than Violet, but she looked closer to Joshua's age. Peggy was as thin as the soup the benevolent societies handed out. She kept her fine, wispy blonde hair pulled back in a cap, which meant her pale face looked stark and vulnerable. But she was strong and honest and hardworking.

Still, even the usually unflappable Peggy looked shocked by the pub's interior. "Well," she said, after taking it all in. "At least there's no damage to the outside."

"Are other buildings damaged?" Violet asked. She hadn't been out and hadn't thought about what other havoc the rioters in the street might have caused.

"Oh, yes. Broken doors, smashed lamps, cracked windows. Mrs. Littman said she will send a bill for the damages straight to the marquess himself."

Violet straightened. Mrs. Littman ran the boarding house across the street. It was little better than a flash house, considering it was filthy and frequented by thieves and whores, but Mrs. Littman was a large, fearsome woman whom no one ever dared cheat. But that wasn't what had caught Violet's attention. "What marquess?" she asked. She knew *marquess* was some sort of title—like prince or duke. It was entirely possible one of the nobs in the Silver Unicorn last night had been a marquess. And everyone knew a man with a title had piles of gold.

"Let me think." Peggy pressed a finger to the center of her forehead, pressing hard enough to make a red mark. She always did this when she was asked to remember something. It was as though she was pushing the information out of the depths of her brain box. "She said something about no one broke her windows without paying for them, and she would send the bill straight to the Marquess of Kingston."

"The Marquess of Kingston," Violet murmured.

"He'll never pay her a cent," Joshua said.

"Why not?" Violet asked. "If he was here last night, he should pay."

"And who will make him?"

*I'll make him,* Violet thought. She wasn't sure where the idea came from, but as soon as she thought it, the rock in her belly felt lighter.

"Can't Mrs. Littman make him pay?" Georgie asked.

"No." Joshua crossed his arms over his chest and sat back.

Georgie imitated his brother, down to the dejected look on his face. "God loves the markiss more," he said with authority.

"It's mar*quess*, and no, He doesn't love him more. God loves everyone the same," Violet said, only half believing it herself. But she couldn't have Georgie thinking God didn't love him. And she couldn't stand sitting here and doing nothing for the rest of her life. She was so tired of keeping her head down and working hard, just to have all her hopes and dreams smashed. It seemed to happen every few years, so often that she all but expected it now. But that didn't mean she had to accept it meekly. Why hadn't she put up a fight before? The answer was obvious—she'd been too young or too scared or too desperate.

She was still all of those things, but she was also something else—determined. And she would not sit here and do nothing. She was taking matters into her own hands today. Right now, in fact. She hadn't realized she'd stood until Joshua said, "Vi, where are you going?"

"I have an errand," she said absently, untying her apron and smoothing her hair.

"An errand?" Peggy gestured to the wreck of the Silver Unicorn. "Now?"

"Yes. I'll be back as quick as I can to help with the cleaning." First, she had to change into her best dress and coat and smooth her hair. She had better scrub her face and hands as well.

She started toward the back and the stairs to their flat above, but one look at the three forlorn faces she was leaving behind gave her pause. She couldn't simply leave them in the midst of this mess without any hope. She didn't know that she had any real hope to give, but then again, she didn't make promises she couldn't keep. And so she'd better keep this one.

"When I come back, I'll have good news," she said. Then she left them behind, hoping her words were true.

# CHAPTER THREE

T HE KNOCKING WOKE him. It started far enough away that King could ignore it. But then it grew closer and louder, and he tried to pull the pillow over his head to drown it out. But he had no pillow, he discovered when he opened one eye, because he was lying on the rug before the cold hearth.

"My lord?" came a voice he knew, followed by more knocking.

"Go away," King croaked, and put his throbbing head back on the rug.

"My lord! I must speak with you urgently." The voice was that of his butler, Churchwood.

King groaned and rolled over, immediately regretting the movement. The room spun and his brain seemed to lurch violently inside his skull. Churchwood was saying something else, but King had to take several enormous breaths to keep from tossing up his accounts. Finally, he called out, "Come in, then, Churchwood. And stop knocking."

Where the devil was Danby? Why hadn't Danby kept Churchwood from waking him?

Then King spied a stockinged foot and followed it to a pantalooned leg and up to the shirted torso of his valet, who was snoring softly on the rug not far away. King shoved the foot, but Danby grunted and kept snoring.

"I cannot come in, my lord. The door is locked, and I cannot find Mr. Danby."

King had a vague memory of making Danby lock the door last night. He didn't want to risk the witch finding a way in, though considering that she had stepped out of the fire in the hearth, he didn't know why he'd thought a locked door would stop her. But, of course, she hadn't really stepped out of the fire in the hearth. She'd been a hallucination brought on by bad rum. A nightmare formed out of his drunken delirium.

King made a valiant effort to sit, but the room spun so wildly that he knew he would never make it to the chamber door. Instead, he elbowed Danby's foot again. "Wake up, Danby."

Danby grunted.

"Door, Danby." King jabbed at the valet's foot harder, and this time Danby seemed to start awake and look about him in confusion. Churchwood's knocking began again, and King felt like growling. Instead, he put his head in his hands. "Make him stop, Danby, or I'll sack you both."

Danby scrambled to his feet, straightened his coat, and stumbled to the door. The knocking stopped, and King closed his eyes and lay back down again. The rug was a plush Aubusson, and he congratulated himself on the wise purchase. He had slept on it many a night when climbing into bed seemed too much effort. He was almost asleep again when something shook him. He swatted it away, but the shaking continued.

King opened his eyes and scowled at Danby. "Go away."

"My lord, you must rise immediately. There is a crisis."

"Deal with it." King tried to roll over, but Danby just scurried to his other side.

"I cannot, my lord. I tried to tell you last night. It's about the duke."

"The duke..." King muttered. He was vaguely aware that his father was in some sort of trouble. He and the duke were estranged, which was to say that they hadn't exchanged more than a handful of words in the last ten years. Still, he heard news of the Duke of Avebury from time to time. It was inevitable, no matter how hard he tried to avoid his sire's name. Someone had even mentioned His Grace last night. In fact, that might have been what started King's heavy drinking. And now Danby was mentioning the duke as well, and Danby knew he was strictly forbidden from ever bringing up Avebury's name.

Gradually, King became aware that though the knocking on his door had ceased, there was still a sound of not knocking, but banging and clanking and heavy thudding. What the holy hell was happening in his house at barely—he squinted at the clock on the mantel—half past nine in the morning? His staff knew he did not like to be disturbed until afternoon.

"Help me up, Danby." King began to feel he might need to rise from the floor for whatever was coming. Danby offered an arm. King tried to stand, found that too ambitious, and sank into a chair. Danby began to speak, but King lifted a hand. "I don't know what you are about to say." He heard more concerning noises coming from below. Men speaking as they seemed to be passing in and out of his house. "I think whatever it is, I shall need a drink first."

"Yes, my lord."

Danby fetched him a brandy, and King drank it down. Thus fortified, he nodded to the valet.

"I have concerning news, my lord. The duke has been found guilty."

"Guilty." King stared at the valet, whose face was white as the cravats he starched. "What do you mean?"

Danby folded his hands before him. "My lord, I know you do not wish to speak of your father—"

"He's the duke. Not my father."

"Yes, my lord. I know you do not wish to speak of the Duke of Avebury, but surely even you are aware of the accusations made against him."

When King didn't answer, Danby swallowed.

"The charges of treason, my lord?"

King had heard, of course. He even knew that the duke was on trial. It wasn't often the entire House of Lords was summoned by the lord high steward to act as triers. It was in all the papers. Everyone knew Kingston and Avebury were estranged, which was the only reason he had not been vilified by the press as well. A charge of treason was a serious matter, but then, Avebury had serious enemies. They would have to concoct quite the story to have any hope of ruining the duke.

"Is the trial concluded?" King asked, putting the snifter to his lips again, even though it was empty.

"It is, my lord."

"That's done, then." And yet the sounds coming from below concerned him.

"Unfortunately, my lord, as I said, the verdict did not go as we had hoped."

The room spun again, and this time it had nothing to do with the amount of alcohol he had imbibed. "Guilty," King said, the word making sense now.

"Yes, my lord, the duke was found guilty of aiding and abetting the enemy. He sold secrets to France and has been placed in prison, awaiting his sentencing."

King stared at Danby. His mind was slow to comprehend what he was being told, but as realization sank in, his body went cold. "It will be death. Execution, no doubt."

Danby pressed his hands together tightly. King watched the skin turn white where Danby's fingers met. "The duke has been stripped of his titles and privileges, my lord."

King found it difficult to draw in his next breath. His throat was tight, and his skin covered with chill bumps. He did not love his father—he did not even like the man—but the duke was his only close relative, and he would prefer the duke lived.

"That's not all, my lord."

King stared at the valet. Of course that wasn't all. When one's life was being smashed to rubble, best to smash it into oblivion. "There will be an attainder by verdict," King said, his lips saying what his mind would not allow him to contemplate.

"Yes, my lord. The matter will come before the lords and commons later this week."

"It will pass," King said.

"Most likely, my lord."

"And then I will be stripped of my title and properties."

"Yes, my lord."

King looked up at Danby. "I suppose you can stop calling me *my lord*."

Danby opened his mouth but didn't seem to know what to say. He closed it again. A crash filled the silence.

"What is happening below?" King asked.

"Er—" Danby shifted from foot to foot.

But King already knew. His creditors had descended like sharks when there was blood in the water. Who could blame them? He had accounts at every merchant on Bond Street and then some. He owed drapers and haberdashers, bootmakers and jewelers. Those merchants had no hope of being paid when the duke's offspring—King—was stripped of his wealth and titles. They had to reclaim what they could now.

Feeling strangely calm, King stood and walked to the bedchamber door. It was open, and Churchwood stood just outside, eyes wide and lips pressed together. As soon as he saw King, he pounced. "What shall I do, my lord?"

"I suppose you ought to grab some candlesticks or silver," King said, voice hard. "I won't be able to pay you. I'll give you a reference, though fat lot of good that will do you." He walked to the winding stairway and looked down at the chaos below. He could feel Danby and Churchwood right behind him. He stared at the large foyer, now crowded with men moving couches and tables and longcase clocks through the open front door. Just outside, wagons lined the street before the house and people stood across the way, gaping at the spectacle.

King started down the stairway just as several men started up. They'd begin to pilfer from the bedchambers and the drawing room now. Nothing to be done about it. Soon his landlord would arrive and want to be paid the money owing for the lease. Then King would be out on the street.

His legs gave out then, and he sank down on the steps about a quarter of the distance from the bottom. A few of the movers gave him curious glances, but they didn't cease their work. There was a line of them waiting to move through the door with whatever booty they could take.

King watched the men file out the door then file back in again like an industrious ant colony. He used to enjoy observing ant colonies on the rare occasion he was at the Avebury country estate. He supposed he would never see that again. Were there creditors in those ancient halls now, stripping the walls of the portraits of the previous dukes of Avebury?

One of the men passing him gave him a pitiable look, and King had to urge to trip the bastard. Let them look at him with pity. He would find a way to fix this. He would find a way to reclaim what was his. He had friends and connections. He had never been in a situation he couldn't find a way out of, and this was no different. He just needed time and a bit of sobering up.

King's gaze sharpened as a figure seemed to separate itself from the crowd of men. Or perhaps they moved apart to reveal her. A woman in a shabby blue coat with a ragged bonnet hanging by the ribbons down her back stood under his chandelier and looked about. She wasn't one of his servants, and yet she looked familiar for some reason. She was pretty, with her dark hair in a neat bun at the nape of her neck and her large blue eyes in a face that seemed too thin. King never forgot a pretty face.

Her dark eyes settled on him, and he felt something inside him shift under her gaze. Judging by her clothing, she was of absolutely no consequence to him or the world, and yet he felt as though he'd just been noticed by the queen.

"You," she said, stepping forward.

With some amusement, King noted that the burly men moving his belongings scrambled to step out of her way as she started for him. She pointed an ungloved finger at him, and King had the ridiculous notion to put a hand to his chest, as though saying, *Me?*

"It was you. I knew it!" She started up the marble stairs, pausing two steps below him. She was even prettier now that she was closer. Her skin was surprisingly smooth and clear for someone of her class. Not a pockmark in sight. He looked down at her, and her cheeks colored under his direct gaze. Belatedly, he realized she was holding something out to him. His gaze lowered, and he spotted the sheet of paper. He looked up again, and she nodded down at it.

He took the paper, feeling vaguely uneasy that he was still seated and she standing. He did not need to rise in her presence. She wasn't a lady. King unfolded the paper and stared at a list of items with numbers beside them. "What is your name?" he asked, looking up from the odd paper.

"Miss Baker. Violet Baker." She narrowed her eyes at him. "I am the proprietress of The Silver Unicorn." She raised her brows meaningfully, as though her words should hold some import.

"Good day, Miss Baker. I certainly hope your day is better than mine thus far."

"It is not, sir—I mean, my lord. Thanks to you, my day has begun very poorly indeed. You may remedy that by paying the sum indicated."

He stared at her until she nudged the paper he still held gingerly between two fingers. As she leaned forward, he caught the scent of her—the smell of yeast and lye and perhaps something lightly floral. King looked at the paper again. His thoughts were a complete jumble. Not only was he still foxed, he felt as though an entire shelf of books had crashed down over his head. The Duke of Avebury was a traitor. Was he in the Tower even now? Would he be executed today? And King, who had always known he would one day be duke, now knew nothing of his future. That future lay like a fathomless maw before him. He scrambled to hold on to the familiar, but he was being pushed into that bottomless blackness whether he wanted to go or not.

The words and letters on the paper swam before his eyes until he blinked and made a valiant attempt to concentrate. And then he frowned and looked up. "You want me to pay you ten pounds?"

"That's right. That's what you owe for the riot you caused last night."

"Riot?" King stood, holding on to the newel post for support.

"Yes, my lord." She looked up at him and squared her shoulders as though refusing to be intimidated. "You and your friends came into the Silver Unicorn last night, caused a riot, and destroyed my tavern."

King gaped at her then realized who she must be. "Are you speaking of that grimy den we stopped in last night? The place with the rum like horse piss?" The rum that had caused him to imagine witches in his chambers.

Her pointed chin jerked up sharply. "I have never tasted horse piss, my lord, but I do believe my publican served you rum." She shifted her gaze away thoughtfully. "In fact, I don't believe you paid for that either. Let me have that paper. I'll add the cost of the rum." She held out her small hand. It was decidedly not the hand of a lady. Her nails were short, her knuckles red, and her skin chafed.

"You may add whatever you like to this…receipt. I can't give you ten pounds." Yesterday he would have ordered Churchwood to pay her, finding the whole exchange amusing. He had a vague memory of tables overturning and chairs smashing last night. He didn't think he was wholly responsible for the damage to her dirty slum tavern, but he would pay it just to make her go away. Today, he didn't think he even had a pound to his name. Really, for the damage the rum had done to his brain, *she* should pay *him*.

"Eight pounds, then," she said, moving to block him even as he moved down a step. "And no less. I won't take no for an answer."

"No," he said. When she wouldn't move out of his way, he took her thin shoulders in his hands and moved her out of his path. King didn't know where he would go, but he did not want to sit on the steps and watch his life carried away.

Miss Baker was not done with him, though. She was right on his heels. "My lord, if you do not pay me, I will be forced to involve the authorities."

King found this threat wholly amusing. The Parliament would vote to attaint the duke and his offspring tonight, no doubt with the full support of the prince regent. Prinny had never liked King, not since King and Rory had played that little joke on him. The prince would be more than pleased to see King stripped of land and titles. And this little chit from Seven Dials thought to threaten him with…what? A constable? A magistrate?

"Go ahead," he said, dismissing her with a wave.

But before King could move away from the stairs, another man approached, holding a sheet of parchment. "My lord, I beg you to take a moment to look at the charges on your account from Schweitzer and Davidson."

King turned to the other side, where another man waited. "Your account from Stultz, my lord. If you would be so kind as to settle it."

Every tailor, hatmaker, bootmaker, and costermonger would be on him in a moment. And he with only—King reached into the pocket of his waistcoat and pulled out a coin—a crown to his name. "This is all I have, gentlemen. Have at it." And he flipped it into the air. The men lunged for it, but a hand reached out and caught it neatly before any of the men could snatch it. King turned and saw the petite tavern owner secure the coin in a flash.

"You still owe me seven pound, fifteen shillings," she said. This began a general outcry of men calling out the sums he owed their various employers. King pushed through them, shouldered past the movers carrying his dining room table out, and stood in the yellow light of morning. How could the day have dawned so sunny when he felt as though he was being swallowed into a dark pit?

Ah, but the vipers in the pit had followed him, and the bill collectors crowded about him even on his own stoop. The sound of them was enough to make King's head pound even worse. He tried to move away and bumped into Miss Baker, but instead of reiterating her demand for payment, she waited until he righted himself then shoved through his creditors and started away. For a moment, King was rather jealous that she could escape so easily. She could disappear into Seven Dials, and no one would find her. God knew he didn't think he could ever again find that little shack of a tavern she claimed to own.

And if he couldn't find it, no creditors would think to look for him there.

"Miss Baker!" King called.

She jerked to a surprised halt and looked at him over her shoulder. "Hold a moment." Now she raised her brows as he fought through the men surrounding him to reach her.

"You said I owe you seven pounds?"

Her hands went to her hips. "Seven pounds and fifteen shillings."

"Right. Well, I'd like to see the damage and verify it myself."

Her gaze slid past him to the men still calling out to him. "You want a place to hide," she said.

He could have denied it, but why the hell should he? He did want a place to hide. Even a wolf needed a den to lick his wounds and recover for the fight ahead. "Just for a day or so," he said. "Until I can put my affairs in order." Until he could rally his friends and reclaim what was his.

"And then you'll pay me?"

A small voice taunted him, saying, *You'll never pay her or any of them. You'll be lucky to convince a friend to loan you enough so that you don't starve.*

King silenced the voice. He had many friends—rich friends. He might be down for the moment, but he could still turn things around. He always did. "Of course," he told her. "I'll pay."

Her brows came together in a skeptical expression. She was not like the ladies of his acquaintance. She wasn't innocent and naïve. She had her doubts that he'd pay. And then something like cunning flashed in her clear blue eyes, and King had half a mind to reconsider his plan. He'd always thought he was the wolf, playing with all the sheep for entertainment. But in that moment, her eyes were every bit the predator's.

King shifted away from her, his instincts telling him to walk the other way, but before he could act on those reflexes, she grasped the sleeve of his coat and yanked him back into her orbit. The shrewdness was gone from her eyes, and she blinked at him sweetly as she pulled him along with her.

But King didn't believe it for a moment. As he glanced over his shoulder at his house, the doors open and his furnishings on the street outside, he wondered if he hadn't just jumped out of the fire and into a raging inferno.

# CHAPTER FOUR

F OR ALL THE trouble he had caused her, she would get her full eight pounds—rather, seven pounds, fifteen shillings. She had the crown in her pocket, one hand fisted around the coin so it stayed there, no matter how many thieves jostled her as she neared home. As they passed the entrance to Seven Dials, where the sundial column had once stood, Violet glanced back at the marquess. He was following her without protest. He'd shaken her hand off his coat sleeve as soon as they left his house behind.

So far, nothing about her plan to force the nobleman to pay for the damage he and his friends caused had worked in her favor. Violet, however, was nothing if not resourceful. If he wouldn't pay her now, then she'd simply keep him in her sights until he did.

Not that looking at him was any great hardship.

He was an extremely handsome man, even as disheveled as he appeared this morning. His brown hair stuck out from his head at all angles, and there were bags under his red-rimmed green eyes. A shadow of stubble covered his jaw, and his clothes, though finer than any she had ever owned, were wrinkled and stained. But even looking shabby and disreputable in the morning light, he stood out like a peacock among pigeons as he strolled through Seven Dials. Violet could feel the eyes on them as she picked her way around the debris and filth on the narrow streets.

"Could you perhaps hunch your shoulders a bit?" she said after seeing two men in an alley elbow each other as he passed. With her luck, they worked for Ferryman and would report she had a nob with her. Then she'd have his whole gang to contend with.

The marquess looked at her then blinked as though waking from a dream. He really had no idea the danger he was in at the moment. "Pardon?" he murmured sleepily.

Violet grabbed his sleeve and pulled him aside. He looked down at her hand on his arm, his mouth twisted with distaste, and she hastily released him. "Do you think you could be less conspicuous? We're attracting attention, and that's not a good thing in this part of the city."

Instead of slouching or casting his eyes down, he straightened and looked about boldly. "Are we being followed?" he asked loudly.

"No. Shh!"

"Come out from where you're hiding," he yelled. "I'm more than happy to give you a taste of my knuckles." And then the idiot raised his fist in the air and waved it about in challenge.

Violet grabbed his arm, pulled it down, and, using the momentum, tugged him into the doorway of a closed shop. From the strong smell of tallow, she guessed the shop owner made candles. "What is the matter with you? You are not in Mayfair any longer, and in case you haven't noticed, your friends aren't with us."

"I can defend myself. Where is my walking stick?" He looked about as though just realizing he had left it behind.

Violet had two brothers, and she knew when a man was spoiling for a fight. Ordinarily, she didn't care if one of the nobs went and got himself killed, but this one needed to survive until she was paid what he owed her for destroying her tavern. She needed those seven pounds, fifteen shillings or she was done for. She couldn't exactly run a tavern without any functioning tables and chairs, not to mention mugs, glasses, or spirits.

"If you want to get yourself killed, go right ahead," she said, poking him so he gave her his attention again. "But do it after you've paid me for the damage you caused last night."

He looked at her, his expression turning serious. Thank God! The man was finally comprehending the danger surrounding them. He cocked his head. "You're very pretty," he said.

Violet closed her eyes in frustration. Did these so-called gentlemen think of nothing but drinking, fighting, and bed sport? She opened her eyes and saw he was still looking at her. She had better put him in his place now, or he'd think he could take liberties. "And you look like a drowned rat and smell like you fell in a vat of rum."

"Ouch." He put his hand to his heart as though wounded.

"If you think that hurts, wait until you feel my knee in your stones. Keep your hands to yourself."

He reeled back as though slapped. Violet wondered if he'd ever been rejected by a woman before. Probably not, which meant it was long past time.

"Are you always so full of sunshine and light?"

"Are you always such an idiot?" she asked. "Try to stay alive until we reach my tavern." And without another word, she marched past him and back onto the street. She walked quickly now, eager to be home and safely behind locked doors, but not so quickly that the marquess could not keep up. Violet was beginning to wonder if perhaps the man was more trouble than he was worth—except seven pounds, fifteen shillings was a lot of coin and worth a lot of trouble. So far, this man seemed to be seven pounds and then some worth of trouble.

She'd been surprised when she arrived at the marquess's address to find the doors open and movers carrying rugs and draperies outside. Though she wondered at the sight of the line of men going in and out, one didn't look a gift horse in the mouth. She went inside. That was one less obstacle to overcome. But the moment she'd stepped into the house, her jaw had dropped. Never had she seen anything like the grandeur surrounding her.

The entryway alone was easily as large as her tavern, and the sun streaming through a large window above the door made the entry light and airy. She'd looked up as the sunlight sparkled on the chandelier above her, and it seemed as though a thousand diamonds winked at her.

Stunned as she was, Violet was not so much a fool as to not realize something was amiss. She had seen enough neighbors tossed out of lodgings to know what eviction looked like, and the marquess was clearly being evicted. The thought gave her a moment's pause about the possibility of collecting recompense for the damage to the Silver Unicorn, but then she pushed the thought aside. Eight pounds was nothing to a man of his stature. Why, the chandelier above her must cost twice that!

But, of course, nothing could be simple. She hadn't been the only merchant there wanting to be paid, and the coward appeared to want to run away from his creditors. That was fine— as long as he couldn't run away from her. At least not until he paid her, and she threw him out. He said he needed a day to put his affairs in order. Fine. She'd have her seven pounds, fifteen shillings tomorrow, then.

"Where the holy hell are you taking me?" he said, sounding tired and irritable. Good. Now he knew how she felt.

"You don't remember my tavern from last night?" She glanced at him over her shoulder.

"Would you be offended if I said no?"

She gave him a long look.

He cleared his throat. "The White Unicorn, was it?"

"*Silver* Unicorn." She blew out a breath. *Seven pounds, fifteen shillings.* "It's just here, as I'm sure you recall." She led him around another corner and into the street just outside the tavern. Broken glass and furnishings, some of which she recognized as belonging to her, littered the ground outside. The damage extended further along the street, where she caught sight of other merchants nailing boards over broken windows or attempting to repair smashed railings and doors hanging off hinges.

"Quick. Come inside," she said. It wouldn't do for one of her neighbors to recognize him and demand payment for their damages before she received hers. She pulled a key from the pocket of her coat, shoved it in the lock, and opened the door to the tavern.

But the marquess, instead of hurrying inside, paused and peered cautiously over her shoulder into the cool darkness within. "How do I know you don't have assassins waiting inside?"

"The only people inside are my maid Peggy and my two brothers, Joshua and Georgie."

"That's what you say now..."

Violet rolled her eyes. "Listen, I don't care if you live or die, *my lord*, just as long as you die *after* you pay me my seven pounds, fifteen shillings." She pushed the door wider and stepped aside. "Now go inside, or I really will leave you to the thieves and cutthroats just waiting for their chance to slit your throat and steal those fine clothes off your back."

That did it. He stepped into the tavern, moving cautiously. Violet pushed in behind him, closed the door, locked it again, then slammed the heavy wooden bar down over it to keep everyone out.

She paused a moment to allow her eyes to adjust to the gloom of the interior. Neither Peggy nor her brothers were nearby, but she thought she heard the sound of Peggy's humming coming from the back.

"Good God, what happened here?"

Violet could have cheerfully kicked the marquess. He was standing with his hands on his hips, surveying the utter destruction of her tavern.

"*You* happened here," she said. "You and your nob friends started a brawl, and this is the result. I suppose you never pause to think about the damage you leave behind after one of your nights slumming."

"Why would I pause to remember this"—he glanced at her and seemed to think better of whatever he'd been about to say—

"establishment?" But his motives were too obvious and his bad mood all but contagious. She, however, was immune to his disease this morning.

"You are trying to make me angry."

"What? You, angry? Not my Miss Sunshine."

"It's Miss Baker, and I have two younger brothers. I'm not so easily baited." She went to a hook and pulled her apron off it. After tying it on, she indicated the table where she'd sat with her brothers this morning. "You said you needed a day to put your affairs in order. You may sit here. I can fetch pen and paper if you need it."

He raised a brow, obviously surprised that she would have pen and paper. He probably didn't think she could read.

"I would like pen and paper, but this won't do at all." He gestured to the table, his nose in the air. "It's far too dark in here, and my head is still spinning. I'll need a nap, a meal, and a desk with more light."

"A nap and a meal?" Violet's hands hurt from clenching them so tightly. "You're not here to take a nap and eat through my larder. If you want a nap, you can have it after you pay me seven pounds and fifteen shillings."

"You do seem quite obsessed with that exact sum."

"Because that's what it will take—at least—to return my establishment to even a semblance of its former self! Thanks to you, my publican is injured, my tavern is destroyed, and I have no way to make an income, so yes, I want my seven pounds, fifteen—"

"Shillings. There's no need to shout, Miss Sunshine. It only hurts my head."

Violet grabbed a broom nearby. "I will hurt your head!" She swung the broom at him, but he caught it neatly, tugged it hard, and brought her stumbling against him. He tossed the broom aside and grasped her about the waist, holding her in a manner she found far too familiar.

"Now, now, Miss Sunshine. No violence."

"Get your hands off me, sir."

He looked down at her. "Do you promise not to attempt to kill me?"

"No."

He grinned. "Do you promise not to attempt to kill me until after I've paid you?"

"Yes," she ground out. "Now let me go."

He released her, and she made a show of brushing herself off and generally looking disgusted by being forced into close proximity to him. The truth was she needed a moment to calm her racing heart. That seeming eternity when her body was pressed against his had caused all the breath to whoosh out of her. Not only couldn't she breathe, but she couldn't seem to force her hands to push away from his chest—his solid, muscular chest. He was warm and he smelled like rum, yes, but he also smelled of brushed wool and clean linen and bergamot tea. She'd had to force herself not to bury her nose in his chest and inhale deeply.

The door to the back swung open and Peggy stuck her blonde hair through. "Is everything—Oh!" The girl's eyes went wide at the sight of the marquess. Peggy dropped her jaw and then her broom, making a loud clatter. "Oh," Peggy said again, not even seeming to notice the fallen broom.

Good. Having Peggy nearby would keep the marquess from touching Violet again. And she could have Peggy show him upstairs. There was paper and light there. She hadn't wanted him in her private quarters, but with the shutters still closed, she couldn't argue that it wasn't too dark in the tavern for him to write, and she imagined he had to appeal to his men of business or his friends for the necessary funds.

"Peggy, this is the man who owes me seven—"

"Pounds and fifteen shillings," the marquess said, giving Peggy a dashing bow.

Violet stared at him. Where had this chivalry been just a few moments ago? Peggy put her hands to her mouth and giggled. Violet felt like banging her head against a wall. Now Peggy would have stars in her eyes all day, and Violet would have to remind her of tasks three and four times before she would hear.

"But I actually have a name," he said, glancing at Violet. "And a title." He made a flourish with his hand. "The Marquess of Kingston, at your service. Of course, my friends call me King, so you must as well."

Violet snorted. Only a man truly full of himself would ask others to call him *King*.

Peggy giggled again, seeming too taken with the marquess to actually speak. "Peggy," Violet said, "would you mind taking his lordship to the flat above? Ask one of the boys to give him pen and ink."

Peggy's eyes widened, and she gave a hasty curtsy then scurried away, looking over her shoulder at the nobleman anxiously.

"There's access to the staircase through there," Violet told him, gesturing to the back room. "I suggest you start on your correspondence immediately. No naps."

"Yes, Miss Sunshine," he said, sounding like an obedient servant. She might have even believed him, if he hadn't winked at her over his shoulder before following Peggy into the back.

Violet gripped her broom tightly. What had she gotten herself into?

KING NOTED THE back room was clean and organized. He supposed the contrast between the neatly arranged casks of spirits and stacked mugs and cups in the back and the complete chaos of the front made an impression. He truly did not remember much of the Silver Unicorn from the night before, but if this back area was any indication, it had not always looked as it did now. Was he really to blame for the destruction in the front? King supposed he and Henry might have broken a table or chair, but Miss Sunshine couldn't blame him for what looked like the aftereffects of a cyclone.

He followed the maid up a narrow flight of stairs. At the top, she opened a door and stepped inside to allow him to pass. King had to duck, and even when inside the room and he stood upright, the low ceiling almost grazed the top of his head.

"Do you need anything else, your lordship?" the maid asked.

"I don't suppose there's anything to eat?" he said hopefully. Now that he was sober again, he was beginning to feel rather hungry.

"Er…" The maid looked about the small flat. "I'm not certain, your lordship."

"Very well." He made a dismissing gesture with his hand and walked across the room. The ceiling slanted down at the same angle as the roof, and he had to duck again by the time he reached the window overlooking the street below. A few people passed by, wrapped in thin shawls or threadbare coats. A woman swept the walk outside her building, and a group of barefoot children raced past.

King dropped the thin muslin window covering and turned to look at the room. At one end was a clothesline with various items of clothing hung to dry. A large tub sat below the line with sponges and brushes and various cleaning materials inside. Behind the line was another door. A closet or another room? Perhaps a water closet, though he doubted a flat this primitive would have an indoor privy. In fact, there was a tattered sheet hung in one corner, and King would have placed bets that behind that was a chamber pot.

Beside the window where he stood was a small table with two mismatched chairs and a three-legged stool. A shelf was against the wall, and it held three wooden plates, one wooden bowl, and three chipped glasses, as well as a porcelain pitcher. King imagined the closed cupboards held a motley assortment of pots and pans.

The dark coal stove squatted on the other side of the room. Beside it was an all but empty coal bucket. The room was chilly, though he imagined in a few months, at the height of summer, the room would be stifling hot. Beside the stove was a mattress with an assortment of ragged blankets. King's gaze moved past it and then back again, and he spotted the small lump and followed it up to the small head of a dark-haired, brown-eyed boy. This must be one of Miss Baker's brothers. The child looked just like her.

"Who are you?" King asked.

The boy pushed off the blankets and stood. "I'm George Baker, sir. Who are you?"

"The Marquess of Kingston." At least for a few more hours. "But you can call me King."

"The markiss who owes Vi blunt?" The boy's brown eyes widened. "Did she take you prisoner? Is that why you're here?"

King frowned. "There's no logic behind that idea, Master Baker," he said. "Your maid showed me in here, and I assure you if Miss Sun—Baker had attempted to abduct me, I would have thwarted her efforts."

The boy looked dubious. "I don't know about that. She can be pretty strong sometimes."

King had no idea about the age of children. This child could be three or ten. Regardless, this one seemed in good health and reasonably intelligent, if a bit misguided. "Is there anything to eat, Master Baker?" King asked.

The child's gaze went to the cupboard with the plates and bowl. "Not much. Joshua sometimes brings food back, but he's not here right now."

Joshua must be another of Miss Baker's charges.

King went to the cupboard and opened it. As he'd suspected, there was a pot and a pan, and also a basket with a cloth over it. King removed it, uncovered a loaf of bread, and set it on the table. He lifted the pitcher from the shelf and poured what appeared to be water into one of the chipped cups. Bread and water. How he'd come down in the world.

He sat in one of the chairs, gingerly testing it before putting his full weight on it. It creaked but held. A moment later, George was kneeling on the stool, elbows on the table, watching King eat.

King didn't have a knife, so he tore a piece of bread off the loaf and took a small bite. Stale and mealy, but it was better than nothing. He had to put something in his belly to soak up the remaining drink.

"Vi won't like that you're eating that," the boy said.

"Don't tell her, then."

The child looked as though he'd never considered that option. He looked to be the sort who couldn't keep a secret. King knew how to deal with that sort. One involved them in the crime to make them complicit. That generally assured compliance.

He broke off another piece of bread. "For you, Master Baker."

The child took it, popped it in his mouth, and said between bites, "You can call me Georgie."

"It would be my honor."

Georgie smiled, and King saw his half-chewed bread and two missing front teeth. "You've lost something," he said. Georgie looked about. When he didn't discover anything missing, King pointed to his mouth. "Your front teeth. Had them knocked out in a brawl, did you?"

"Noooo." Georgie shook his head.

"Fell down the stairs?"

"Noooo."

"You're too young for them to have rotted away."

"They're not rotten. They just fell out. Like my bottom ones did." He pointed to the bottom set of his front teeth, which were uneven and seemed to be growing in at various rates.

King made a sound of understanding. He vaguely remembered that children lost their teeth before the adult teeth grew in. He supposed he'd lost his own at one time. He didn't like to think about his childhood very much. It hadn't been a happy time.

The bread was gone and so was the water, and King was still hungry. Nothing to do about that at the moment. From below he heard the clink of glass and the sounds of furniture being moved. The maid and Miss Baker were obviously working hard at cleaning up the mess. It was an impossible task, but if Miss Baker was engaged in that, she couldn't hound him.

"Is that the only bed?" he asked, pointing to the one Georgie had been lying in.

"No. Vi has her own bed in there." The boy pointed to the closed door behind the clothesline. "But we can't go in there because she's a girl."

"She's not in there now," King pointed out.

"But it's—I forgot what it is. My brother knows the word. Something about privacy."

King furrowed his brow. "An invasion of privacy?"

Georgie pointed at him. "That's it! How did you know?"

"Lucky guess." King rose. "Don't worry. I won't invade her privacy."

He strolled across the room and opened the door to Miss Baker's bedchamber. Well, it wasn't a bedchamber. It was a closet with a bed inside and several garments hanging on hooks. The roof sloped so steeply here that he would have to all but crawl to move from one side to the next. That was if the bed had not taken up almost the entire space.

Still, it was a bed and not a mattress on the floor. He could nap here until a decent hour of day and not be disturbed.

Georgie had come to stand behind him, and peered into the closet. "You're not supposed to go in there."

King looked down at him. "Then don't tell anyone." He hunched down, moved inside, and closed the door. He had little choice but to sit on the bed, but even then his head rubbed against the ceiling, so he lay down. The bed was not uncomfortable. It was long enough to accommodate him, and considering the walls on either side, he wouldn't fall off. He pulled a quilt over him and closed his eyes.

A moment later, he opened them again. The quilt smelled like her—like Violet Baker. It had that faint floral scent mixed with lye and yeast. None were unpleasant. In fact, he rather liked the scents of yeast and flowers, but something about the combination unsettled him. It brought her face to mind. She was very pretty. *Very* pretty. That was something one didn't see often in the lower classes. Any woman with passing good looks was usually snatched up by a protector or the abbess of a bawdy house. Violet Howard, with her thick, dark hair, her blue eyes, and her clear skin, was undeniably lovely. She was also quite without protection. The small child in the other room couldn't keep her safe, nor could that slip of a maid who had shown him upstairs. There was mention of another brother. Perhaps he had shielded her from harm.

Or perhaps she was in very real danger, and that was why she was so keen on collecting money from him. King felt an unfamiliar sensation, like a tug in the middle of his chest.

He ignored it. Violet Baker and her brothers and her maid and her tavern were not his problem. He had bigger problems. Problems someone like Miss Sunshine could never understand. He'd pushed his father's trial and guilty verdict to the back of his mind, but now he had nothing else to distract him.

His father was a traitor. He, King, was the son of a traitor. He knew what that meant. He'd be ostracized. He'd lose everything—his titles, his money, his connections.

Everything.

What was he supposed to do now? Where was he supposed to go?

He'd write to his friends this evening. They would help him. They'd give him blunt, offer him refuge. If there hadn't been a war on, he would have decamped to the Continent. Perhaps he'd go to Canada or the United States for a few years until the scandal died down. Yes, that was what he'd do. He'd ask his friends for blunt and purchase passage on a ship. Once he reached the New World, he'd put all of this behind him—the creditors, his father, and, most importantly, that witch.

# CHAPTER FIVE

J OSHUA WAS CAREFUL to keep out of the way of Ferryman and his
gang. That was as much commonsense as self-preservation.
Ferryman was always looking to add to his gang, and even
though Vi paid him extra to leave her brothers alone, he wasn't
known for keeping his promises.

Joshua should have been at the Silver Unicorn helping to
straighten up, but Vi had gone on a fool's errand to find her
marquess, and Joshua hadn't wanted to waste the chance to
embark on his own errand. Once she returned, he'd be cleaning
for days. He'd followed her out of Seven Dials and set up his
thimbles in Covent Garden. There were always a few people
willing to risk a coin or two there on a game of thimblerig. He let
a few of them find the pebble under his thimbles, and then, when
he had a bit of a crowd, he offered double or nothing. A young,
well-dressed man took him up on the offer, and Joshua did what
he'd practiced a thousand times. He palmed the pebble so no
matter which thimble the man picked, he wouldn't find the
pebble. Then Joshua neatly replaced the pebble when he turned
over all the thimbles so it would seem to be a fair game.

He might have played longer, took in more coin, but he had
other plans. So he pocketed his money and his thimbles and
disappeared back into Seven Dials.

Ferryman's territory was comprised of three streets—well,

two and one that was contested by Resurrection Man, another arch rogue, and his gang. There were frequent fights over who was allowed to collect taxes from the shops and taverns on that street, and it had become so treacherous that most of those establishments had closed. The Silver Unicorn was located on Clover Lane, a small offshoot of one of Ferryman's streets. The Black Bear was at the other end of the other street. If Joshua had gone directly, it would have taken him about five minutes to walk from one tavern to the other. But he didn't go directly. He took a long route through back alleys and inside abandoned buildings, over fences and roofs, and finally into the first-floor window of a room above the Black Bear's public room.

At this time of day, the tavern was quiet. The owner served coffee and tea in the morning, but there wasn't much call for that sort of fare in Seven Dials. Business picked up when the fancy came slumming and the locals returned home from their work in the factories and shops outside of Seven Dials.

The quiet of the tavern suited Joshua just fine. If the place had been busy then Lizzie would have been needed downstairs. At this time of day, he expected to find her working upstairs.

Joshua crept out of the room he'd entered and into a corridor. The other doors along the corridor were closed. Most of those rooms were rented by prostitutes, so he wasn't about to start opening doors. Whores did not like having their sleep disturbed. He was wondering how long he'd have to stand here, and if Lizzie was even around, when a door opened and she stepped out. Joshua slunk back out of instinct, then poked his head out the door again. He waved to her, and she waved back, though she looked over her shoulder in a way that let him know she was concerned.

Joshua ducked back into the room where he'd entered. There were blankets on the floor and a few items of clothing strewn about. Lizzie had told him once this was where she and some of the younger members of Ferryman's gang slept. The other gang members were no doubt already at their jobs, the legal and illegal.

Joshua was glad he had Lizzie to himself for once.

She stepped into the bedchamber and, with a quick look over her shoulder, closed the door behind her. "Ye shouldn't be 'ere," she said quietly, but she was smiling.

"Can't I visit a friend?"

"Not if Ferryman finds out. 'E'd kill both of us."

Joshua didn't doubt the truth of that statement. That was the reason Vi had forbidden Joshua from talking to Lizzie, but though he respected his sister and thought most of her decisions sound, he couldn't give up Lizzie. She was his friend. Secretly, he hoped one day to marry her. He'd made the mistake of telling Vi this one time, and she had acted as though the ceiling was falling down on their heads.

"Marry her? Joshua, the girl will be lucky if she lives to see fourteen." Vi had jumped up and grasped the back of one of the chairs in their flat. "She's Ferryman's dell. You know what that means."

Joshua did know what that meant. A dell was a woman who hadn't yet lost her virginity and whom the arch rogue of a gang claimed as his own. Once Ferryman tired of a dell, she became the property of the gang and was passed around to all the members. Lizzie's parents had died when she was nine or ten, and she'd been snatched from the orphanage by Ferryman, who had an eye for a pretty girl. Lizzie had deep brown eyes and dimples when she smiled. Although she was dirty, too thin, her unwashed hair limp, she was still pretty.

"He hasn't touched her," Joshua had said, hunching his shoulders.

"He will," Vi said with a certainty Joshua didn't like. "Remember Molly Rogers? She was dead of the pox by age fifteen. God knows what happened to the brats she birthed." Vi closed her eyes, and for an instant, Joshua saw the pain in them. She didn't show emotion very often. She said it was because there was so much sadness in the world that if she allowed herself to feel too much of it, she would drown in a lake of her own tears.

When he'd been little and cried over something, Joshua some-times imagined his own tears would create a lake. Since he couldn't swim, he usually wiped his nose and dried his tears.

"Vi, can't we do something to help Lizzie?" Joshua had asked, taking advantage of her rare show of emotion.

Vi opened her eyes. "No. I can barely keep you and Georgie safe. I can't do anything for Lizzie. I'm sorry for her, but there's nothing I can do."

Joshua hadn't been angry with Lizzie. He knew he'd asked the impossible. Vi could no more help Lizzie than she could the one-legged beggar on the corner, the prostitutes sleeping in the room next door, or the children who dwelt in the room where he stood with Lizzie. Those children were undoubtedly wading into the cold Thames right now in search of bits and bobs.

"He won't find out," Joshua told Lizzie now. "No one saw me."

"Good." She sighed then set down her bucket full of rags and polish and lye. She worked at the Brown Bear cleaning and serving ale to pay for her room and what little she got to eat. If she made anything more than what was needed to cover those expenses, Ferryman took it. No one received special treatment from him, not even the girls he chose as his special companions.

"I have something for you," Joshua said.

"Ye do?" Her dark brown eyes lit up in a way that made all the effort it had taken to see her worth it.

He reached into his pocket, pushed the thimbles out of the way, and withdrew a tattered red ribbon. He held it out, wishing it was new and clean.

"Oh!" Lizzie's eyes widened.

"I thought red would look pretty in your hair," he said.

Lizzie nodded, but she didn't reach to take the ribbon. Joshua pushed his hand closer to her, but she shook her head. "I can't take it."

"Why not?"

"If 'e sees it, 'e'll ask where it came from."

"Tell him you found it."

"Ferryman will say I'm lying and beat me. 'E don't allow me anything 'e 'asn't given me."

Joshua pulled his hand back. "Lizzie, he hasn't…touched you yet, has he?"

She shook her head. "Not yet. 'E says I'm worth waiting for."

Joshua fisted his hands, crumpling the ribbon he still held. "I hate him. I wish I could take you away from this."

"And where would we go? Ye think there's anywhere in London 'e couldn't find us? Besides, ye need to worry about yerself. I 'eard Ferryman talking about yer sister."

He straightened. "What was he saying about Vi?"

"Something about a fight at yer tavern and 'ow it was like to ruin 'er. Then she'd 'ave no choice but to come to 'im on 'er 'ands and knees, and wot 'e would like 'er to do on them 'ands and knees."

Joshua could feel his face heating, knew his cheeks were red. "If he dares touch her, if he even looks at her—"

"Ye'll do wot? 'E'll kill you without a thought. 'E won't even bother to do it 'isself. 'E'll have one of the gang slit yer throat and toss ye in the river." She must have seen something on his face, because she reached out and put her hand on his arm. "I'm sorry, Joshua. I know ye mean well. And—well, thank ye for the ribbon. Even if I can't take it, it means a lot that ye thought of me. But it might be better if ye didn't."

His gaze had fixed on the hand she'd placed on his arm. It was small and red, raw from hot water and lye. "If I didn't what?" he asked.

"If ye didn't think of me," she said.

Joshua wanted to say that was impossible. He wanted to say that Lizzie was all he thought about some days—most days. But it wouldn't help her to hear that. It wouldn't help Vi if he said it, and he now realized Lizzie was right. He should be home helping Vi. "I'd better go," he said, turning abruptly. "Vi needs me."

Lizzie nodded. "Be careful."

Joshua put a foot out the window and reached over to grab the ledge he could use to hoist himself back up to the roof. He grabbed on to the ledge, and Lizzie poked a head out of the window. "Goodbye, Joshua," she said.

It sounded final.

"You'll see me again," he said.

"No, I won't." She closed the window with a final bang.

*I won't give up that easily,* he told himself as he climbed to the roof and started on the winding path back to Clover Lane. He always wondered why it was called Clover Lane. He'd once asked Vi what clover was, and she told him it was a small green plant. There wasn't anything green and growing on Clover Lane in Seven Dials.

Twenty minutes later he entered the Silver Unicorn through the back door and pushed into the public room. From the piles of debris in the rubbish bin out back, Vi had made good progress. She looked up now, her face streaked with grime, and the hair she'd piled on her head coming out of its pins. Her eyes narrowed. "Where have you been? I thought you were upstairs." She nodded at the wrapped pies he carried.

"I bought us something to eat." He gave one meat pie to Vi and the other to Peggy, who gave Vi a pleading look.

"Go ahead and eat it, Peggy. We'll start again in a quarter hour."

"I have another for me and one for Georgie."

Vi put her hands on her hips. "Where did you come by the money for those? Don't tell me you were running a game of thimblerig."

"I won't tell you, then."

"Joshua!"

"I was careful, Vi. I promise."

The back door opened again, and this time Georgie came tumbling through. "Meat pie!" he sang out. "I thought I smelled food!"

Joshua handed him a wrapped pie. "You must be starving."

"Not really," Georgie said, his mouth full of pie already. "The markiss and me had bread."

"Who?" Joshua asked at the same time Vi screeched, "What?"

Georgie took another large bite of pie.

"He ate the bread? I was saving that for supper," Vi said.

"That's not all he did," Georgie said.

"Who?" Joshua asked again. "Who ate the bread?"

"The markiss."

Joshua looked at Vi.

"He's upstairs," she said. She explained about going to his home and finding him overrun with creditors and how he promised to pay her seven pounds, fifteen shillings once he reached out to his friends. "I was hoping you could take the letters he's written and deliver them, Joshua."

"Oh, he ain't writing any letters," Georgie said.

"What's he doing?" she asked, her eyes narrowing again.

"Sleeping," he said. "In your bed." He pointed at Vi.

Joshua had seen her angry before. He knew the signs. Her cheeks went pink, her eyes went dark blue, and her lips thinned. But this time her cheeks went bright red, her eyes black, and her lips all but disappeared. She muttered something under her breath and, still clutching her pie, stomped across the public room and through the back door. Joshua and Georgie glanced at each other and ran to follow.

VIOLET MARCHED INTO the flat, immediately spying the open cupboard where she'd stored the bread, followed by the crumbs and unwashed glass on the table. The gall of the man. Not only had he eaten her bread, but he also hadn't even cleaned up after himself. She strode across the room and pulled the door to her closet open. There he lay, on his back, her quilt thrown over his midsection, snoring softly. Her gaze roved over him, and she drew in a sharp breath. He hadn't even removed his boots.

Georgie was behind her. "See. I told you he was sleeping."

"Give me something heavy," she said.

Joshua handed her a scrub brush from the pail under the clothesline. She aimed and threw, hitting King smack in the middle of the chest. He came awake with a start, sat up, and knocked his head on her low ceiling. Served him right.

"What do you think you are doing?" she demanded.

He put a hand to his head, turned bloodshot eyes toward her, and promptly bumped his head again. This time with less force. Unfortunately.

"What the holy hell?"

"Get out of my bed or I'll show you holy hell."

His red-rimmed eyes seemed to focus, and he studied Violet then seemed to dismiss her. Anyone who knew her would have told him that was a mistake.

"Go away. I need to sleep for another hour or two."

The marquess lay back down.

"Joshua, hand me another scrub brush."

King sat up again, this time careful not to hit his head. "Listen, you little termagant. Do not throw anything else."

"What did you call me?"

"Whatever it was, it didn't sound like a compliment," Joshua said. He'd hefted another brush into his hand and was holding it menacingly. "Say the word, Vi, and I'll show this fellow what for."

King tried to rake a hand through his hair and ended up just stroking the ceiling. "This is ridiculous. A farce."

Violet held out her hand, and Joshua placed the brush in her palm.

The man held his hands out in surrender. "Fine! Fine! You want me out of bed, then I'll rise." He made a shooing motion with his hands, crouched, and stumbled out of her room. Of course, then he rose to his full height, and Violet was forced to look up at him, as were Joshua and Georgie. She'd forgotten how tall he was, and how imposing. In these cramped quarters, she could feel the warmth of him, the pull of him, and her body swayed toward him before she forced her feet to stay in place. She began to wonder if bringing King here had been her best idea.

"This is my brother Joshua," she said, pointing to him with her hand. "And you met my brother Georgie. Joshua has offered to deliver the letters you wrote, King."

Joshua snorted, showing what he thought of her characterization of his part in all this.

"What letters?" King said. He sniffed and looked about. "Do I smell meat and pastry?"

Violet looked down at her left hand, where she still held the wrapped meat pie. "You came to the flat to use pen and ink. You said you would pay me after you had a chance to sort out your affairs."

"Right. I do plan to write several letters to my friends and my solicitor, but there's no point in rushing. My friends don't wake until afternoon. So you see"—he turned back toward her closet— "there's plenty of time for a nap."

"Oh, no you don't." She grasped his sleeve with the hand that held the pie. "Your man of business will be awake and at his offices, so you may start with him. And when your friends wake, they will find your correspondence waiting for them."

King looked at Georgie. "Is she always like this?"

The boy nodded. "There's no point in arguing with her. If you keep it up, she'll start yelling."

"We wouldn't want that."

Georgie shook his head. "It hurts my ears."

King eyed her. "I can imagine." Then he sniffed and grasped the hand on his sleeve. Vi tried to pull it away, but she wasn't fast enough, and he caught hold of the pie. "I knew I smelled pastry and meat."

"That's for Vi," Joshua said, neatly snatching the pie back. Violet hoped Ferryman never saw how agile Joshua was with his hands. He'd put him to work as a pickpocket in a snap.

"Georgie, let's sit at the table and eat while King begins his letter writing. Joshua—"

"I know. Fetch a quill and parchment." He went to a drawer in the cabinet that held their dishes and pulled out two precious sheets of parchment as well as her ink and a quill. Her ledger was inside as well. She winced to think about all the expenses she'd have to tally now that she had an idea of what she'd need to replace. Setting the mirror aside, she needed new tables, new chairs, new glasses, and bottles of spirits. Many bottles of spirits.

She and King took chairs at the table, while Georgie balanced on the stool. He unwrapped his pie and looked up at King, who was studying the quill with a frown.

"Do you want half of my pie?" Georgie asked King.

Violet paused in the act of unwrapping hers and stared hard at King. His gaze met hers, and she shook her head.

"No, thank you, Master Georgie. I find I have no appetite all of a sudden." He gave Violet a meaningful look. She smiled and took a big bite of her pie.

King opened the jar of ink, dipped the quill inside, and attempted to write the date on the parchment. He frowned at the results. "How am I supposed to write with this? The quill is dull, the ink all but dry, and the parchment—"

Joshua stuck a knife in the table so the handle quivered and the blade sank into the scarred wood. "You can sharpen the quill, if you like," he said.

"You know what I find writes well?" Violet took another bite of the pie. "Blood."

King gave Joshua then Violet dubious looks and dipped the quill in the ink again. He scratched away for some time. Georgie finished his pie and hopped down from the stool.

"Joshua, you and Georgie go down and help Peggy sweep and carry the last of the rubbish to the yard," Violet said. "Then she'll need water and help with the mopping and washing."

"Come on, Georgie," Joshua said, holding out a hand. The two of them tromped downstairs, and soon Violet heard the sound of their chatter as they moved in and out, carrying the broken pieces of furnishings.

"I wouldn't have taken the half of the pie," King said, looking up at her. "I wouldn't take food away from a child."

"You ate the bread that was to be our supper," she said. "So you've already taken food away from a child."

"I'll replace it."

"With what coin? You said that crown was your last."

King patted the folded parchment before him. "My friends will loan me money. I'll be flush before nightfall. You'll see."

"Well, if that's the case, you can buy us all supper."

"Gladly." He handed her the letters. "Now, if your brother will be so kind as to deliver these as directed, I will just lie down for a moment and rest my—"

"Oh, no you don't." She jumped in front of him before he could start for her bedchamber. "After all the damage you caused, you can help with the tidying up."

King looked down at her, his green eyes full of amusement. She wished he did not have such lovely eyes. They distracted her. "You want me to sweep," he said, and it was an incredulous statement, not a question.

"Sweep, mop, wipe the counters and walls. I must open to-morrow, and it will take all of us working together to make that happen."

"I admire your drive, but I am still a marquess. I do not sweep tavern floors."

"And you still owe me seven pounds, fifteen shillings. Until you pay me, you'll sweep, mop, and wash windows, if I say. March, my lord." She pointed to the door and tried very hard not to show her surprise when he actually complied with her order.

# CHAPTER SIX

T HIS WAS NOT the first time someone had tried to force King to engage in manual labor. He'd had any number of headmasters who had attempted to beat him into obedience, and when that didn't work, they'd impose punishments of backbreaking work. Henry, Rory, and he had always found a way out of those punishments. Today was no different. An hour after Miss Sunshine had put a mop in his hand, King was outside the Silver Unicorn attempting to juggle three corks. He just needed to stay out of the way until the work was done for the day, or until one of his friends came to retrieve him.

"What are you doing?" came a small voice.

King looked down at the little boy, Georgie. "What does it look like?"

"It looks like you are tossing corks in the air."

"I'm juggling."

"That's not how you juggle."

King bristled. "You think you can do better?"

Georgie held out a hand. King dropped the corks into it. Georgie began by tossing one then added the second and finally the third. Apparently, the boy *could* do better.

"Where did you learn that?" King asked.

"Joshua taught me. He knows all sorts of tricks."

King wondered what those tricks might be, but just then

another small child appeared. This one looked to be of a similar age to Georgie. "Georgie, come play kick the ball with us!"

Georgie caught each cork neatly. "I have to ask Vi."

"Aww. She'll say no." Then the little urchin looked at King. "Ask your new pa."

King took a step back at the words. "I'm not—" But he caught Georgie's pleading look. He didn't know why, but it seemed the child wanted him to pretend to be his father.

"Er—Pa?" Georgie said.

King just stared at him.

"Pa?" Georgie cleared his throat. "Can I go kick the ball with Danny?" When King still didn't speak, Georgie nudged him with a foot. "You have to give me an answer," he said out of the corner of his mouth.

"Erm—yes?"

"Thanks, Pa!" Georgie gave him an enormous smile and ran off to follow Danny. A moment later, he returned, dropped the corks, which were now sticky, into King's hand, and took off running.

That had felt good, King thought. No harm in telling the young lad he could go play with friends. The boy was too young to be stuck inside a tavern cleaning.

"Georgie!" came a distant voice from inside. King winced and moved a little away from the door, hoping Miss Baker wouldn't see him if she poked her head out.

He was attempting to juggle again when Joshua returned from delivering his letters. "No circus would hire you," the young man said.

"You say that as though it's a bad thing."

"When I get old enough, I plan to run away with the circus. I know a few tricks."

"So I hear." King knew Joshua was older than his brother, but he was again at a loss as to what age this person might be. "And how old must one be before he runs away to join the circus?"

"Sixteen, I figure. That means we only need to wait three

years."

"Who is we? Certainly, you don't mean to take your siblings."

The boy looked as though he'd been caught with his hand in a rich man's pocket. "I didn't say *we*. I said I only need to wait three years."

King raised his brows. "My mistake. Did you deliver my letters?"

"I did. I went to the back door of all the fancy houses and handed the letters to a footman."

"I told you to give them to the butler."

Joshua rolled his eyes. "No butler will give someone like me the time of day. But the footman will give them to the butler. If he can read your writing. It's all but illegible."

"That's not my fault. The ink—Never mind. What about my solicitor? Did he send a reply?"

"I have it here somewhere." The boy reached into one side of his coat and then the other. King had to refrain from grabbing the child and turning him upside down to shake loose the contents of his pockets. He needed that letter. He'd instructed the solicitor to send him an advance on his allowance. By now his stomach was growling rather impatiently, and he needed that blunt, lest Miss Sunshine starve him.

"Here it is." Joshua handed him the letter. King took it and turned it over, dismayed to see it bore no wax seal. The solicitor couldn't be very worried about the contents if he hadn't even sealed it. King opened it and read the missive quickly. The words blurred together after he saw the phrase *accounts frozen*.

"This can't be right," he said. "Did he give you a bank draft or a tenner?"

"A tenner? In my dreams!"

"Did he say anything to you?"

"Not really. But I heard him speaking to his clerk, and he mentioned a trial and...something else." Joshua scratched his head.

"Attainder by verdict?"

"That was it."

"Bloody hell."

"Don't let Vi hear you talk like that. She once washed my mouth out with soap when I said blo—" He glanced around. "When I said that word."

"She may have a few choice words of her own when I tell her this news. It means I don't have the money I owe her. Not yet, at any rate."

"Make sure I'm somewhere else when you deliver that news," Joshua said. "Say, what are you doing out here? I thought you were supposed to be helping to clean."

King snorted. "I'm a marquess. I don't clean taverns."

Joshua shook his head.

"I don't know what the solicitor told you, but for a few more hours, I *am* a marquess. And there's nothing that little termagant can say or do to make me get on my knees and scrub floors."

"Is that so?" came a feminine voice from behind him.

King glared at Joshua. "You might have warned me," he muttered.

"I tried."

"I wondered where you'd disappeared," Miss Baker said as King turned around. "If you aren't working, I assume you can pay your debt?"

He scratched his head. "Not yet."

Her blue eyes slid to Joshua. "You delivered the correspondence?"

"I did, and I even brought a reply from his solicitor."

Miss Baker glanced at the letter King held. He quickly tucked it behind his back, but Joshua plucked it out of his hands and passed it over to her. "I beg your pardon," King argued. "That's private."

She merely turned her back on him and read the letter anyway. That gave him the chance to study her backside. It was nicely rounded. A moment later, she turned back, and he looked up at the sky as though he'd been doing that all along. "Your accounts have been frozen. Does that mean you cannot access your finances?"

"For the time being," he said. No need to panic her—or himself.

"What does your man of business mean by *your present situation*? Does this have something to do with the swarm of creditors at your house this morning?"

"My father, the duke, is in a spot of trouble," King said. That was certainly one way to describe being found guilty of treason.

"There's an attainder by verdict," her brother chimed in helpfully.

Miss Baker's eyes narrowed. "What's that?"

"Nothing good," King said.

"Don't you think it's time you explained exactly what you're hiding from?" she demanded. "Why are your creditors closing in? Why are your accounts frozen? I'm beginning to think whatever you've done will cause your friends to desert you as well."

"I haven't done anything."

She stared at him, those blue eyes beautiful and piercing.

"I give you my word as a gentleman."

She sighed. "I've known enough *gentlemen* in my life to be unimpressed."

King straightened and began to object.

"But I'll take it because I see the title of gentleman means something to you. But you cannot stay here. I assumed you'd have the seven pounds, fifteen shillings by now and be on your way."

"I'll have it soon," he said. "My friends will be here any moment." At least Carlisle would be here. His other friends might value their reputations more than their friendship, but King knew he could count on Carlisle. If only Rory was in England, he'd come to his aid as well. But Rory had been on the Continent since his wife's death earlier this year. King had no way to reach him in a timely fashion.

"If you don't have it yet, then you'd best earn your keep. The area behind the bar is still sticky with spilled spirits. Peggy could use your help." She looked about. "Where is Georgie? I thought he would be outside with you."

"He was. I gave him permission to play with his friend Danny."

"You *what*?" Both Joshua and Miss Baker practically yelled at him.

King took a step back. "Boys need time to play. He wanted to kick the ball."

"And what if Ferryman sees him? What if he decides to snatch him and charge me a ransom?"

"Who is Ferryman?" King asked.

"Never mind! This would never have happened if you'd stayed inside and worked as I'd asked. Joshua, go find your brother and bring him back. Hurry."

"I'll find him, Vi." Joshua put a hand on his sister's shoulder. "Don't worry." He took off running through the now waning afternoon sun.

King looked at Miss Baker and saw the way her shoulder stiffened as her brother disappeared into Seven Dials. He had the feeling he should be the one comforting her. Instead, he had caused her more distress. Carlisle couldn't come soon enough. He wanted out of this slum and away from Miss Baker and her family. He wanted clean clothing and something to eat.

"If I'm to be put to work," King said, following Miss Baker back to the door to the Silver Unicorn, "might you advance me a small sum so I may purchase something to eat?"

She gave him an incredulous look over her shoulder. "You want *me* to give *you* money?"

"I'll pay you back."

"That I'd like to see."

King clutched his belly and gave her a mournful look. "I'm starving. A man cannot survive on bread and water alone. I know you have a crown." He knew because he'd given it to her. "I'll buy food for our supper and bring you the change."

She shook her head. "I'll buy food for supper. You stay here and scrub, and if you don't do your part, you won't get anything for supper."

"That seems rather harsh."

She made a sound of dismissal and turned on her heel.

King stepped into the tavern and spotted the maid behind the bar. "I've been sentenced to hard labor," he told her. "What should I do?"

The maid giggled and stammered. Finally, she calmed enough to give him the mop while she went on her knees with the scrub brush. King mopped at the sticky floor, privately thinking it would never be clean, but he was hungry enough to do anything at this point.

The bell of a distant church chimed five, and the maid rose, dried her hands on her apron, and dropped her brush in the pail. "Well, I'm off, then," she said, peeking at him from under her lids.

"What do you mean, you're off?"

"I stop work at five. I go home and make supper for my ma. She's a healer and forgets to eat most days. She'll be hungry as a horse." She smiled and added, "Usually I come back at night to help Vi with the washing and cleaning, but she won't be open tonight."

King looked about the tavern. It was in better shape than it had been this morning, but it wasn't yet ready for patrons. "No doubt Miss Baker will blame me for the loss of business."

"She does have a bit of a temper, but if she was all soft and weak, she'd never have survived this long. Nor those brothers of her, neither."

"Why is she all alone?" he asked. "No husband? No father? Her brothers are too young to protect her."

"Joshua tries, but he's only thirteen, and little Georgie is barely six. Vi has to be mother and father to them since her pa passed away."

"When was that?"

Peggy scratched her head and drew her hand away, examining her finger to see if anything came with it. "Maybe three years ago? But he were sick longer than that. She's been running the Silver Unicorn for almost five years now. Least, that's what Archie told me."

King would have asked who Archie was, but he didn't know when Miss Baker would return, and he wanted more of her story before the maid left. "And her mother?"

"Oh, her mother died when she was a baby. I don't think she ever knew her."

"How is that possible, if she has two brothers?"

"Those are her stepmother's boys. She moved in with young Joshua and the baby when she married Mr. Baker. But it wasn't long before she took ill with cholera."

King leaned against the counter. So Violet Baker was not only on her own, she was caring for two boys who were not even technically related to her. She could read and write and do sums. She could have worked in a shop or applied to become a teacher. The pay might not have been much, but she might have escaped Seven Dials and had some measure of security. Instead, she was stuck here with the burden of two young boys tied about her neck.

And now he had added to that burden as well.

King shook his head. He'd offered to pay her for the damage to the tavern—even if he wasn't exactly responsible. And he'd mopped at least a foot of the floor. If anything, he was helping her.

"May I go, my lord?" the maid asked. "My ma will be very hungry."

"You're dismissed," he said, giving her a wave of his hand.

She scurried away, and King was tempted to put the mop down. He swished it about one more time then leaned on the bar. Underneath, Miss Baker had stacked the unbroken bottles of spirits. He found a half-full bottle of sherry and peered about for a glass. Finding one, he held it near a tallow candle, trying to determine if it was clean or not. Then, with a shrug, he uncorked the bottle.

"Pour me a glass too," said a voice from the doorway.

King looked up and spotted the figure of Carlisle in the entryway. He set the glass down and came around the bar. "Henry, thank God."

Henry raised his brows. "That's probably the first time anyone has thanked God for me. Things must be worse than I thought."

"Much worse. You heard about my father."

Henry, the Duke of Carlisle, strode into the tavern and looked down his nose at the place. "This seems vaguely familiar. But your father, yes. It's all over the papers. He's in the Tower, and everyone says he'll be hanged for treason. I'd offer you my condolences, but I know you hate the man."

"That doesn't mean I wanted him labeled a traitor. The old fool is taking me down as well."

Henry nodded. "Corruption by blood. If the attainder by verdict goes through, the duke will be barred from inheriting or transmitting property, and you will be barred from inheriting his property and his title."

"I have little doubt he won't be attainted. My solicitor informed me my accounts have been frozen, and I had a line of creditors at my door this morning."

"What brought you…here?"

"The taverness claims we started a riot last night and are financially responsible for the damage."

"Riot?" Henry waved a hand. "It was barely a brawl."

"That's what I said, but I offered to pay her so I could follow her here. I needed somewhere to hide from the tailors and haberdashers. But now that you're here, I can finally be free."

"About that—"

"If you don't want me at your house in Town, I'll go to one of your country estates. I should lie low for a few months. Until all of this blows over."

THE KING AND VI

"It's treason and corruption of the blood, King. I hardly think it will blow over."

"It's not as though *I* sold secrets to the French. I couldn't even tell you the last time I spoke to my father."

"And no one in the *ton* will care one way or another. You're a pariah."

"It will pass."

"No, it won't. This isn't like one of our school pranks, Kingston. Your father is to be executed. You are to be thrust out of Society. It won't pass."

King crossed his arms over his chest and gave his friend a long look. "What are you saying? You won't help me?"

Henry looked away. "Of course I'll help you."

"Then why won't you meet my eyes?"

Henry looked at him. "Because I can't do what you asked in your letter. I can't offer you shelter. That could reflect poorly on me. I consulted my lawyer—"

"Not a *lawyer*." King wanted to groan in frustration. If there was anything he hated, it was lawyers.

Henry shuffled, looking rather sheepish. "My debts are rather more numerous than I like to admit, and my lawyer thinks if I'm seen providing you succor, that might propel the gentlemen holding my vowels to demand payment."

King wanted to argue, but what could he say? Henry was right. King was tainted, and if Henry was seen associating with him, the taint could bring him down too.

"I just need to pay off my debts, and then I'll be able to help you."

"How long until you can do that?"

"A few good nights at the tables, and voilà!" Henry snapped his fingers.

King resisted the urge to pull out his hair and scream. Carlisle was in debt *because* of a few nights at the tables. Though he usually had good luck, the duke often lost enormous sums. King enjoyed the gambling tables himself, but he never bet more than a couple hundred pounds. If he lost, he walked away. Henry couldn't seem to walk away. He often continued playing even after he'd lost thousands.

King felt that awful sinking feeling in his belly again. He didn't want to think about it. Didn't want to consider his bleak future. "Isn't there *anything* you can do?"

"Of course. I brought your clothes."

King brightened at this. "You did?"

"You know my valet and Danby are good friends. My valet snatched up several items of your clothing before Danby could sell them to the pawnbrokers. I have them in the coach." Henry walked outside, and King followed.

He refrained from commenting on what he'd like to do to Danby. How dare the man sell his clothing?

As soon as the outriders saw the Duke of Carlisle, they jumped down and opened the door to the coach. By now, the presence of such a large and expensive conveyance had attracted a crowd, and several people called out to the duke. Henry ignored them and signaled to a footman, who leaned into the coach and emerged with a handful of garments. King recognized coats, breeches, shirts, and waistcoats. "Carry them inside the Silver Unicorn," King directed the footman. Another reached in and retrieved footwear. King gave him the same directive. "I don't suppose you managed to get a hold of any plate or silver?"

Henry shook his head. "I imagine the butler and footmen were selling that—if your creditors didn't take hold of it before they had a chance. I heard there was quite a scene after you left your townhouse. Danby said he almost lost his wig running for the back door."

King smiled despite his dire circumstances. He would have liked to see Danby fighting his way through the shop owners and debt collectors. "I don't suppose you can loan me some blunt," he said. It wasn't the first time he'd ever asked a friend to give him money, but it was the first time he actually needed the money. It was also the first time he had no way to pay it back.

"Of course," Henry said, reaching into his coat. He reached into one side then the other and finally produced a fiver. "All I have, I'm afraid. I'm making do on credit at the moment."

King understood this. He paid for almost everything on credit himself. If only he had seen his father's guilty verdict coming, he would have prepared and had a stash of pounds on hand. It was his own fault. He hadn't taken the charges seriously and preferred not to think about his father, rather than plan ahead.

King took the fiver just as Miss Baker and her brothers appeared at his side. "I'll take that," she said, snatching the note from his hand.

# CHAPTER SEVEN

VIOLET TUCKED THE fiver into her bodice before King could try to snatch it back. His expression was unmasked shock at her audacity, but it was only a moment before his mask fell back in place. She'd rather liked seeing him without his haughty, upper-class mask for a moment. He seemed like a real person rather than one of Cruikshank's caricatures of a marquess.

"Why are you two standing in the street exchanging blunt?" she demanded. "Do you want to be robbed of all your possessions?" She looked over her shoulder. "I see some of Ferryman's gang right over there. They're just waiting for an opportunity."

King met the other man's gaze. "Your Grace, may I present Miss Violet Baker and her brothers, Master Joshua Baker and Master George Baker." He looked at her. "Miss Baker, the Duke of Carlisle."

The duke gave her a bow. "Charmed, I'm sure."

"I remember you," she said. "You were less than charming when you started the riot last night."

The duke's brows went up. "I remember you now. You're the little blue-eyed vixen from the tavern."

King cleared his throat. "Miss Baker is the proprietress of the Silver Unicorn."

"It looks as though it's seen better days," the duke remarked.

"No thanks to you!" she retorted. "Have you come to take

him away?" She aimed her thumb at the marquess.

"Not just now," the duke said. He looked at his friend. "King, I leave you in very capable hands. Shall I write to you here if I have—er, news?"

"Yes, do. And, Henry, make it quick."

The duke hopped into his coach, and a moment later, his coachman was urging the horses through the crowded streets. Violet was already inside the tavern. "If you don't want the clothing stolen right off your back, you'd best come inside," she told King.

He seemed to wake from his reverie, looked about, and strode inside. She closed the tavern door and barred it. Spying the pile of clothing on the bar, she moved to examine it. "What's all this, then?"

"Nothing of your concern," King said, scooping it into his arms. "That five pounds you took was all I had. I'd like it back, please."

"This tavern is all I have. I'd like all the bottles and tables and chairs you broke back. Not to mention my publican."

The marquess glared at her.

"You realize that even with these five pounds, you still owe me two pounds—"

"Fifteen shillings. Yes, I know. I too can subtract."

"When will you pay me the rest?"

"Vi." Joshua took her arm and pulled her into a corner. "Look at the man." She glanced over her shoulder to look at King. He was leaning against the bar, clutching clothing to his chest. "He looks as though he's had a shock. He may need a day or two to come up with the blunt."

"You're on *his* side?"

"I'm not on anyone's side. I'm just saying, if you look past the money, you'll see something is wrong. He wouldn't be here if it weren't."

"If I look past the money?" Violet shook her head. "If I forget about the money, then we can forget about the tavern. And if we lose that, we're out on the street. I don't have to tell you what happens if we're forced to live on the street."

She could imagine it only too well. Joshua would be forced to join Ferryman's gang and Georgie would be put to work as a mudlark. She'd either have to leave them and find work at another shop or stay with them and become one of Ferryman's whores. Within a year, they'd all be either dead or wishing they were.

"One day won't put us out on the street. He can stay here tonight, and we'll figure out the rest tomorrow."

"No." She shook her head. "He cannot stay here tonight." She said the last loud enough that Georgie, who was standing near the marquess, heard her.

"But you can't make him leave, Vi," he protested. "Danny says if you show him your charms, he might become our new pa." Georgie looked up at the marquess. "Don't you want to be our new pa?"

"Ahhh." The marquess looked as though he wasn't sure how to answer.

"I'm not showing King any of my charms," Violet said.

"You have charms?" he asked, raising his brow.

She ignored him. "He will not be your new pa. He's not staying."

King finally looked as though he'd woken from a bad dream. Something about the charms comment had spurred him out of his stupor. "What if I work for my keep?" he asked. "I can repay you from my wages."

"You? Work?" She raised her brows. "Not possible."

"I can work," he said. "I mopped behind the bar."

Violet sniffed and marched across the tavern to peer behind the bar. It looked exactly the same as it had when she'd last seen it.

"That corner there," he said, pointing to a small area.

Violet looked at him. "That corner is clean?"

He nodded.

"Georgie, hop over and see."

Georgie hoisted himself onto the bar as he had a thousand times and hopped down on the square indicated. "Looks clean to me!" he announced.

Violet gave him a long look. "Pick up your feet," she said.

"Why?"

"Just do it, Georgie."

With a frown, he picked up one bare foot—or at least he tried. It stuck to the floor so that Georgie had to tug until it came free. "See, Vi! Clean!"

She looked at King. He scratched his head. "Maybe it was that corner." He indicated another small area. Georgie tried to move that way, but his feet kept sticking. Joshua took pity on him and lifted him out. "Very well. Mopping isn't my strong suit. But there are other things I can do."

Violet put her hands on her hips. "Name something else you can do." She put a hand up. "Besides drink, fight, and dance at fancy balls."

"He can act as publican," Joshua said before King could answer. "With Archie hurt, we need someone behind the bar. He's big enough to intimidate the troublemakers, and you just said he knows how to fight."

"I do know how to fight," King said, seizing on Joshua's words. "And I can be very intimidating."

Violet couldn't argue with this, even if she wanted to. King was an objectively tall and well-built man. That alone was intimidating, but he also had a presence about him. He had an air of authority that would discourage most men from crossing him. And Joshua was right. They were in need of a publican and protector with Archie injured.

King seemed the perfect solution, but she didn't want to agree. She didn't want him here. She didn't want him in her life or that of her brothers.

If she were brutally honest with herself, she didn't want him here because every time she was near him, her body seemed to thrum with awareness of him. She found herself stealing glances at him and her cheeks growing warm when he looked at her directly. "No," she said. "He goes. Even if it means we never recover the two pounds, fifteen shillings."

Joshua and Georgie stared at her open-mouthed. "*You're willing to give up two pounds?*" Joshua said. "Vi, are you feeling well?"

She scowled. "I don't like him. He's trouble."

"He's not trouble," Georgie said, hugging the marquess's leg.

"Yes, he is. Look, you're already getting attached to him."

King set the clothes down on the bar. "What are you really afraid of, Miss Baker? First you said I wasn't helpful. Then I was trouble. Then your brother is becoming attached to me. I think no matter what anyone says, you'll find an excuse."

Yes, she would. Because she did not want him here. She didn't know what she really was afraid of.

Well, yes, she did. She was afraid of him and of her body's reaction when he was close. Moreover, she was afraid *she* would become attached to him, need him, and she knew he would never stay. He'd disappear as soon as the opportunity arose. She could not afford to rely on anyone but herself.

But when she looked at her brothers, at the hope in their eyes, she couldn't be the one to dash that hope. She was always the one delivering bad news, the one telling them they couldn't have this or that. It was exhausting.

She closed her eyes. "I will certainly regret this," she said. "You can stay." The boys cheered, and she held up a hand to silence them. "Only until the two pounds, fifteen shillings is paid. And I'll take room and board out of your wages too."

"That means you'll be here a long time," Georgie told him. "It will take years to pay all that back."

"Not years," Violet said. "But a few weeks, at least." She couldn't trust him to stay here longer than that or trust herself not to do something stupid, like throw herself at him.

"I accept," King said. "That's the word of a gentleman. Once

I've given my word, I keep it."

Violet snorted. "If you say so."

He started for the back room. "Now, I'll just take these clothes upstairs and put them away."

"You're not sleeping upstairs," she said.

King paused and looked back at her. "You have another bed somewhere?"

"You can sleep in the back room. That way if anyone enters the tavern when we're sleeping, you'll hear and chase them away."

He narrowed his eyes then moved into the back room and looked about. "There's no bed in here."

"It's a good thing you have all those clothes, then. I'm sure the pile of them will be comfortable. Plus, there's a small stove we use for heating water and cooking. If you can find coal, you can use it to keep warm."

"Find coal? Am I to work in a mine? One buys coal."

"No money for that," she told him.

"You have five—"

"Now, excuse me while I purchase something for supper. I'll be back shortly. Bar the door behind me."

She grasped a basket on her way past the bar and walked quickly through the tavern, eager to be back before full dark fell. It was strange to have the Silver Unicorn quiet and dark at this time of the day. Now that she had King, she'd be able to open tomorrow. She'd use the blunt she had to purchase spirits, and the customers would have to stand until she could afford more tables and chairs.

She walked to the corner, keeping her head down, and her money in her fist in her pocket. A small but sharp dagger was strapped to her thigh just below where she'd tied on her pockets. Both were accessible through the slit in her skirts. At the corner, she spotted Charlie Apples. She supposed his name wasn't actually Charlie Apples, but everyone called him that because he sold apples.

SHANA GALEN

"Hullo, Charlie," she said. "Three apples, please." Then she remembered King. "Make that four," she said, grudgingly.

Charlie lowered the sack on his back and produced four small, bruised apples. "Here you are, Vi. Look at these beauties."

She gave him the coin and waited while he made change. Then she placed the apples in her basket and put the change in her pocket, inside her fist.

"Looks like the Silver Unicorn is closed tonight," he said.

"Archie didn't feel well," she said, aware passersby might be listening. "But I have a new publican until Archie feels better. We'll be open tomorrow."

"Who's the new man?" Charlie asked.

"No one you'd know," she said, and started away.

She had to travel further to find someone selling sausages, and by the time she was on the way back into Seven Dials, it was dark. She held her basket tightly, her wrapped sausages and four apples hidden away under a worn tea towel. She was nearing home when two men stepped out in front of her. She stepped back, sliding her hand out of her pocket and down against her leg.

"Out of my way," she said, pulling her dagger free of her skirts.

"Now that's not very nice," said a voice behind her.

Violet tensed. She recognized that voice. Adjusting course, she moved to put her back toward the building beside her and glanced over at Ferryman.

"It's not nice to have your boys scare me like that."

"Oh, I doubt very much you're scared, Vi. Nothing much scares you," Ferryman said, smiling. He had thin lips and large teeth yellowed from tobacco. He wore a black hat tipped back on his greasy brown hair, and his coat was a muted purple. His clothing looked expensive enough to belong to King, especially the ruby jewel glinting from his neckcloth.

He was wrong that nothing scared her. She had a long list of things that scared her, and he was at the top of that list. "What's this about?" she asked, lifting her chin. "I paid my taxes."

80

"That protected you last week. What about this week?"

"I have two more days left in my week. Unless weeks are only five days long now."

Ferryman inclined his head. "A little mouse told me you won't be able to pay in two days."

"I wouldn't believe what you hear from the mice. They like to squeak, but they can't be trusted."

"And you can? Be trusted?"

"I've always paid you before."

"Yes." He looked disappointed in that fact. Violet thought he probably was. If she didn't pay, he could take payment in other forms, and that was exactly what he hoped for. He reached out a hand gloved in black and touched the tip of her dagger with one finger. "There's a first time for everything."

"May I pass?" she asked.

"There's something else," Ferryman said, leaning close enough that she could smell the tobacco on his breath. "Another squeak from a little mouse."

"What's that?" Violet asked, trying not to breathe too deeply.

"One of my little mice told me your brother was at the Black Bear today."

"Joshua was with me all day. He had no reason to go to the Black Bear." No reason at all, but she would have a few words with him if she ever got back.

"I didn't say which brother," Ferryman said. "And yet you knew immediately who I meant."

Violet wanted to kick herself for making such a stupid mistake. "I assumed. But except for a game of kicking the ball, Georgie was with me as well."

"I advise you to keep them both close. I have little mice watching everywhere and quite a few rat traps ready to spring." He clapped, and Violet jumped. Ferryman stepped back. "Hurry home, Miss Baker," he said. "It's dark, and I can't spend all of my time protecting you."

He waved a hand, and his two boys stepped aside. Violet

forced her legs to move. She wanted to run. She could feel Ferryman's strange ice-blue eyes boring into her back, but she made herself walk quickly.

She rapped on the door to the Silver Unicorn. It seemed to take years as Ferryman and his gang moved slowly up the street, coming closer and closer. Finally, Joshua opened the door, and she shoved inside, pushed him aside, and slammed the bar down on the door again.

"What happened, Vi?" he asked.

The next moment, King was beside her, taking her basket. "You're white as snow. Sit down." He offered her a chair, but she waved it away and glared at Joshua.

"You."

"What did I do?"

"You went to the Black Bear again, didn't you?"

He shook his head, but she'd surprised him and saw the flicker in his eyes. "No."

"Don't lie to me. You know Ferryman has spies everywhere. Someone saw you and told him."

"I didn't go there!"

"What's the Black Bear?" King asked.

"Stay out of this," Violet told him.

"No chance," he said. "You come back looking like you've seen a ghost and then you start ranting about the Black Bear. I can't protect you if I don't know what's happening."

She glared at him. "You think you can protect me or anyone from Ferryman? You can't. He'll slit your throat and gut you like a fish."

She heard the sharply indrawn hiss of air, and her gaze fell on Georgie. His mouth was open, and his brown eyes were big and round.

"I'm sorry, Georgie. I didn't mean for you to hear that."

Georgie wiped his eyes, trying not to cry. "Ferryman wants to hurt our new pa?"

Violet closed her eyes, and though she'd refused the chair

King had brought her a moment before, she needed it now. She reached back, and he drew it behind her. Violet sank into it. Everyone was talking at once—Joshua lying about the Black Bear, Georgie crying about his pa, King saying he wasn't in any danger and to stop wailing.

"Silence!" she said, and the room fell quiet.

She looked at each of the males in turn—Joshua with the stubborn set to his jaw, Georgie with tears in his eyes, King with—Well, he was altogether too handsome. She'd do better not to look at him.

"Georgie, take this basket upstairs and set everything on the table. Wash your hands, and we'll be up for supper shortly."

Food was probably the only thing that could have distracted Georgie in that moment, and it worked. She handed him the basket, and he took it then raced past the bar and into the back. She waited until she heard his feet on the steps before she glanced at King. A quick glance.

"I'll talk to him about this idea he has of you being his pa. In the meantime, you can eat with us upstairs tonight. Go ahead."

King folded his arms across his chest. "I think I'd rather hear whatever you're about to say to Master Joshua."

"I didn't go to the Black Bear."

King let out a snort. "Here's a tip when you're lying and want to be believed. Don't talk so much. The more you claim you're innocent, the more guilty you seem. So out with it—why did you go to the Black Bear?"

"I know why he went," Violet said. "He went to see Lizzie."

King's brows went up. "This is about a girl? I'm assuming the Black Bear is a tavern. Does Lizzie work there?"

"She does," Violet said. "She's Ferryman's dell, or will be soon, and Joshua thinks he can save her."

"I *can* save her, Vi! At least I have to try."

"No, Joshua." She stood and took his face in her hands. He was almost as tall as she was now, but still lanky and thin. "You have to stay alive for your brother and me. I can't lose you, and if you try to cross Ferryman, he will kill you. Both of you. How is that helping Lizzie? If she's dead?"

"Your sister has a point," King said.

Violet looked at him with shock. She hadn't expected him to support her.

"You can't help this girl if you're dead. And you have a duty to your family first and foremost. What about your sister? If you run off with Lizzie or are killed, who will care for her?"

Violet opened her mouth to say that she didn't need anyone to care for her, especially not a thirteen-year-old boy, but she saw the look on Joshua's face. She closed her mouth again and let King keep talking. Not for the first time, she realized that now that Joshua was growing older, he didn't want her telling him what to do. But here was a man, a wealthy and powerful man, giving him advice. Joshua was clearly listening.

"I hadn't thought of that," he said. "But I..." He looked at Violet. "I care for Lizzie. I want to protect her too."

Violet knew Joshua thought Lizzie was a pretty girl, but she hadn't considered that he had feelings for her. She'd had soft feelings for boys when she'd been thirteen too. She'd imagined silly scenarios, where the boys asked her to marry them or revealed she was a long-lost princess they'd been searching for. Foolish childhood fantasies that she grew out of. She wanted to tell Joshua he would grow out of this foolishness for Lizzie too.

"I see," King said, nodding as though this was all very serious. "Then we should talk more about her and what can and cannot be done to help her."

"You'll help her?" Joshua asked.

"No," Violet said.

King raised a hand. "I don't know. I need more information, but if there's something I can do—*we* can do"—he looked at Violet—"I think we should consider it."

"Yes!" Joshua smiled broadly. Violet blinked. She hadn't seen him smile like that in so long. "Thank you." He surprised her again by embracing King before rushing out of the room, presumably to the flat upstairs. King looked surprised too. He straightened his coat and cleared his throat.

Violet crossed her arms. "And how exactly do you think you're going to help the girl one of the most powerful gang leaders in Seven Dials has laid claim to?"

"I don't know yet. I probably can't help her."

She pointed to the ceiling. "You have him thinking you can. What do you think he'll do when he realizes you're just smoke and mirrors?"

"Is that what you think of me?"

"Do you claim to be genuinely interested in helping Lizzie? To be genuinely interested in helping us? I know your type, my lord. The only person you want to help is yourself."

"I don't deny that," he said.

"That's a start."

"But it doesn't follow that helping myself and helping your brothers is mutually exclusive."

"It does when Ferryman will kill you if you so much as look at Lizzie. If you really want to help Joshua, then be honest with him. Tell him she's a lost cause."

"But young love, Miss Sunshine!" His voice dripped sarcasm when he used the name he'd given her. "That would break his heart."

"And while you're at it, tell Georgie you'll never be his pa either."

"And break *his* tender heart? I think you're better at that than I am."

She laughed and looked him up and down. "I'm sure you've broken your share of hearts, my lord. What's two more?"

"Maybe I'm done breaking hearts."

Violet turned and walked away. "That, I very much doubt." She was absolutely certain he'd end up breaking all three of theirs.

# CHAPTER EIGHT

S INCE MISS SUNSHINE, who was no ray of sunshine at all, had deigned to allow him to eat with her upstairs, King ducked his head and trudged upstairs. For the first time he thought of his father, a duke, sitting in the Tower while the lords debated stripping him and King of all his lands and titles. Were they passing the attainder by verdict at this very moment? He could just imagine the chatter at White's—his *former* club, as he would surely be stripped of membership if he hadn't been already. His so-called friends would be saying things like *oh, how the mighty have fallen* and *how the tables have turned*.

And they'd be right.

In a single day he had gone from a powerful peer with dozens of servants and hundreds of tenants to a man who couldn't even afford a loaf of bread. He'd lived in Mayfair, slept on the softest sheets, had his every whim catered to. Now, he would sleep on the floor of the back room of a tavern.

What had he done to deserve this?

*Stolen from the witch.*

He jerked his head up at the unwanted thought and smashed his forehead on the lintel. "Damn!" he cursed, putting a hand to his head and stumbling into the flat.

"Uh oh," said a little voice. "Vi doesn't allow that sort of language, Pa."

"Georgie," came a female voice. "Come here a moment."

Still holding his head, King stumbled to a chair at the table. In the corner, he could hear Violet telling Georgie that she knew he wanted a new father, but that King was not that man and would never be that man, and not to become attached. The description of him was entirely accurate, but for some reason it made King sad to think he'd never be the sort of man who could be a father to little Georgie. He was thirty years old. Old enough to be a father.

"The washbasin is over there," Joshua said. King's head was still throbbing violently, but he lowered his hands and looked at the screen the boy pointed to.

"I'll go wash my hands, then," he said. He rose, careful to hunch over so as not to hit his head again, and stepped behind the screen. He poured water into the basin and used the sliver of soap to wash his hands, then dried them on a rough cloth. When he turned to leave, Joshua was blocking his path.

"If you want coal for the stove and straw for the floor, wake up early tomorrow and I'll help you acquire it."

King narrowed his eyes. "Do you mean steal it?"

"Shh!" Joshua looked over his shoulder, but apparently his sister was still telling Georgie what an awful father King would make. "That's a last resort. We can pick up loose bits of coal that fall off the delivery wagons, but we have to go early."

"And the straw?"

"Oh, that's easy. We stop at a few shops and beg for the straw their shipments are packed in."

"I can't wait." Now King would have to resort to begging for straw and chasing after bits of coal fallen from wagons. It seemed every day brought a fresh hell.

"Come and eat," Miss Baker called, and King followed Joshua to the table where Georgie was already seated on the stool. Joshua took a chair, and that left nowhere for King to sit. Unless he was willing to take the chair Miss Baker might occupy, and he wasn't ready to stoop that low yet.

"I'll just stand, then," he said.

No one even looked at him. The boys were watching as their sister placed apples on their plates and then took two sausages and cut each in half. She handed King an apple and half a sausage, and he waited for her to produce more, but instead she sat and put her hands together. The boys lowered their heads too.

Apparently, they were praying over this food.

"My lord, would you like to say grace?" Miss Baker asked.

King looked at her. He wanted to ask God to give him more food, and something edible at that, but he kept that to himself. He'd dined with enough bishops to know what to say. "For these thy gifts we are about to receive, let us be truly thankful."

"Amen!" Georgie said, and bit into his apple.

Since he'd been given no fork or knife, King lifted the sausage and took a bite. It didn't taste like any sausage he'd ever had, but he didn't want to think about what that might mean.

"Do you think I might have a bath after supper?" he asked.

All three of them looked at him as though this was the most ridiculous request they'd ever heard.

"Why would you want a bath?" Georgie asked, wrinkling his nose. "Vi makes me wash once a week, and it's the worst."

"Shh," Miss Baker said. "My lord, I'm afraid we don't have a bathtub. We usually pull water from the common well down the street and wash with that."

"I suppose that will have to do," King said, biting into his apple. "Heat up the water after supper, and I'll wash downstairs."

Joshua gave him a look of warning, and King shook his head as though to say, *What is it now?*

"I think there's been a misunderstanding, King," Miss Baker said, voice icy. "I don't work for you. *You* work for me. That means I don't fetch water or heat it for you."

King sighed. "Fine. I'll do it myself."

"Not with my coal, you won't. If you want warm water, buy your own coal. You'll have to fetch your own water, too."

"There's an entire bucket behind the screen," King protested.

"I saw it a moment ago when I washed my hands."

"Joshua fetched that this morning for our use."

"He can use it, Vi," Joshua said. "We'll draw more tomorrow. Then I can show him where the well is. He'll never find it tonight and probably get his throat slit if he goes walking about."

"We wouldn't want that," the termagant said. She really did not give any quarter. King was either beginning to hate her or admire the hell out of her.

"I'll just take the bucket with me when I go downstairs, then," he said, and took another bite of his apple.

Miss Baker met his gaze and held it, her blue eyes full of ice. He'd always thought he liked sweet, biddable females, but he was finding himself rather more attracted to Miss Baker than he expected. Something about her spirit, her backbone, her sheer grit, made him want to inflame her further. And when her cheeks were pink and her eyes sparking with anger, he started thinking about kissing her.

King bit his apple again.

"Did your pa really name you *King*?" Georgie asked.

King slid his gaze away from Miss Baker. "No. That's a shortened version of my title." Possibly his former title at this moment. "I am"—*was?*—"the Marquess of Kingston. I have other titles, but as that is the highest ranking one, my friends called me Kingston, and then just King."

"Like we call Violet *Vi*."

"Exactly."

"Your Christian name is Markiss?" Georgie asked.

"No, that's part of my title. My Christian name is the same as yours. My full name is George Oxley, Marquess of Kingston."

Georgie dropped the apple core he was gnawing on. "Your name is George too?"

"It is."

"Vi, did you hear that? We have the same name!"

"I heard," she said. Smiling, she ruffled her little brother's hair. She was so pretty when she smiled. King wished she'd do it more often. Maybe he liked the look of her smiling even more than angry. That meant it was better if she didn't smile. He'd rather think of her as a termagant than a pretty young woman, especially when she got that hazy look in her eyes and her mouth softened. King could imagine, in quite a bit of detail, kissing those lips.

"I'll go downstairs to bed now," he said abruptly. It was probably no later than eight o'clock, but what else did he have to do? Anything was better than standing here and fantasizing about kissing Violet Baker. She'd probably bite his lips if he tried. King thought he might not mind that—

"The water," he said, turning his back on them and moving behind the screen. Once shielded, he took a moment to breathe and tell his cock to behave, then he lifted the bucket and carried it out of the flat, down the stairs, and into the tavern's back room.

It felt colder than it had earlier. Perhaps because it was now empty. The stove upstairs hadn't been lit, but with four people, it was warmer. Dare he say it—almost cozy?

But he wouldn't think about Miss Baker and her cozy flat. He'd wash and lie down and sleep. God knew he was exhausted enough to sleep for a week.

A tallow candle sat on a table well away from the casks of ale, and he used the tinder box to light the wick, giving him enough light to survey the room. Miss Baker had suggested he sleep in the space under the counter. The stove was at one end of that space, and if he'd had coal, he might have been reasonably warm. The wall on the other side was stacked high with casks, the row of them only broken by the stairwell leading to the flat. At the far end of the room were shelves of glasses and mugs, and beside them a door leading to the yard behind the tavern, which was really just a square of dirt between the tavern and another building.

Well, he had slept in worse places. Of course, he'd usually been drunk and only half-conscious, but he supposed he would survive this. He looked about the room again. He had little choice but to survive it.

Weary to his bones, King removed his boots and stockings then stripped off his coat, neckcloth, waistcoat, and shirt. He'd dropped all on the ground but remembered he didn't have a valet, and stooped to pick them up and fold them neatly. He placed the clothes on the floor to use as a pillow. Look at him! Surviving already.

Bare-chested, he looked about for a basin to pour water from the bucket into but found nothing of use. He didn't have a cloth or soap either. He'd acquire those tomorrow, he told himself, and dipped a hand in the cool water. He splashed the water over his face and shivered when the icy droplets landed on his bare shoulders. He'd acquire coal tomorrow as well. What he wouldn't give for a steaming bath right now.

Using his wet hands, he scrubbed his face, feeling the stubble of the day's growth of beard. He supposed he needed a razor, and shaving soap too, or he'd soon look unrecognizable. On the other hand, perhaps that was preferable. He slid his fingers through his hair, slicking it back, then dipped them into the water again and repeated the gesture. He was feeling better already.

He repeated this several times, shivering when the water splashed on his back or shoulders, until finally he had to grit his jaw and splash his chest. Holy hell that was cold. He scrubbed and dipped again. He was cold and covered in gooseflesh now, but the worst was yet to come. He reached for the fall of his breeches. He'd do this quickly and put on clean clothes. But just as he slid the material over his hips, he heard a gasp from behind him.

King glanced over his shoulder, expecting to see Joshua or Georgie, but his brows rose when his eyes met Miss Baker's wide blue ones. She'd obviously been in the act of walking down the steep stairs, one hand on the wall for balance and the other holding a basin. But now she stood, statue-still and slack-jawed, staring at him. King felt a tingle skitter up his back at the look in her eyes. He knew that look, and knew what it meant as well. She might treat him with cold disdain in public, but privately, she desired him as much as he did her. Her cheeks turned a rosy shade of pink as she realized she was staring at him and he back at her.

"I—" She held out the basin and stepped down, almost losing her footing.

King moved quickly to grasp her arm to steady her. Her skin was warm beneath his cold hand, and surprisingly soft.

"Thank you," she said, her gaze dipping to his waist, where he held his breeches just high enough to protect her modesty. She thrust the basin at him. "I thought you might need this."

King released her arm and took the basin, which contained a strip of linen and a sliver of soap. "That's surprisingly thoughtful of you," he said.

Her blue eyes went flinty, and he was sorry he'd spoken. The look of arousal in them was gone in a snap. "Goodnight, my lord."

He didn't want her to go. He wanted to see that look of desire in her eyes again. "You needn't rush off," he said. "You can stay and watch." He raised a brow in invitation.

Her mouth parted then closed.

"You're a grown woman. It must get cold and lonely in that bed of yours. Don't you ever want company?" Twelve hours ago, King had barely known this woman existed, but now he wanted nothing more than to be the man in her bed.

Her gaze flicked to his chest again, then she drew in a breath and fixed her gaze on his face. "I don't want company, no. Especially not *your* company."

She was lying. He could see it in her eyes. "I think you'd enjoy my company. I think you're blushing because you *know* you'd enjoy it."

"Goodnight, my lord," she said again, this time giving him her back.

"I'll be here if you need me," he said, his hope beginning to fade.

"I won't," she said, opening the door at the top of the stairs and then closing it behind her. King heard the bolt slide home and smiled. Was she locking him out or herself in?

Maybe he wasn't doomed to sleep on the floor for the next few weeks after all. Maybe he could persuade Violet Baker to share her bed. He certainly wouldn't mind seeing those lips that scolded him all day soften and beg him for more at night. He'd give her more, right after he stripped off her ugly dress and put his hands on the warm, soft flesh beneath it.

King shifted uncomfortably and blew out a breath. Maybe one night, but not this one. With jaw clenched, he finished washing with the cold water, trying to feel grateful for the soap and the rough cloth.

When he was as clean as possible in this place, he dressed in unsoiled clothing, crawled under the counter, and tried to get comfortable on the hard wooden floor. Though he hated to wrinkle his coats, he finally gave in and laid a few on the floor then dropped his greatcoat over himself as a blanket. Thank God for Henry having retrieved his clothing. King offered up a prayer that his friend was winning at the tables right now.

But Henry couldn't save him from a witch's curse. King fisted his hands. Why the devil was he thinking about that witch? He'd been drunk and half-asleep the night before. She was nothing more than a figment of his imagination. But why think about her after all these years, and why imagine her ranting about a curse?

Was that his problem? *Was* he cursed?

King threw an arm over his head. Ridiculous. A curse didn't make his father sell secrets to the French. He was being punished for his father's sins, not his own. Not for stealing that cask of whiskey and dropping it so it spilled upon the ground.

There had been many times in the seventeen years since he, Henry, and Rory had pulled that prank that King had wished he had not gone along. He'd been the leader of their trio and all the underlings at St. Andrew's Preparatory for Boys. He could have suggested another prank. He could have simply said no. He and his friends had engineered many pranks in their lives, but King only regretted a handful. Stealing the Scottish witch's cask of whiskey was one of them—not because he believed in curses. He didn't. But because she and her sister had been poor, and that whiskey was valuable to them. When the prank had gone wrong and the cask broke, they'd probably watched the liquid flow away and saw their food, kindling, and means of survival washed away.

He hadn't thought that way when he was thirteen. He rarely thought that way as a man, but since he'd reached adulthood, he'd seen his share of beggars and unfortunates thrown on the street. He pitied them, and he was sorry that he had been the reason the witch might have suffered.

Not that being sorry would change anything. He had lost everything. He was suffering and would suffer more.

Maybe before Miss Sunshine kicked him out, he could help her and her brothers. He knew how he wanted to help Violet specifically, but perhaps he could also protect her and her brothers from this Ferryman and make sure they had the means to stay afloat.

King rolled over, and his back gave a twinge of complaint.

What was the matter with him? Had hunger and poverty warped his mind? He didn't usually want to help people. He might feel sorry for a beggar, but he never gave them any coins. He'd stick his neck out for Henry and Rory, but that was it. Why should he help Violet?

No answer came to him. There was no reason he should help her...except that he wanted to.

It was lust, he decided. Hunger, cold, and lust were working together to turn him into some sort of philanthropist. The word was like a curse in his mouth.

Considering his present circumstances, the word was also not one he was likely to claim. He had to think of himself. He was only here until Henry returned with some blunt. Then he'd walk away and never have to think about hard floors, empty bellies, and Miss Baker's blue eyes.

No. He pulled his thoughts away from her eyes. *Think about yourself.* That was what he was best at. No point in changing now.

# CHAPTER NINE

V IOLET WOKE IN the morning when she heard Joshua moving
about. He tried to be quiet, but she'd learned that young
boys were about as quiet as a drove of pigs. She knew it was
Joshua because Georgie was not an early riser. He'd lie abed half
the day if permitted. She and Joshua often teased him, saying he
should have been born a lord, since he liked to keep the same
hours as the rich and titled.

The Marquess of Kingston was most certainly still sleeping. It
was his fault she'd had a restless night. She should have sent
Joshua down with the washbasin last night, but she hadn't
thought that King would be half-naked already. And then when
she'd seen him—well, she hadn't been able to think at all. She'd
seen plenty of naked males, mostly her little brothers, but a few
adults as well. She was generally unimpressed by the species.

But she had never seen a man who looked like King. The way
the muscles of his back had rippled when he turned to look at her!
His shoulders had been so broad and his waist so narrow. His
breeches had dipped down, giving her the most tantalizing
glimpse of his firm bottom. She'd tried not to look at him below
the waist, but dear God, even his bare arms had tempted her.
How did he have arms that looked like that? She thought the
upper classes lounged about all day eating candied violets.

And then when he'd touched her, she'd had to use all her

willpower not to wrap her arms around him and feel that powerful chest against her own. His hands had been cold, but she thought she could warm them up quickly enough.

Of course, he'd had to ruin everything by opening his mouth. As soon as he'd spoken, the spell was broken. Well, not completely. She was almost ashamed to admit she'd considered his suggestion to join her in bed. But she'd only entertained it for a split second. The last thing she wanted was an arrogant, entitled lord in her bed. Not only did she not want to risk pregnancy, being with King in that way would send the wrong message to Joshua and Georgie. King was not staying, and she wouldn't pretend otherwise. Besides, he'd probably behave in bed exactly as he did outside of it and think only of himself.

Violet sat up and opened her door, peering out. "Joshua!" she whispered.

He peered around the clothes on the line a moment later. "Did I wake you?"

"Where are you going?"

"I told King we'd gather coal this morning, maybe some straw too."

"Don't steal anything, no thimblerig, and be back by noon." He made a face at her, but she ignored his disappointment. "I thought I'd ask Mrs. Littman if we can borrow an extra table and chairs. I'll need your help to carry them over."

"I wanted to visit Mrs. Archie and see if Mr. Archie is improved."

She'd wanted to do that as well. "We'll go together after we move the table and chairs. It will have to be a short visit, as we must open tonight, even if our patrons sit on the floor." She would take Georgie this morning and buy spirits and what furniture she could afford with the money she had from King. Peggy could finish mopping behind the bar, and with any luck, people would hear about the new publican at the Silver Unicorn and stop in. She'd make enough tonight and tomorrow to pay Ferryman his taxes.

If not…well, she wouldn't think of that.

"I'll see you at noon, Vi," Joshua said, ducking out of sight.

"Be careful! And, er, Joshua?"

His head appeared from behind a sheet again.

"I love you."

His face brightened at the unexpected words. "I love you too, Vi."

She listened as he opened the door and took the stairs to the back room. She heard him speaking softly to King, and King's deep voice in reply. It sounded as though the marquess was none too happy at having been woken at such an early hour. For some reason, thinking of him grumpy made her smile.

She lay in bed a little longer, listening as Joshua cajoled the marquess up and out of bed. Strange and oddly comforting to hear his deep baritone voice drifting upstairs. It had been years since she'd lived with a man—since her father died—but she hadn't forgotten what it felt like to be taken care of, to know that if there were a crisis, she would not have to face it alone. King's deep voice reminded her of that time.

She pushed out of bed and pushed the memories away too. No point in dwelling on the past. She had too much to do in the present. She washed and donned her second-best dress—of two—then pinned her hair up and out of her face and pulled a cap over it. Taking her apron from its hook, she tied that on and tiptoed downstairs, leaving Georgie sleeping.

The back room was in disarray with King's fine clothing strewn about, water on the floor, and her basin tipped over. She straightened everything then opened the back door and found two full pails of water waiting for her. Violet smiled. Joshua must have shown their guest where the well was and brought the pails back.

She carried one upstairs and set it inside the flat, then took the other to begin mopping behind the bar. By the time Peggy showed up with another pail of water, Violet had made good progress. The two finished cleaning then moved the still-intact

SHANA GALEN

tables and chairs back into place. She'd had eight tables, and five were too badly damaged to use. She and Peggy moved those to the back room, as well as the chairs that were broken. Violet then sought out a carpenter, persuaded him to come back to the tavern, and asked him to repair what he could and chop the rest into kindling.

She also hired him to make her a new table and set of chairs, though she didn't yet know how she would pay for it.

She went out again and used the last of her coin to buy several bottles of gin, one of brandy, one of sherry, and one of whiskey. These were sold by a member of Ferryman's gang, which Violet found unforgiveable. Not only did she have to pay Ferryman taxes, she lined his pocket by being forced to buy spirits from his men.

When she returned to the tavern, she and Peggy set up the bar, rolling out casks of wine and ale and placing the spirits safely away from reaching hands of patrons.

Peggy went out to draw more water from the well so they could have water for tea and coffee, and Violet went back to check on the carpenter. He'd chopped up a couple of chairs, repaired others as well as a table, and told her he would come back the next day with the tools and materials he needed to repair the other furnishings, in so much as it was possible. He'd done all he could with what he had.

He left, and Violet muttered, "That's why I didn't pay you in advance."

She could hear Georgie's footsteps in the flat. He was awake and probably playing. She'd go up and see him after she carried the repaired chairs into the tavern. She lifted the first and hauled it through the door. She set it down to survey the area and determine where to place it, then let out a squeal of fright.

An old woman with long white hair, almost to her knees, stood in the center of the tavern. She was thin and bony, dressed in clothing that might have once been colorful but had now been washed so much it was devoid of color. Her dress swept the floor, the tattered hem floating when she turned to look at Violet.

Violet glanced at the tavern door. She'd barred it when Peggy left, and she'd been in the back room. The bar was still on the door, and no one had come in through the back. "How did you get in here?"

The woman's green eyes crinkled as she smiled, showing a full set of teeth inside her thin, cracked lips. "Are ye the owner of this establishment?" she asked, her accent heavily Scottish.

"I am. I'm Violet Baker. Who are you?"

"Miss Baker," the woman said, moving closer to Violet. She had the urge to shrink away but gripped the back of the chair. This woman was no threat to her. Violet could knock her over with a puff of breath. "I am a friend of Lord Kingston."

Violet's eyes widened.

"Ye have been kind tae him."

Violet wouldn't have put it that way. "He owes me money."

"I believe it," the old woman said. Violet wondered how old she was—seventy? Eighty? Older? "The lad has heavy debts, and ye're nae the only one he owes."

"I can't say I'm surprised. I suppose you've come to collect what he owes you?" Violet didn't wait for a reply. "Unfortunately, his luck has taken a turn for the worse, and he is without funds right now. He's working to pay what he owes me."

"Oh, I imagine the lad's luck has turned. That's why I'm here."

Violet frowned, her gaze flicking to the barred door again. How had this woman gained entrance? "You've come to help him?"

"Mayhap. Would ye be so kind as tae give him this for me?" The woman held out a bony hand with what looked like an ancient scrap of paper between two gnarled fingers. Violet did not want to move closer to the old woman, but she swallowed and stepped forward, taking the paper. It was dry and felt almost brittle. Hastily, she tucked it in her apron pocket.

"I'll give it to him. Is there anything else I can do for you?

Would you like a drink?"

"Oh, nae. That's verra kind of ye, lass. I'll come back another time when Kingston is here. He owes me a whiskey." The old woman started for the door, and Violet hurried ahead of her, pushing the heavy bar back and opening the door. The day was foggy and gray, but warmer than the spring had been of late.

"Good day, then, er—" Violet realized she still hadn't been given the woman's name. "I'm so sorry. What was your name again?"

But the woman only waved distractedly and stepped into the fog, soon disappearing into the gray shroud.

Violet blew out a shaky breath. "That was odd."

"What was odd?" came a small voice behind her. She turned to see Georgie, dressed and looking at her expectantly.

"And good morning to you," she said, ruffling his hair. "I imagine you are hungry."

"Starving, Vi."

She patted her pockets and realized she had nothing left to purchase anything to eat. She'd figure something out. "We'll eat soon."

"Where's Joshua and Pa—I mean, King?"

Violet gave him a sidelong look. "They went out early this morning. I imagine they will be back shortly. Here—help me with this chair and the table in the back."

Just as they had the public room arranged as best as they could, Violet heard the back door open. "Peggy?" she called.

"It's Joshua, Vi! We have coal and straw and bread."

"Bread!" Georgie squealed, and ran back to greet them.

Violet sat down at one of the tables and tried to tidy her hair. Then she realized what she was doing and made herself stop. The door opened again, and she expected to see Georgie, but King walked through. He wore tight buff breeches and a dark blue coat with a blue waistcoat and limp neckcloth. His coat and breeches were dusted with coal, and he had bits of straw in his dark hair—and yet he looked every inch the gentleman. And a breathtaking one at that.

Violet swallowed, ignoring the flutters in her belly. She was hungry. That was why her belly flipped when she saw him.

"That was the worst day of my life," he said, taking a seat beside her. "Well, the second worst. Do you know what I had to do?"

Violet bit her lip to keep from smiling. "Gather coal?"

"We chased after delivery carts and picked coal up from the ground. Tiny pieces." He showed her with his finger and thumb, which, she couldn't help but notice, were blackened. "And there were others doing this as well. I had to fight them off for a piece of coal the size of my thumbnail!"

"You fought women and children for coal?"

"No!" Joshua said, coming through the door to the back room with Georgie right behind him. Georgie held a piece of bread and was chewing. "We would have been back sooner, but he kept giving coal to women and children." Joshua sent a withering look at King.

"I didn't give it to them."

"*I didn't see that piece, Master Joshua,*" Joshua said, mimicking King's upper-class accent.

"Am I supposed to grab the coal from under their fingertips?" King demanded. "It's unseemly."

"See how unseemly it feels when you're shivering again tonight," Violet said.

"Luckily, he had *me* there with him," Joshua said. "I managed to gather almost a half bucket."

"Impressive," she said, ruffling his hair as he sat on her other side. She glanced at King. "It looks as though you also gathered straw for bedding," she said, nodding to his head.

He reached up and pulled straw out of his hair, cursing under his breath. "I don't even want to discuss it," he said. "Too demeaning."

Joshua rolled his eyes. Violet didn't need to ask. She knew he asked shopkeepers for packing straw. If he had no luck there, he went to the mews behind some of the finer houses and begged for handfuls of straw the grooms cleaned out of the horses' stalls. Most of it was still reasonably clean.

"How did you manage the bread?" Violet asked, taking a piece when Joshua offered it. King shook his head, but Joshua ignored him.

"He sold two buttons for it."

"What?" Violet's gaze flew to King's coat, and she noticed that two gold buttons were missing.

King's hand moved to cover the area. "Desperate times and all that," he muttered.

"You could sell the rest of your clothing for blunt," she told him. "I imagine you'd make enough to pay me back."

"Madam!" He looked affronted. "I would hope I'd make enough to pay you back twenty times over."

"Not with the pawnbrokers in Seven Dials," Joshua said. "There's still time before we open. Can we go see Archie?"

Violet rose. "Yes, let's visit him, then it will be time to open for the evening."

KING FOLLOWED MISS Baker and her two charges through the narrow alleys and winding streets of Seven Dials. It seemed every doorstep was full of barefoot children dressed in rags. He passed more women with infants strapped to their chest, reaching out for coin he didn't have.

This was not the Seven Dials he was used to. He had always come after dark and kept to the main thoroughfares. There he was used to seeing prostitutes and flashy pimps, as well as vendors hawking their wares or tavern owners calling for patrons to step inside and have a pint. He'd never seen the starving women, the bony dogs, or the masses of homeless children before. Or maybe he just hadn't wanted to see.

They finally arrived at a building that looked as though it should be condemned. He started toward the door, but Miss Baker indicated that they should go down the steps to the door on the ground floor. King hesitated, not certain he wanted to go down into that gloom, but the boys had already gone ahead, so he followed Miss Baker down.

King ducked to enter the dark room and stood still for a moment until his eyes adjusted.

"Rose," Miss Baker was saying, "I'm so sorry I didn't come sooner."

"Never ye mind," said a woman with a strong lower-class accent. "Ye've come now, and I'm grateful to ye. Joshua 'as been 'ere, and it's always a pleasure to see Georgie."

King looked about the room. It was dark and cramped. On the opposite wall was a bed, low and close to the floor. A man lay there, arms folded on the sheets, and his head wrapped in a bandage. A table was in another corner with a chair. A few rags lay scattered about on the floor. One had a face painted on it, so he assumed it was a doll of some sort. He didn't see any children other than the Baker boys. But there was a blanket nailed across what might have been a doorway to another room.

The woman who looked at him now had red hair and pink cheeks. She was young, probably not even eighteen, but she had the look of someone much older. It was the eyes, King decided. They were brown and hard and weary.

"This is…King," Miss Baker said, indicating him. "He'll be working as publican until Archie recovers. King, this is Rose Garrett, Archie's wife."

King inclined his head. He hadn't asked questions about this excursion, hadn't asked who Archie was, but now he understood the man in the bed had been the publican at the Silver Unicorn.

"Mrs. Garrett, I wish we could meet under better circumstances," King said. He knew he looked and sounded out of place here, but if he'd needed any further confirmation of that, Rose shot a look at Miss Baker, who gave her a tight smile.

"What happened to him?" he asked, moving closer. The man looked familiar. He was a big man, almost too big for the bed. He had a broad chest and thick arms. His breathing was slow and steady, but his eyes were closed.

"Has he opened his eyes yet?" Joshua asked.

"Open your eyes, Archie!" Georgie said, shaking the publican.

"Georgie, Meg and Jenny are in the back playing. Why don't you join them?" Miss Baker said.

Georgie made a face. "I don't want to play with girls."

"Georgie, go back and say hello at least."

He crossed his arms over his chest and thrust out his chin at his sister. "I want to stay with Archie."

"Don't argue with your sister," King said.

Georgie's arms dropped, and he bowed his head. "Yes, sir." A moment later he disappeared behind the blanket.

King moved closer to the bed then looked about, aware the room was too silent. Miss Baker and Joshua were both staring at him with mouths open.

"What's wrong?" he asked.

Miss Baker shook her head and closed her mouth. "Not a thing. I've just never seen Georgie agree to anything so quickly."

"Or say *sir*," Joshua said.

"How was Mr. Garrett injured?" King asked.

"'E was 'it in the 'ead at a brawl at the tavern," Mrs. Garrett said. "Some young scamps caused a riot, and I don't know for sure, but I think one of them 'it 'im with a bottle."

King's gaze flew to Archie again. No wonder the man looked familiar. He'd been the publican at the Silver Unicorn that night. King felt his cheeks heat as he remembered trying to order champagne from the man. *Idiot*, he thought, looking back on his behavior that night. He'd thought he was the funniest man in the world, and all this man was doing was trying to support his wife and two children.

"Has he seen a doctor?" he asked.

Mrs. Garrett snorted. "Ye must not be from 'ere. Even if a

doctor would come 'ere, I 'aven't any coin."

"Mamma?" came a small voice. King glanced at the hanging blanket and saw a red-haired girl looking out. She was smaller than Georgie and had large brown eyes like her mother.

"Polly, go play now."

"'Ungry, Mamma."

"I'll make you something soon. Here is Susan." Mrs. Garrett picked up the rag with the painted face from the floor. "Play with her."

King didn't like the feeling churning in his belly. He didn't like the way his chest clenched or his throat closed up. Thousands of children made do with rags for toys. Men were injured all the time. King had always told himself there was nothing he could do. Even if he helped one beggar or orphan, there were a thousand right behind that one with a hand out.

But he felt somewhat responsible for this situation. He and his friends had been enjoying themselves, but they'd also been very drunk, and King had been spoiling for a fight. He'd needed some way to release the tension building since his father was accused of treason. What if he had started the brawl? What if he had thrown a bottle? Even if his bottle hadn't hit this man, someone else might have taken a cue from him and thrown another bottle.

King clenched his fists. Was Miss Sunshine right all along that he owed her for the damage to the tavern?

He could acknowledge now that perhaps she was, but his situation wasn't what it had been that night he'd visited her tavern. Truth be told, now his situation was far worse than hers.

And yet he couldn't leave that little girl to go hungry, because it was patently obvious that Mrs. Garrett had no food nor coin.

"I wanted to give you this," Miss Baker said, holding out a small piece of cloth tied with a knot on top. King heard the coins clink inside.

"I can't take that from ye," Miss Garrett argued.

"Yes, you can. It's not nearly enough considering what a good

SHANA GALEN

friend Archie has been. I'll try to bring more."

Mrs. Garrett looked like she might refuse again, and King said, "Take it." Then he did something he couldn't explain, something he told himself not to do. But his body seemed to be working independently of his mind, and he was powerless to stop himself from removing his coat. "Take this too."

"Oh, no, sir. I can't take yer fine coat. It wouldn't fit my Archie anyway."

No, it wouldn't. He could put the coat back on now.

But instead, King watched as his arm reached out, and he took the woman's hand and pressed the coat into it. "Sell it. It's worth a pound or two, at least."

The woman was shaking her head, but she didn't release the coat.

"And I'll send Joshua to fetch a surgeon I know. He's stitched me up a few times, and he owes me a favor."

"Thank ye, sir."

"Not sir. Call me King. Excuse me." He turned and fled the room. He needed fresh air and sunlight and space. Not to mention, if he stayed much longer, he might take off his waistcoat or his boots.

Neither fresh air nor sunlight awaited him outside. The air was stagnant with the scent of coal and cooking onions. The fog had lifted somewhat, but the day was still gray and dreary. Joshua stepped out a moment later and stood beside him.

"What do you want?" King said, tone surly.

Joshua shook his head. "You said you wanted me to fetch the surgeon."

"Right."

"That was a nice—"

King held up a hand. "Don't say it. I'm not nice. I don't do nice things."

"Understood." Joshua nodded. "Where do I go to find the surgeon?"

"I'll tell you, but first, we need to have a chat." King looked at

Joshua. "About Lizzie."

Joshua's eyes went blank just a moment too late.

"Don't pretend you weren't thinking of taking this opportunity to go see her. I was a boy of—How old are you?"

"Thirteen."

"I was thirteen once. I spent an inordinate amount of time thinking about girls."

"Lizzie isn't just any girl."

"No, she's the one the gang leader, Ferryman, has his eye on. I know you want to help her, but right now, you need to keep your brother and sister safe. Making this gang leader angry will put them in danger."

"You're one to talk. You're the reason Archie is hurt, and our tavern was all but destroyed."

King hadn't expected that response, and he'd certainly never expected a thirteen-year-old boy to speak to him in that tone of voice. He glared at the lad, but Joshua just glared back, all but daring him to do something.

"If you are so worried about my family, you shouldn't have put us in the position of not being able to pay Ferryman."

King's anger at Joshua's tone faded. "What's this, then?"

"You think you know so much, but you don't know anything."

"Tell me, then."

"We have to pay taxes to Ferryman. Everyone in his territory pays him taxes, and if we don't, he levies a fine."

"What sort of fine?"

Joshua shrugged. "Depends on the business. I've seen him burn them down or come in and allow his boys to take whatever they want. Sometimes he beats the owner bloody. If it's a woman…" He trailed off.

King clenched his hands. "Has he ever touched your sister?"

"No, but he'd like to. He'd like to get his hands on me and Georgie too. Bring us into his gang. Vi has been late paying the government her taxes before, but she always pays Ferryman on time."

"So he's a bully," King said. He knew something about bullies, having been one himself. He looked back at Joshua. "Let me tell you something about bullies—they inspire loyalty out of fear. There's no question in my mind if this Ferryman catches you with Lizzie, he will hurt you or even kill you. It scares anyone else who might challenge his authority."

"I don't want to challenge his authority," Joshua said. "I just want to help Lizzie. You know what's coming for her. She's my friend. I have to help her."

King blew out a breath. Joshua was looking up at him with wide, pleading eyes as though King could help him, as though he was some sort of savior who could stop a gang leader and save a young girl's innocence. He wanted to tell Joshua he had it all wrong. King couldn't even help himself, much less this Lizzie.

But how was he supposed to say that when Joshua was looking at him with those eyes?

"I can't promise anything," King said. Joshua smiled and grabbed his hand. King shook him off. "I said I can't promise, but I'll try to find a way to help."

"Thank you!"

"Don't thank me." King gave him the directions to find the surgeon then leaned on the building again, waiting for Miss Baker to finish. He would have liked to go back to the tavern, but he didn't think he could find the way on his own.

"I'll be back as soon as I can," Joshua said, moving away. "And King? Thank you!"

"Don't thank me," King said again. "I haven't done anything yet."

"But you will," Joshua said. "I just know it."

King watched Joshua run off then dropped his head in his hands. He had to get out of here before he turned into one of those do-gooders. Where the devil was Henry?

# CHAPTER TEN

Violet didn't trust King. He was unpredictable, and she didn't trust people she couldn't predict. One moment he was arrogant and entitled, the next, he was giving a woman he didn't know the coat off his back.

*What is he playing at?* she wondered as she watched him draw ale at the bar. She wiped tables and delivered drinks quickly and efficiently, skirting the wandering hands of those patrons who felt entitled to a pinch. King had taken an hour or so to get his bearings behind the bar, but she and Joshua had helped him, and now he looked as though he'd been born to be a publican.

Of course, the night was young and the crowd thin. It would grow as word of the new publican—a handsome man with pretty manners—spread.

King seemed to play up those manners, doing everything with a flourish and generally charming almost every man or woman he spoke with. She supposed all the time he spent in Society had trained him in social interaction. He was much better at that aspect of the job than Archie or her. On the other hand, that wasn't all the job entailed. As the night went on, men became drunker and more prone to violence. He'd have to manage that aspect of the tavern too.

Violet had little faith in his abilities on that front. He was used to causing difficulties, not preventing them. Speaking of causing mayhem, she couldn't understand why he was still here. She knew he had some personal misfortunes. From what she'd seen of the merchants at his house the other morning, it looked like financial trouble. But surely he had other properties where he could escape and where he wouldn't be required to serve ale and gin. Violet was under no illusion that King was staying because he felt obligated to repay her.

She stepped into the back room to wash a few glasses and found Joshua already there handing glasses to Georgie to dry. "You're one step ahead of me, I see," she said.

"Always." Joshua grinned.

Violet emptied her dirty glasses into the soapy water and started placing clean glasses on her tray. "Did the surgeon agree to go take a look at Archie?" she asked.

"Yes, but he didn't look happy about it. King said he owes him a debt. When I mentioned that, the surgeon went red with anger and said he'd go."

"Good." She placed more glasses on the tray.

"He's not half bad out there," Joshua said.

"No, he's not," Violet agreed. "But I can't help wondering—"

"Why he's still here?"

"Exactly. Do you know anything? You saw his man of business."

"And King wasn't happy with the reply I brought."

"Did you read it?"

"My reading isn't that good."

Violet nodded. There had been little time for learning of late, and she was usually too tired to do much teaching. When she'd been young, her father had enough money to send her to school every day. She'd learned reading, writing, and numbers. She needed to find more time to tutor her brothers, especially Georgie.

"But the solicitor did say something that seemed to upset King when I told him."

"What was that?"

"It was a phrase. Let me think."

Peggy came in. "I need more—Oh, I'll take those." She took Violet's tray of glasses and went back out again. Violet reached into the soapy water and began to scrub.

"I can't be sure I have this right."

"Go on," she told Joshua, handing a wet glass to Georgie to dry.

"It was something like tainder by verdict."

"Verdict is a word I know, but not *tainder*."

"Maybe it was *attainted*?"

"I don't know that one either." She continued scrubbing.

"Whatever it was made King unhappy. You came up behind him while we were talking. He said, 'I'm still a marquess for a few hours and that termagant can't make me scrub floors.'"

Violet ceased scrubbing. She remembered the termagant slight, but she hadn't heard the first part. "What does that mean *for a few hours*? You're sure that's what he said?"

"It was something like that."

"But how could his title be taken away? Is that possible?"

He shrugged. "I don't know. But I say, if he wants to stay, let him. Even when Archie comes back, we could use him."

"Hmm." She went back to scrubbing. "We'll see."

A couple hours later, Violet finished tucking Georgie into bed and came back down to find the Silver Unicorn so full that men spilled out into the streets. Joshua was furiously washing glasses, and when Violet stepped into the tavern, she found Peggy red-faced and sweating. "They're thick as thieves tonight," she panted.

Violet went right to work, sliding behind the bar and helping King. Despite the crush of men and women, he hadn't broken a sweat. He had an air of authority about him that she envied. No one was jostling, and everyone seemed content to wait their turn. He'd hand out one drink, take the coin, and nod to the next person in line. Still, when he saw Violet, he gave her an appreciative smile that made her heart pound a bit harder. She told herself she was excited about the coin in the money chest. She'd caught a glimpse of the coins inside when King opened it. But she knew it was his smile. He was so handsome, and those green eyes were pretty enough to make any woman's heart flutter.

"Yes, sir?" she asked, and began to draw ale. They worked in tandem for two hours, until the crowd thinned a bit.

"Might I step away for a moment?" King asked her as she wiped the bar.

"Of course. You haven't had a moment all evening."

"You'll be all right?"

"I was fine before you came, and I'll be fine when you're gone," she said. Her tone was harsher than she'd intended, but King winked at her.

"You'll miss me when I'm gone," he said, and walked away before she could think of a retort.

Violet scrubbed the bar harder, practicing retorts in her mind.

*I'll throw a party when you're gone.* No. Too weak.

*You're the last person I'd ever miss.* No, that didn't have much of a punch.

*I'd miss a rat more than I'd ever miss you.* That seemed promising, though a bit insulting to rats. She smiled.

"You're about to scrub a hole in that wood," said a voice on the other side of the bar. Violet looked up into the face of a man about ten years her senior. He was familiar. She didn't know his name, but he'd been in here before.

She ceased scrubbing. "Good to see you, sir. What are you drinking this evening?"

"Oh, I'd say it's well past evening," he said, smiling at her. She smiled back, though he was right. Evening had faded into night, which was quickly turning into the wee hours of morning. She was weary and ready for her bed.

"Then something before you head home and to bed."

"I'd like to go to bed," he said. Violet took his meaning and ignored it.

"Ale? Or do you want something stronger?"

"Ale," he said.

She drew it from a cask and told him the price. He slid the coin onto the bar, and she put the glass in front of him. But as she moved to lift the coin, he put his hand over hers. Violet was no stranger to this trick. She palmed the coin and tried to slide her hand free. The man closed his fingers over her wrist. She looked up at him. "Let go," she said calmly and quietly.

"I meant what I said about bed. I don't want to go home alone tonight."

"Then find a whore. Now let go."

"I found you. Pretty girl like you must get lonely sometimes."

Violet's gaze flicked to the crowbar under the bar. It was out of reach, and the patron had her wrist clasped firmly. She might be able to wrench free, but not without causing a scene. Then she'd have to grasp the crowbar, and enough men were well in their cups and might be spoiling for a fight. That was the last thing she needed on the first night she was open again.

"Sir, I don't want trouble. Release me, and we'll talk." She'd tell him to get the hell out of here.

"I like how we're talking now," he said. "Lean forward and give me a little kiss."

"The lady asked you politely to release her," came a deep voice from behind her. Violet almost jumped. She whipped her head to the side and saw King standing, arms folded, and a thunderous look in his eyes. "I'd do as the lady asks."

"And what if I don't?" The patron's fingers tightened on her wrist. Violet looked past him to those men standing nearby. A few sidled away, sensing the tension and wanting no part of it. Others were quiet and moved closer, nudging and elbowing each other in anticipation of violence.

"Then I'll break your fingers," King said, voice calm and still low enough not to carry far beyond the bar. Still, did he not see the way those nearby leaned in? They needed only the smallest provocation to start throwing punches and breaking glasses.

"Is she your woman?" the man asked, his fingers loosening

slightly.

"As much as she's any man's," King said. It was a pretty play of words, and the patron took it the way King wanted. He loosened his grip, and King lifted Violet's hand from the bar and kissed it. His gaze never left the crowd. "We're closing. Come get your last pint or glass. Half price for the last one."

A cheer went up, and men rushed forward and began to shout their orders. Violet yanked her hand out of King's and glared at him. "We will talk later, sir," she threatened.

"I'll look forward to it."

KING CLOSED THE door and barred it as the last patrons left, singing a bawdy tune. Joshua had wiped their few tables and placed the chairs on them, but Miss Baker told him to leave the sweeping for the morning and sent him to bed. Peggy had left before the incident with Violet, and King dearly hoped she'd be here early in the morning, so he wasn't forced to sweep.

Now he slipped behind the bar and poured a quarter glass of brandy. He sipped it, wincing at the taste. It was a crime to call this brandy. He should stick to the beer, though if he never saw another glass of the stuff, he wouldn't complain. He'd spent enough time in taverns to know what to do, and he'd acquitted himself well. Miss Sunshine wouldn't give him a compliment if her life depended on it, but he didn't need her to tell him what he already knew. He was good at the job of publican. He was probably better at it than he was at being a marquess. And since he was almost certainly not a marquess any longer, maybe that was a good thing.

He heard water splashing in the back room and knew Miss Baker was back there washing glasses. King sighed. He owed her an apology. Not for his performance behind the bar tonight, but because the incident with her and the patron had shown him something. When that idiot had put his hand on her and tried to proposition her, King hadn't thought twice before stepping in. He could see now that had been a dangerous choice. The air had changed as soon as he challenged the man, and the winds of violence had started to blow. A fight or a riot might have easily broken out.

For the first time, King had realized why Miss Baker blamed him for the brawl at the Silver Unicorn the night he and his friends had visited. King might not remember much of the events of the night, but he could see now that it didn't take much to light a fire in the dry tinder of Seven Dials. He should have been more careful. Then her tavern wouldn't have been damaged. Archie wouldn't have been injured.

He owed her an apology—not that he would give her one. Hell could freeze over before he bended a knee. Working in her tavern was apology enough. In fact, she should not only thank him for working here, she should thank him for saving her from that idiot who'd propositioned her. The man had actually touched her. The sight of it had infuriated King. He couldn't say why. It wasn't as though she had small, delicate hands. She had red, callused hands. And yet King didn't like seeing that man touching them. Looking at her—no, *leering* up at her. If he'd been a man of less restraint, he really would have broken the man's fingers, and his nose as well.

He couldn't finish the brandy. It was too awful, so he carried the glass to the back to give to Miss Baker to wash with the rest. As soon as he walked in, he realized his mistake and started back out.

"Oh, no you don't," she said, grabbing his arm with a wet hand. "We need to have a word."

"You've been back here waiting for me," he said, giving up on escape. "Seething with anger." He could see that clearly enough. Her cheeks were flushed pink and her blue eyes dark. Her little bow of a mouth pressed into a thin line as she looked up at him.

"I don't know who you think you are," she began, releasing

his arm and wiping her red hands on her apron, "but this is my tavern. Not yours. I make the rules." Using her wrist, she pushed a stray piece of hair off her cheek. At the beginning of the day, her hair had been pinned up, but as the day had worn on, he'd noticed pieces of it escaping and her topknot falling lower and lower. Now her dark hair fell down her back in a long, dark ribbon, secured only by a piece of twine.

"If it wasn't for me, you might not have a tavern to call your own. Those men were looking for any excuse to start trouble."

Her glare turned sharper, if that was possible. "*You* are lecturing me about brawls in my tavern?"

He shrugged. "Ironic, isn't it?" He rubbed a hand over his chin, feeling the bristle of stubble. Now would be the time to apologize, if he were to do it.

He kept silent.

"Let me make one thing clear, King," she said, moving closer. The clean scent of soap clung to her. "I don't need your help. I don't need you to rescue me from grasping men. I don't need you to give my ale and spirits away—"

"It was half price. That's hardly giving it away."

"—and I don't need you to tell me how to run *my* tavern. Just serve the beer. Pour the gin. And if someone starts trouble, bosh them over the head."

"Bosh them?"

"Yes."

"You make me sound like a mindless brute."

"That's what I need."

"No, it isn't."

She looked as surprised as he did. Why had he said that? He had no idea what she needed. But he knew what he needed, and just maybe, for once, they needed the same thing. He reached out and took a lock of her hair, running it through his hand then winding it about his fingers until she moved closer to avoid having her hair pulled.

"What are you doing?" she asked as he put his other hand on

her waist and tugged her against him. Her voice was still hard, but he heard the way it hitched.

"I'm about to kiss you," he said.

She shook her head "No, you're not."

"Yes. I am." He released her hair and slid his hand through it to cup the back of her neck. "Last chance to tell me to stop." He lowered his lips, pausing just a fraction from her mouth. She tensed, and he thought she would come to her senses and shove him away. Instead, her arms went about his neck, and she closed the distance between their lips.

And yet, when their lips touched, it was soft and almost tender. He brushed his mouth over hers, taking in the feel of her softness, admiring the shape of her mouth, now that it wasn't pressed into a thin line. She explored him as well then pressed closer until their mouths met again. They kissed, pulled back, kissed again. King growled low and claimed her mouth, deepening the kiss and taking what he wanted. He was aware of her heat, her softness, the faint scent of beer and the stronger tang of the soap. He moved his hand on her waist lower to curve it around the fullness of her hip. From there he couldn't help but slide a bit lower to take hold of her bottom. It was round and firm, a good handful.

She made a sound between pleasure and dismay and closed her hand in his hair, tugging his mouth down so she could taste more of him. She tasted of wine, the sweet wine that cost a penny and that the lower classes drank watered down. He pushed her back against the counter he slept beneath and lifted her onto it, sliding between her legs. She closed them around him, and he pressed close. The heat of their bodies colliding shocked both of them. King's heart beat so loudly he couldn't hear his own thoughts, which were basically a chant to *take her now* and not very profound. He supposed there might be a smaller voice telling him he would regret taking this further, but he was good at ignoring that voice.

Apparently, Miss Baker had the same voice, and she was less

skilled at ignoring it, because she pushed him back and broke the kiss. "We can't do this," she said, voice breathless. Her entire face was flushed now, and her eyes were bright and so very blue.

He moved to kiss her again, but her hand was between them. "Yes, we can," he said. "We'll just regret it in the morning." He dipped his head and kissed the pulse beating rapidly at her throat. "Then we tiptoe around each other and pretend it never happened until tomorrow night, when we do it all over again."

She let out a small laugh, and the sound surprised him. He'd so rarely heard her laugh. "That's a horrible idea."

"I'm known for my horrible ideas, and here's the thing about horrible ideas—they're only horrible after the fact. At the time, they're usually extremely enjoyable." He bent to kiss that fluttering pulse again, but she pushed him back. Obviously, she wouldn't be persuaded. And he was not the sort of man to coax a woman to his bed. She either wanted him and came willingly or not at all.

King stepped back, raking a hand through his hair. "Give me a minute," he said, stepping aside and putting his hands on the counter. His cock was hard and eager, and he had to think of cold baths, ice, and snow. He reminded himself he didn't even like this termagant.

Beside him, Miss Baker jumped down and smoothed a hand over her skirts. Then she gasped. "I cannot believe I forgot!" He gave her a sidelong look, slightly annoyed at how easily her ardor faded, and she pulled a slip of paper from her skirts. "This is for you," she said. "An old woman came in this morning and left it for you."

King took the yellowed paper, carefully, as it was particularly thin and brittle. Something about the feel of it, the ancient scent of it, sent a shudder skittering up his spine. "You said an old woman gave this to you? What did she look like?"

Miss Baker frowned at him. "She was thin and bony, with long white hair, and very old, seventy or eighty at least."

"Had you seen her before?"

"No."

"What else?" He took hold of her shoulder, and she began to look concerned. "Tell me everything you remember."

"She had a Scottish accent, rather thick. She said she was looking for you and that I had been kind to you." She looked up at him then, perhaps expecting him to argue.

"Go on."

"I said you owed me money, and she said she could believe that. She said you owed her a whiskey."

King's fingers tightened on her shoulder. "Anything else?"

"She said to give you this and that she'd come back when you were here. Do you know her?"

He released her and held the slip of paper with two shaking hands. "She's a witch," he said.

Miss Baker laughed then, when she saw he wasn't joking, became sober. "You can't be serious." Her gaze went to his hands, which were still trembling. "King. What's wrong? Sit down."

She directed him to a chair in the corner and pushed him into it. Then she took a few pieces of coal from the bin and put them in the stove. Still, the warmth didn't penetrate the ice running through his veins.

"Do you want me to open it?"

He wanted to throw it in the stove and pretend he'd never seen it. And yes, he wanted anyone but himself to open the folded paper. But what if it was cursed? He couldn't allow Miss Baker to be cursed on his account.

"I have it," he said. Willing his hands to cease shaking, he unfolded the paper, which had been folded at least eight times. It was badly creased and fragile with age. He carefully smoothed it then moved close to the lamp to read the words scrawled in black.

*Procure petal of flower, dash of dust of the fae.*
*Combine now in this goblet, please if you may.*

*Hear me now, great goddess of good and light.*
*Take mercy on these children. Ease their plight.*
*Lose they may all they hold dear,*
*But open a path to clean the smear.*

The bottom of the paper had been torn and the message ended there.

"What does it say?" Miss Baker asked.

He looked up. "It says I can change the curse."

# CHAPTER ELEVEN

V I WAS SUPPOSED to be in bed. Joshua knew he might wake King when he came in, and he rather hoped that was the case. He wanted to talk more about Lizzie. But when he eased the door open and stepped in from the yard, he found his sister and King standing by the counter staring at him.

King held a piece of parchment, and both of them looked as though they'd just seen a ghost. "What's the matter?" Joshua asked, forgetting he was supposed to be in bed asleep.

"Nothing," King said, folding the paper and sticking it in his waistcoat. He was the perfect picture of a guilty man.

"We'll talk about this tomorrow," Vi said to him, and then her gaze fell on Joshua. "And where have you been, Joshua Baker?" Her hands went to her hips.

"I just stepped outside to use the privy," he said, which was the excuse he had practiced in case she woke up and caught him sneaking back in. Perhaps he hadn't waited long enough to sneak back in.

"No, you didn't. King and I have been in the back room and would have seen you. I sent you up to bed more than an hour ago."

"I went to bed, but—"

King shook his head. "A little advice, Master Joshua. Once you're caught, tell the truth. If you add lies, it just compounds the offense." He leaned a shoulder against the wall. "Besides, I think we all know where you were."

"Joshua Baker." His sister spoke through a clenched jaw. "If you were with Lizzie, so help me God—"

"I wasn't with her, Vi. I just went to see her. I spied on her. No one saw me, not even Lizzie. I just had to make certain she was well."

Vi gave him an exasperated look, but Joshua didn't care. He knew he'd put her and Georgie at risk going to see Lizzie, but how was he supposed to stay away? How was he supposed to sleep, worrying that Ferryman might be... Well, he didn't want to think about that. He just needed to see Lizzie, to reassure himself she was still whole and unharmed.

"How many times do I have to tell you to stay away from her?"

"I can't. I love her, Vi."

She rolled her eyes. "*Love.* You are thirteen! You know nothing about love."

"I know how I feel. King understands, don't you, King?" King was shaking his head, but Joshua was too upset to curb his tongue. "He said he'd help me. He'd help Lizzie."

Vi rounded on King now and shot daggers at him. "Tell me that's not true."

He squared his shoulders. "I said I'd do what I could."

"You will both be the reason we are killed, or worse. Why don't you think about Georgie?" she demanded of Joshua. "Do you want him to be forced to wade into the freezing water in the Thames, diving in that muck for bits of copper and plate? And what do you think will happen to me?"

"I won't let anything happen to any of you," King said.

Joshua had hung his head low, but now he looked up at King. The way he'd spoken sounded utterly convincing. Looking at him now—tall and strong and full of authority—Joshua truly believed King wouldn't let anything happen to them.

"And how will you stop Ferryman?" Vi demanded, skeptical

as always. "He has an entire gang of criminals at his beck and call. Your own friends haven't even come to help you. Speaking of which, don't you have enough on your plate without adding our problems?"

"I'm used to managing others' problems," he said. "That's what the nobility is for."

Vi raised a brow in a mocking expression she never showed to Joshua or Georgie. "Somehow I doubt before you came here you were helping old ladies cross the street and solving tenant disputes. If that was the sort of man you are, you wouldn't be in whatever trouble you're in now. Are you ready to reveal that trouble?" She paused, and King said nothing. "I didn't think so."

The look on his face was the sort the sky got before it poured rain. Joshua actually took a step back, wondering now if Ferryman was the real threat. King looked like he might strangle Vi, and then Joshua would have to jump in and protect her. But King slid his hands into his pockets and didn't move.

"You don't know what sort of man I am, Miss Baker. All you've done is judge me on the actions of one drunken night."

Joshua thought about mentioning how that wasn't quite true. King had behaved rather badly the next morning as well, but he seemed to be changing. After all, he'd made the surgeon come to help Archie, and he'd worked at the bar all night.

"If I say I will protect you from Ferryman, I'll protect you."

"Well, you will have the chance to prove that," she said. "He'll be here tomorrow wanting his taxes. We had a good night, but it won't be enough."

Joshua drew in a breath. "You mean we're short?"

Vi nodded. "I did a quick count of the money we made tonight, and it's not enough. I knew it was a stretch to think we'd make it all in one night, but I thought we had a chance. Until someone had the idea to make the last round half price."

Joshua looked at King, who closed his eyes and sighed. "I'll handle Ferryman and the payment tomorrow," he told Vi. "It will all work out."

"How?"

"You'll have to trust me."

"Ha." She tossed her hair. "Never." And then she stomped upstairs. Halfway up, she paused and looked back at Joshua. "I expect you in bed in five minutes, and don't think there won't be a punishment for running off to see Lizzie. *Love*." She muttered this last word under her breath.

When she was gone, Joshua looked at King, who raised his brows and looked back at him. "Sorry," Joshua said. "I shouldn't have told her you said you'd help Lizzie."

"No, you shouldn't have. Always protect your confederates."

"My what?"

"Your partners. In this case, me."

"Will you still help me help Lizzie?"

"I said I would. A gentleman is only as good as his word. I'll meet this Ferryman tomorrow, and then I'll know better how to go about it. In the meantime, maybe don't go about professing your love to her. I said I'd help her, not that the two of you can play Romeo and Juliet."

Joshua frowned, trying to puzzle King's meaning.

"She won't be safe in Seven Dials," King said. "I'll have to get her out of here, which means you won't see her again."

Joshua opened his mouth to protest then closed it again. "I understand," he said.

King gave him a nod. "Maybe you really do love her."

"I *do*. Why is that hard to believe?"

"I believe it. I was probably your age when I first fell in love."

"You fell in love?"

King shrugged. "Well, I thought it was love. Her name was Mary Thatcher, and she was the daughter of the vicar in Avebury. That's where my family's ancestral home is." He cleared his throat. "She was the prettiest girl I'd ever seen, with long, dark hair and blue eyes."

"That sounds like Vi."

Surprise flickered across King's face. "I suppose there is a passing resemblance."

"Did you tell Mary Thatcher you loved her?"

King's mouth curved into a small smile. "No, but I spent hours pining over her."

"What's that mean?"

"It means thinking about her and wishing I were with her and writing poetry about her."

"Poetry?" Joshua had thought he finally had something in common with King, but writing poetry must be one of those noble things.

"I made any excuse to see her, which I'm sure sounds familiar."

Joshua smiled. "Did you ever kiss her?"

"I kissed her hand. Once. I didn't want to wash my lips for days."

"Was her hand soft?"

"It was gloved, so I have no idea," King said.

Joshua wondered why he wouldn't wash his lips if they hadn't even touched Mary Thatcher's skin, but the nobility was strange.

"Do you still pine for her?" he asked.

"No," King said. "I haven't thought about her in years. I imagine that's how it will be for you. When you're thirty, you'll look back on Lizzie with fondness, but you'll fall in love a dozen times or more between now and then."

Joshua shook his head. "I'll always love Lizzie."

"Then she's a lucky girl. Now, you'd better go to bed before your sister comes looking for you. I don't think either of us want another tongue lashing tonight."

Joshua laughed. "That's a funny way to say it. Goodnight, King." He had the urge to throw his arms about the man, but he wasn't a baby anymore. Instead, he held out his hand. He thought King might ask him what he was doing, but instead, he drew his hand out of his pocket and shook Joshua's. It was a firm handshake, but not the sort that hurt because the other man squeezed too hard.

Joshua ran up the stairs two at a time, smiling.

VIOLET CLOSED THE door to her closet just as Joshua bolted the door of their flat. He'd almost caught her eavesdropping. She wasn't proud that she'd resorted to such measures, but if King and Joshua were plotting, she needed to know.

Now she wished she hadn't listened in, because what she'd heard had tugged at her heart. She could hardly imagine King as a boy, mooning over a young girl. Somehow, thinking of him that way made him seem all too human—as though he wasn't becoming human to her quickly enough. The way he'd kissed her tonight had certainly been human—it had been full of passion and need and a heat that she could still feel pooling in her belly.

He hadn't disguised his desire, and he'd made her feel it too. Desire was something she didn't allow herself to feel, something she didn't have the luxury of indulging. And yet the one man she hated had made her hot and achy and heavy with longing.

But then she didn't hate him, did she? She tried to hate him, but every minute she spent with him chipped away at that feeling. He was right that she didn't know him. If she did, perhaps he wouldn't continue to surprise her by his actions. Even listening in just now, she thought she'd hear him tell Joshua something about Lizzie she'd object to, but King hadn't encouraged him to go see her. In fact, he'd pointed out that if he were to help Lizzie, Joshua wouldn't see her again. To her surprise, Joshua didn't argue on that point. No, she didn't believe her brother was in love with Lizzie, but he definitely cared for her enough to want what was best for her, even if that went against his own best interests.

And what of her own feelings for King? Did she care for him? Could she fall in love with him? Could she fall in love with anyone? She'd never allowed herself to be that vulnerable before. She didn't like feeling helpless, and if she cared that much for another person, her heart would be in his hands. Georgie and Joshua already held pieces of her heart. That was dangerous enough. She'd loved her father, and she'd hurt so much when he died, she thought she'd die too. She'd persevered because she had two young boys who needed her, but she certainly didn't want to feel that pain again.

She heard Joshua settle in beside Georgie then quietly undressed and climbed under her own covers. They were cold, and she wondered what it might feel like to curl up beside King. He wouldn't be cold. Every time she touched him, he seemed to have his own fire burning inside, making his skin warm to the touch.

Violet let out a shuddering breath and tried not to think about his kisses and the heat of his hands on her. She wouldn't allow that to happen again. She no longer believed he would run away at the first sign of trouble. He would help with Lizzie and Ferryman, but after that, he would go. Whatever his trouble—had he called it a curse?—he would certainly have it worked out in the next few days.

THE NEXT MORNING, Violet woke early. She was hungry, but she didn't have money for food unless she took more out of what she owed Ferryman. She'd have to send Georgie to beg for his breakfast, and she hated doing that.

She opened the door and descended the steps into the back room, expecting to see King sleeping under the counter, but he wasn't there. Maybe she'd been wrong about him after all. Maybe he *had* run at the first sign of trouble. But she saw he'd left all of his clothing, and she rather doubted he would leave it behind. He seemed particularly fond of it.

She pushed through the door into the tavern and found him sitting at the bar looking down at the parchment the old woman had given her to pass on. She was about to chastise him for wasting her candles when she caught the look on his face. His eyes looked red and his cheeks a bit hollow. He had two days' growth of beard, which she rather liked, but it made him look even more haggard.

"I see I need to send you begging for food as well," she said. "You're looking thin."

He glanced up at her, and she saw a flash of pain in his eyes before he masked it with that annoying smugness.

Violet's eyes narrowed. "What's the matter?"

"I'm not begging," he said.

She waved a hand. "Don't change the subject. What's on that paper that's upset you?"

"It's nothing."

"It's clearly something." She moved around the bar and took a seat on the stool beside him. "It's been three days. Don't you think it's time you tell me what's going on?"

"Why, Miss Sunshine, I didn't think you cared."

She was about to hit him and tell him she *didn't* care, but that was what he wanted. He wanted to push her away, so he didn't have to reveal anything of himself.

"My name is Violet, and I don't know if I care yet. Start talking. Begin by telling me why there was a crowd of merchants trying to collect on debts the morning I came to your house. Does it have something to do with tainder by verdict? That might not be right. I heard it from Joshua."

He sighed, and it was a long sigh. The kind of sigh that made her chest tighten a little with fear. He raked a hand through his hair, disordering it, and with the mussed hair and the stubble, he was almost irresistible.

"It's attainder by verdict," he said. "And yes, it has almost everything to do with that."

"What is attainder by verdict? It sounds like something to do with the law."

He looked down at the bar, and she noticed he traced the scarred wood with one finger. "That's correct. The night I was first here with my friends, my father was tried in the House of Lords and found guilty." He looked up at her, his green eyes full of pain. She hadn't expected that. "Of treason."

Violet gasped. "Treason? Surely that was a mistake."

"I don't think so. I don't have much of a relationship with my father, but I didn't doubt the charges when I first heard them. Rather, I read them. My father and I aren't on speaking terms, and I saw in the *Times* he had been accused of selling secrets to the French."

Violet grasped the bar, shaken by this news. She did not know very much about the war between France and England, but she knew she wanted England to defeat Napoleon. "Why would he want to help our enemy?"

"He was helping himself. That's the only person he's ever cared about. I'm sure they offered him money and titles and land, and that's all the duke cares about."

"What about your mother? Your siblings?"

"My mother is dead. She died in childbirth." Violet put a hand on his arm. She couldn't help but want to comfort him, but he moved his arm away and looked down at the bar again, at his finger tracing a deep scar. "My father never married again. I don't have any siblings. I was the heir to the dukedom, but that's where the attainder comes in."

Violet took a breath, but a knot had formed in her belly, and it sat there, tight and hard and nauseating.

"I won't bore you with the details of attainder, but the consequences are forfeiture and corruption of blood. When my father was found guilty of treason, his title and lands were forfeited to the king. Last I heard, the Parliament was set to vote on whether to strip the duke's heirs of their lands and titles due to corruption of blood. I have no doubt it passed."

"Corruption of blood? The Parliament thinks that you are

corrupted because of your father's actions? You just said you don't speak with him."

"And that's the only reason I wasn't implicated in the treason. Everyone knows we aren't on speaking terms, but I assume I have lost everything." He looked up at her. "I'm no longer a marquess. All I have are the clothes on my back."

"And the pile in the back room." She raised her brows, and he gave her a rueful smile. "What about your friends?"

He opened his hands. "It doesn't appear I have any. Well, that's not true. I have two friends who would never desert me— Henry and Rory. You saw Henry. He'd help me if he could, but he's in debt and somewhat in denial about it. And Rory has disappeared. No, it's not like that. His wife died and he left for the Continent. No one seems to know how to reach him."

"There's no one else?"

He shook his head. "In my world—well, it's not my world any longer—everything is about title and status. I'm a pariah now. No one wants to be associated with me."

Violet sat up straight, hoping the knot would loosen now. "Well, you'll just have to make the best of it, then."

"Make the best of it?" King stared at her.

"Yes. Look at you. You're young, healthy, educated. You aren't without resources. As long as you don't decide to drink yourself to death, you can make something of yourself."

"Oh, God. That sounds so *bourgeois*."

"I don't know what that means, but I would assume *bourgeois* is better than lying in the gutter, begging for food."

"Yes, well, that might be how I end up. I told you this has *almost* everything to do with the attainder. There's more."

Ah, this was why she still felt sick to her stomach. She'd somehow known there would be more. King opened his mouth to tell her, then closed it, stood, walked across the room, and turned to face her. When he still didn't speak, she raised her brows. "Go on."

"I don't know how to say it."

Violet turned to face him fully. "It can't be worse than the treason."

"It's not worse, it's... I don't think you'll believe me. You'll think me mad."

She was intrigued. "Well, now you must tell me. I have all sorts of ideas racing about my mind."

He sighed and stuck his hands in the pockets of his trousers. "I'm cursed."

Violet thought for a moment and resisted the urge to ask him to repeat himself. "Cursed? Like a spell?"

"Exactly. A"—he looked about as though wanting to make sure they were alone before continuing—"a witch put a curse on me."

"Does this have to do with the old woman who left that scrap of paper for you?"

"Yes." He strode over to her and sat on the stool again. "I think that was the witch's sister."

Violet took King's hand, surprised it was so cold. "In my experience, witches are usually women of learning whom men fear. A woman has knowledge of healing, and men accuse her of witchcraft rather than acknowledging her talents. I don't think I believe in *eye of newt* and cauldrons and broomsticks and the like."

"Neither did I, but I can't explain this away. I tried, and then the witch's sister—hell, she's probably a witch too—found me yesterday. Explain that."

"I don't know how to explain anything. You'd better start at the beginning."

King told her about the lark he and his friends had perpetrated when they'd been at school. He told her about hearing the witch curse them and then forgetting about it.

"Except the curse was supposed to come to fruition when we turned thirty. Do you know what happened when Rory turned thirty?"

"He left for the Continent?"

"Because his wife and son died in a carriage accident. On his thirtieth birthday."

"People die in carriage accidents all the time. Children are run down in the street daily. That's why I won't allow Georgie to go out on his own. But they are accidents, not curses."

"Violet—you said I can call you Violet?"

"I suppose you ought to after these shared confidences."

"Violet, you don't think it's something of a coincidence that on Rory's thirtieth birthday he loses his wife, and on mine, my father is found guilty of treason?"

"But you said your father did sell secrets to the French. Did the curse make him do it?"

"No." He stood. "Yes? I don't know how the witch does it. But two birthdays and two life-altering events. And there's more."

"If I were Catholic, I would cross myself." She did not want to know what he would say next, and yet she was insatiably curious.

"You should, because when I arrived home the night I met you—the night I first came to the Silver Unicorn—I saw the witch in my fire."

Violet stared at him. She had not doubted his sanity until now, but she was beginning to think he just might be daft. "In your fire?"

"Yes! I was sitting by the hearth, having a drink, and she appeared in the fire."

"You were drunk, and sometimes the flames can look like shapes—"

"She stepped *out* of the hearth, Violet. She spoke to me." He grabbed her by the shoulders, and Violet looked into his green eyes, which were surprisingly lucid. And yet even through the fabric of her dress, she could feel how cold his hands were. He had truly been frightened, and he was frightened now remembering it.

"What did she say?"

"She said she wanted a look at me now that it has begun."

"The curse."

He nodded. "And I said something like *holy hell*, and she said hell isn't holy. Then I called for my valet, or perhaps I called for him before that—I don't remember. She said he couldn't hear me, and I tried to wake up. I thought it was a dream, but when I closed my eyes and pinched myself, she was still there. She said to remember the curse. And she said—I will never forget this—she said, *I'll enjoy watching ye suffer*."

His voice took on a malevolent tone with what she assumed was supposed to be a Scottish accent.

"Then the next morning, my father had been found guilty of treason and I woke up to find every merchant and debt collector in London at my doorstep."

Violet did not know what to say. It was an amazing story, fantastical and not to be believed.

"I entertained every single thought you are having right now," he told her, still holding her shoulders and looking intently at her face, almost as though he could read her mind. "And I had almost talked myself out of believing any of it happened. And then you gave me this."

He released her and pulled the slip of yellow paper from his waistcoat. He slapped it down on the bar, and Violet peered at the spidery writing on the yellow parchment.

"If there's not a curse, how do you explain this?"

# CHAPTER TWELVE

KING WATCHED AS Violet leaned over the paper and then, with a fingernail, slid it closer to the candle, presumably so she could read it. She squinted and placed her finger so it hovered just above the first line. He noticed she was careful not to touch the paper, and her lips moved as she read. He didn't need to see the parchment to know what she saw. He had the words immutably etched on his brain.

*Procure petal of flower, dash of dust of the fae.*
*Combine now in this goblet, please if you may.*
*Hear me now, great goddess of good and light.*

"This certainly sounds like some sort of spell," she said, pausing after the mention of the great goddess. "But she's calling on powers of good and light. See, here?"

"Yes, this is the spell from the sister. Not the curse."

"Do you think she actually took a goblet and mixed flower petals and fairy dust?"

"I don't know. At this point, I will believe anything."

The expression on her face told him she certainly agreed with that statement.

"The next part is important," he added.

She looked down, and her lips moved again as she read. She

read too slowly for his taste, and he recited it to her. "It says, *Take mercy on these children. Ease their plight. Lose they may all they hold dear but open a path to clean the smear.*"

"The children would be you and the other boys? What is a plight? A burden?"

"I assume it's the witch's curse. She's looking for a way to counteract it. She's easing our punishment. We'll lose all that we hold dear"—he pointed a finger at her, giving her a moment to remember what had happened to Rory and himself—"but there's a path to clean the smear—the, er, stain of our wrongdoing. There's a way to reverse the curse." He lifted the paper. "This is torn. There's more. Where's the rest of it?"

"That was all she gave me," Violet said, patting her dress, which was the same one she had worn yesterday. "There wasn't any more."

"Was it torn when she gave it to you?"

"I don't remember. Possibly. It was in my pocket all day. I forgot about it and didn't take it out until you—we—"

"Check your pocket. I must read the rest of it if I'm to know how to reverse the curse."

She reached into her skirts, but her hand came out empty. No, that was not true. She opened it and showed him a hairpin. "That's all I have. No paper inside."

"Damn it." He pounded a fist on the bar, and she jumped slightly. He hadn't meant to scare her. "I'm sorry. I need that paper." He gripped the bar and closed his eyes. Then he was the one to jump when she put a hand on his shoulder.

"King, I know you want the rest of the poem, but do you really think any spell could reverse what has happened? How could magic, if it even exists, change that your father committed treason?"

"It can't." He didn't dare move now. Her hand was warm and her touch comforting. King hadn't realized how much he needed that comfort, and the last thing he wanted was for her to move away. "But the attainder might be challenged."

"How is that accomplished?"

"In court."

She took his shoulders and turned him to face her. Rather, he allowed himself to be turned. She was strong but petite, and he could have easily resisted her. He looked down at her and her pretty blue eyes, made all the prettier by the way they softened as she looked at him. He'd rather that softness wasn't the result of pity for him, but he supposed he wasn't in any position to inspire lust. "Don't you think your time would be better spent planning how to challenge the attainder?"

"I'd like nothing better than to do that, but I need a lawyer, and not just any lawyer, one familiar with arguing before Parliament. I need money for that, and I have none. Even if I did, not many lawyers of that caliber would take my case. Prinny— the prince regent—has never liked me, not since I played a small joke on him, and no one wants to incur his displeasure."

"You played a prank on the prince?"

"It was harmless—quite funny, actually. How was I to know he would fall over and split his breeches?"

"Oh dear." She covered a smile with her hand. "And you wonder where your friends are?"

"Once Henry has blunt, he'll come. I just need to go to the country and regroup, make a plan."

"What about your father? You can't go to the country until—"

"If you are about to suggest I should visit my father, don't. You imagine some sentimental scene, where we embrace and forgive each other. It won't be like that. He hates me as much, if not more, than I hate him."

"I don't think that's true, and I do think you should visit him, for your own sake, if not his. You might not think this now, but when he's gone, you'll wish you'd told him goodbye."

Her words landed like an arrow in his heart. She hadn't said anything he hadn't thought before, but he'd always shoved the thoughts aside before he could examine them. It was easy to remind himself he hated his father and leave it at that. But now

Violet's words hung between them, and King had to acknowledge that deep down he did want to see his father. Inside of him was still that young boy hoping his father might magically come to love him.

*Idiot.*

"But that isn't what you must do before you leave for the country," she said.

"Don't tell me this is about the pound I owe you."

"Two pounds and—"

King kissed her. Ostensibly, he'd done it, firstly, to get his mind off his father. Secondly, kissing her was the only way he knew to make her shut up about the two pounds, fifteen shillings. She was like a dog with a bone. But there were advantages to kissing her as well—namely, that he had another opportunity to claim that lush mouth and taste her. This morning she tasted of peppermint and smelled of soap. He'd expected her to object to the kiss and pull away. He probably deserved a slap across the face for his impertinence.

But she didn't pull away, and she didn't slap him. Instead, she moved closer, deepening the kiss, leaning into him.

King had to hold back a groan. Was it possible she wanted this as much as he? She thought he hated her, and King had let her believe that even as he himself realized he rather liked Violet Baker. Liked her more than he was comfortable admitting. He was almost certain she hated him, but perhaps he could turn that hate to something else.

His hands left her shoulders and moved, seemingly of their own accord, to her hips. He wanted to cup that bottom of hers again, feel its plumpness in his hands.

The banging on the door to the tavern caused them to spring apart. Violet let out a small cry of surprise.

"Vi! It's Peggy. Open up."

Violet took a breath, looked at King, and then smoothed her hair. He could have told her that all the hair smoothing in the world wouldn't change the color in her cheeks or the swollen look of her lips.

"I'll open it," he said, and strode across the room before she could argue. He lifted the bar and cracked the door. The maid looked at him in surprise but pushed her way inside quickly enough. The air outside was cool and damp, and beyond the doorway, a thick fog lay low to the ground. It was the sort of day a witch might roam the world, and King wished he didn't believe in witches.

"Close the door, then, my lord," Peggy said. "We don't want to let the chill inside."

King closed the door and barred it, feeling an icy finger skittering down his back.

"What do we have to break our fast?" Peggy asked, looking about.

King heard Violet sigh. "I haven't any food or any coin to buy it. Everything I have, I need to give to Ferryman when he comes to collect the taxes. I can't even pay you, Peggy. You should go home—"

"I'll sell a coat," King said. He'd decided last night that was the best course of action. He might have preferred to sell a waistcoat or a pair of breeches, but the coat would bring in the most coin.

"But you love your clothing," she said.

"I love staying alive even more. Just point me to the nearest pawnbroker, and I'll be on my way."

"Oh, no." Violet shook her head. "If you really want to do this"—she waited until he nodded—"*you* cannot go to the pawnbroker. We'll send Joshua. He is the best negotiator."

King put his hands on his hips. "I can negotiate."

Violet put her hands on her hips, mirroring him. "And how much is one of your coats worth?"

He named what he paid for it, and Violet's jaw dropped. Peggy whistled. "Holy Mother of God, but that's a fortune." Violet shook her head. "But you won't get that from the pawnbroker."

"I'll allow a few pounds for wear," he said, "but to take less would be an insult."

Violet and Peggy exchanged a look. "That's precisely why you can't go," Violet said. "Joshua knows what the brokers will pay and where to get the best deals. Plus, he's not emotionally involved."

"I'm not emotionally involved. It's a coat."

"I see. Then you won't be upset at the price Joshua is likely to get?"

"What's that?" She named a number so low that King uttered a curse. "That's practically theft!"

"Not in Seven Dials. Here that's a small fortune."

"I'll not sell for pennies."

"You don't have to sell at all," Violet said. "We'll figure out something."

King could imagine what that something would be—begging or stealing. "Wake Joshua," he said. "I'll get my coat."

He pawed through his clothes. He had three coats left, including the one he wore. He lifted a blue one and a black one, trying to decide. If it hadn't been for this Ferryman, he wouldn't have to sell at all. They had money from the night before. Violet could do well for herself if she wasn't bled dry by the likes of this gang leader. Obviously, Ferryman had to be dealt with.

Joshua came down, and King handed the black coat to the boy, resisting the urge to caress it with one last goodbye. Henry's luck had better change soon, or King would be walking about permanently in shirt sleeves.

Violet entered the back room and gave Peggy the mop and Joshua instructions for selling the coat, what food to buy, and how much to spend. He admired her ability to determine the cost of everything down to the smallest penny. He'd watched her count their profits from the night before, and count again. She knew how much they had, how much they needed, and what they could spare without even touching a pencil and paper.

King had never paid much attention to the cost of anything. If he wanted something, he bought it. If he didn't have any money, he had the merchant send the bill to his father or give it to him on credit, to be paid at a later date. But no one would give Violet or her brothers credit. Her world didn't work that way.

"Should I have given you a moment alone with your coat?" she asked when Joshua had left and it was only the two of them in the back room.

"You had to ruin it," he said. "I was just thinking how clever you were."

"And I was thinking how sad you looked to see your coat go."

"I have good memories in that coat."

"King." Her voice held a serious tone, and he glanced at her sharply. He didn't think he could take another crisis at the moment. But then he saw the expression on her face—firm but gentle.

"Is this about the kiss?" he asked. "I should have asked before I kissed you, but to be fair, you didn't seem to mind it once we—"

"This is *not* about the kiss. And since you've brought it up, I'll remind you we decided that sort of thing was a horrible idea."

"You decided that. I rather like kissing you." To his surprise, her cheeks flamed bright red and she seemed unable to think of what to say in reply, though her throat worked like she wanted to say something. "Why, Miss Baker, does this speechlessness mean you like kissing me too?"

"No." Her words came out choked and thick. "I do not."

"You're not a very good liar. Perhaps we should test it one more time to be sure..." He reached for her, and she yelped and moved out of his range.

"You are such a man!"

He frowned. "Was that in doubt?"

"I mean, how can you think of kissing at a time like this?"

"I can think of a lot more than kissing. There's undressing and sucking and nibbling and fu—"

"King. I had a thought about the curse."

Well, that ruined the mood.

"When I saw Peggy, it reminded me that her mother is a healer. She knows herbs and poultices and the like."

"I don't have a bellyache," he said. "I have a curse."

"Shh. You'll wake Georgie. Peggy's mother knows more than just medicines, but we don't talk about that," she said, voice low. He moved closer, liking the warmth of her when his arm touched hers. "I think you should take your spell to her and ask her opinion."

"Is the woman a witch?"

"Shh! They don't burn women at the stake any longer, and let's not give them a reason to start. I'd better go with you. Give me a moment."

She ran up the stairs to the flat and returned seconds later, throwing her threadbare shawl over her shoulders. She took one more moment to give Peggy instructions then led him out via the back door. In the fog and gloom, Seven Dials seemed even more dangerous and dreary. Figures appeared out of the gray like phantoms, their faces wan and drawn. King followed Violet, but when he almost lost her in the fog, she grasped his hand as though he were a child. He didn't mind touching her. She wore no gloves, and her rough hand was cold and thin in his.

Finally, she led him up a creaky wooden staircase to a door-way that looked as though it had been built for elves. Even Miss Baker would have to duck her head to enter. She knocked on the door. "Mrs. Greene, it's Violet Baker. May I come in?"

The silence dragged on so long that King thought Mrs. Greene was either not at home or not willing to answer, but finally a voice said, "Who is with you?"

Violet looked at him.

King hardly knew how to introduce himself. He wasn't the Marquess of Kingston any longer, but he'd never gone by his Christian name, George. Still, he might have to get used to it. "George Oxley, Mrs. Greene."

The door opened, and a tiny woman with gray hair and hazel eyes looked up at him. "You don't look like a George," she said, raising her gray brows.

"His friends call him King," Violet said.

Mrs. Greene made a sound somewhere between acknowledgement and derision, but she moved aside so Violet could enter. King followed, stooping low so as not to hit his head. The interior of the room was more spacious, but he had to keep his head at an angle so to not hit it on the low ceiling. It took a moment to adjust his eyes to the darkness. If the room had windows, they were closed and shuttered. A single candle burned on a table that was spread with dried herbs. More plants hung from the ceiling. A mortar and pestle were in front of a low stool, and it was clear Mrs. Greene had been working at grinding something when they knocked. King looked behind him, at the low-burning hearth, and saw two bedrolls stowed in the corner.

He turned back and saw Mrs. Greene had taken her seat on the stool again and was regarding him coolly. "What is it you need? Willow-bark tea for a headache? Or perhaps your ailment is somewhat lower?" She looked down at his trousers, and King had the urge to put a hand over his genitals to keep them safe.

"Actually, we need your advice on another matter," Violet said.

"I've been cursed."

Mrs. Greene's eyes widened, and Violet glared at him over her shoulder. "Shh! Let me speak." She smiled reassuringly at Mrs. Greene. "What he means is—"

"I know exactly what he means," Mrs. Greene said. "Come here, boy."

King almost looked over his shoulder. He hadn't been called *boy* since he was eight years old. But he moved closer to the table, and when the old woman held out her hand and beckoned him, he offered his own. He thought she might pretend to read his palm, but instead, she stared at his face. With those hazel eyes of hers, it was rather unnerving. "It's a powerful curse. I sensed it even before you came inside. You made a powerful witch very unhappy."

"Yes, well, I was young and foolish. Her sister brought this." He was happy to have the excuse to withdraw his hand from her bony grip. He placed the torn paper with the spell on the table.

Mrs. Greene moved her candle closer and peered at the words. She looked up at him. "Where is the rest of it?"

"That's all she gave me," Violet said.

Mrs. Greene looked at the paper again then sat back. "This is a counter-spell, and a powerful one, but the witch who made it does not want it enacted yet. Else she would have given you the rest."

"But I need the rest."

"You will have it in time."

"I don't have time. I've lost my name, my fortune, my friends. I need the rest of that spell."

"It sounds to me as though you have nothing but time. But," she added after she caught a glimpse of his expression, "you could appeal to the witch to give you the rest. Perhaps there is some quest or boon she requires."

"And how am I supposed to find her? She could be anywhere in London. She might be on her way back to Scotland."

"You should seek her in the place where you were cursed. That is where the counter-spell will be strongest."

King closed his eyes. Now he was supposed to go to Scotland? He couldn't even afford to travel to Richmond. He grasped his paper and shoved it back in his pocket. "I'll wait outside," he told Violet, and thought it a victory when he only hit his head once on the way out.

Violet joined him a moment later. She gave him a rueful look. "It's no wonder you have a curse, if this is the way you treat all conjuring women."

"This was a waste of time," he said, and started down the stairs, careful to negotiate the broken sections.

"Not at all. She told us you will receive the rest of the spell in time. If you're so impatient, you could go to Scotland."

"Even if I had the means to travel to Scotland, why would I

want to return to the scene of the crime? I'll probably be cursed again. That is if the old hag is even still alive."

The fog had lifted slightly, and he could see four to five feet in front of him now. He still had no idea where he might be or where he was going, though, so he paused and waited for Violet to catch up. Maybe he could hold her hand again on the way back.

"There's no need to be short-tempered with me," she said. "I didn't curse you...yet."

King took a breath. "I apologize. You can't understand what it is to have your entire life changed in an instant."

Immediately, he realized he'd misspoken. Of course she understood. Her father was dead, and she had charge of two young boys and a tavern.

"Violet, I'm sorry."

"Don't be," she said, pushing past him. "You are so self-centered, you can't see anyone but yourself and your hardships. You think no one else has ever suffered loss, or if they have, it couldn't possibly compare to yours."

"Violet."

She held a hand up and walked on, disappearing into the fog. King hurried after her, having no desire to be lost in Seven Dials and wandering for several hours. He plunged into the fog ahead and almost ran into her.

She'd stopped and stood still as a statue as a man with a ruby jewel in his neckcloth smiled down at her.

# CHAPTER THIRTEEN

VIOLET INHALED SHARPLY at the predatory look on Ferryman's face. "Miss Baker," he said. "How convenient." He looked over her shoulder and cocked his head. "And this must be Mr. King."

"Just King," King said. Violet elbowed him in the stomach, and he let out a quiet *oof*.

"I heard you had a good night at the Silver Unicorn," Ferryman said, placing both hands on the head of his cane and seeming to rest them there. "But did you make enough to pay your taxes?"

"I'll pay them," Violet said. "The money is at the tavern. You'll have to come there."

"I don't have time to run about all day. You come to the Black Bear and pay me tonight. And come alone, Miss Baker," he said with a look at King.

Violet didn't like the sound of that, but she could handle herself. "Thank you," she said, just as King said, "Miss Baker won't be coming to see you tonight, or any other night."

She tried to elbow him again, but he'd moved out of her reach.

"If someone needs to pay, I'll do it."

Ferryman raised his brows. "Is that right?"

"Shut up, King," Violet muttered.

"That's correct," King went on, ignoring her. "I'm her protector now, and I find this whole requirement she pay you taxes not only illegal but unnecessary."

"I see. Are you saying you will not pay the taxes?" Ferryman looked at Violet.

"We'll pay them. King, let's talk about this alone."

"There's nothing to talk about." King stepped in front of her, which would have been noble if it hadn't been so stupid. "From now on, you'll leave Miss Baker alone or you'll answer to me."

"You are new here, King," Ferryman said. "So I won't kill you for your insolence. Not yet." He snapped his fingers, and half a dozen men stepped out of the fog and into view.

"Ferryman," Violet said, scrambling in front of King. "He is new to Seven Dials. I'll speak with him, and I'll come to the Black Bear. I'm sorry. Just let us pass."

"Too late for that, Miss Baker." Ferryman gestured to her, and one of the men grabbed her arms and pulled her away.

"King, run!" she cried, struggling to free herself. But of course, the idiot man didn't run. It was five to one—six if she counted Ferryman—but King crouched into what she recognized as a fighting stance and stood his ground. She supposed he thought the men would fight him like gentlemen, coming one at a time. But he wasn't in Mayfair any longer. The men rushed him.

Violet struggled to free herself from the man holding her arms pinned behind her back. She kicked at him, but he was agile and much stronger than she. With a sob, she watched as King threw punch after punch, but he was no match for a group of men, and she let out a cry when he went down. The punches and kicks continued, and she cried out. No one paid her any mind. The blows continued until Ferryman raised a hand. Then the men stepped back, and she gasped at the curled form on the ground. Using his boot, Ferryman pushed King onto his back. "I only give one warning," he said. "Next time I'll kill you." He spat, and the spittle landed on King's chest.

Ferryman approached Violet and paused to stroke her cheek.

She looked away, but she couldn't move until he snapped his fingers, and his man released her.

"Come tonight," he said. "Alone."

Then he was gone, and Violet rushed to King, who still lay on the ground. "King?"

Seeing him on the ground, bloody and broken, made her chest tight and her breath short. Violet hadn't prayed in a long time, but she prayed now—a constant chant of "Please, God, please, God" under her breath.

King opened his eyes and gave her a bleary look. "Ow."

She laughed and had the urge to kiss him. "Are you hurt badly?" She felt down his arms and pushed his hair back off his forehead to see a gash. Blood dripped down his temple.

"I'll survive," he said, pushing up with a groan. "Help me stand."

"Go slowly." Relief rushed over her, making her eyes sting with the promise of tears. She pushed them back. "I should leave you here," she said gruffly, but she offered her hand and pulled him to a standing position. He stumbled, and she rushed to place an arm about his waist to steady him. "You're an idiot."

"I said I'd protect you."

How could she keep her heart from melting when he said that? It had been years since anyone wanted to protect her, and no man had ever stood in front of her and taken a blow.

"Yes, you're doing an excellent job so far. Come on, let's get back before you decide to *protect* me further."

She supported him through the alleys of Seven Dials until they finally reached Clover Lane and the Silver Unicorn. Georgie opened the door to them and gasped. "What happened to Pa?"

Violet was too tired to remind him King was not his pa.

"Ferryman's gang beat him up. Where is Joshua?"

Peggy appeared and supported King's other side. "He's not back yet."

They led King to the back room, but when Peggy would have helped him down to the floor, Violet shook her head and motioned up the stairs. That was more trouble, but she didn't want him on the floor. She led him to the small closet with her bed, and she and Peggy helped him down. Peggy left to warm some water and fetch clean linens, and Violet pulled off his boots and helped him shed his coat.

Finally, he lay back and sighed. "If I'd known this was all it took to get into your bed, I would have done it sooner," he said.

"Hush. You're not staying." The words didn't feel as true as they would have a day or two ago. King had dug his way into...if not her heart, close to it.

Peggy returned with the warm water, and Violet cleaned the blood on King's face and hands. "We should see how bad the rest is," she said. She leaned forward and unknotted his ridiculously intricate neckcloth and then unfastened the buttons of his shirt. "You'll have to sit so I can pull the shirt over your head."

She helped King sit, and he obediently lifted his arms so she could pull the garment off him. She tossed it aside and then glanced at his chest. Her breath caught in her throat, as it had that night she'd caught him bathing. Even with the splotches of red now going purple, he was a prime specimen. The muscles of his shoulders and arms strained as he lay back down, and she couldn't stop herself from imagining how that belly ridged with muscles would feel under her fingertips.

"Georgie, come help me downstairs," Peggy said.

"But I want to stay with Pa."

"I need your help."

Without looking away from King, Violet said, "Go with Peggy."

"Aww!" But Georgie rose and followed the maid, slamming the door of the flat behind him.

"How bad is it?" King asked.

"I've seen worse." She took a deep breath and ran her hands over his chest. It was indeed as nice as she thought it would be. She skated up to his broad shoulders and then down to his biceps.

He cleared his throat. "My arms don't look injured."

"Right." She moved her hands to the bruised area on the right side of his chest and felt for broken ribs.

"Ow."

"I don't think they're broken," she said. "Maybe cracked."

She moved her hands away, and he prodded the ribs himself, wincing. Her hands traveled down to the purpling skin to the right of his navel. It looked like the shape of a boot. She poked it, and he inhaled sharply.

"Careful now!"

She glanced up at his face and saw that the blood from the cut on his forehead was running down his temple again. Taking the clean linen, she sponged it off then took each hand and cleaned his bruised and cut knuckles. "At least you got in a few blows."

"One or two of them will be feeling it tonight."

"Not as much as you," she said wryly.

"It was worth it. You're worth it."

Violet pulled back. "Aren't you the charmer?"

"I can be," he said. "But I mean it. I've never met a woman like you before. All the women I knew were peers' daughters who had as much personality as clotted cream."

"I thought men liked women who were pretty and sweet."

"Not all men," he said.

"Well, as much as I appreciate the compliments, let's get one thing straight between us. I don't need your protection. Your actions today only made things worse with Ferryman."

"I apologize for that."

Violet's brows rose. She knew King was not the sort of man who apologized easily.

"But something has to be done about him."

"You're not the one to do it. With the sale of your coat, you can consider your debt to me cleared. You are free to go to Scotland or the countryside or wherever you desire. In fact, I think it would be wise if you left Seven Dials first thing in the morning."

"You want me to go?"

"I don't want your death on my conscience."

"I'm not leaving until I deal with Ferryman."

"He is not your problem to deal with." She stood. "Rest and recover. I'll pack your things, and you can be away first thing in the morning."

"Violet—"

"No arguments." She picked up the basin of red-tinged water and walked out, closing the door to her closet behind her. In the flat, she dumped out the water and rinsed the linens, hanging them on the clothesline to dry. Then she started downstairs, taking a moment to close the door to the flat and lean on it to slow her heart.

She didn't want King to leave. A couple of days ago, she couldn't wait to see the back of him. Now he seemed part of the Silver Unicorn—as much a part of it as Peggy or Joshua.

But he had to go. Not only because he had incurred the wrath of Ferryman but because the way he made her feel was unwelcome. It had been a long time since she'd felt any attraction to a man, and she'd never felt the sort of attraction she felt to King. She didn't know what was wrong with her. The man caused more trouble than he was worth. He'd destroyed her tavern, upended her world, and now caused more strife with Ferryman. The sooner he was gone, the better.

But oh, how she would miss those stolen kisses and the way he made her feel when he pulled her into his arms. During those moments she forgot she was a poor taverness with rough hands and unwashed hair living in the armpit of Seven Dials, and instead felt like the most desirable woman in the country.

"Vi! Vi!" It was Joshua's voice, and Violet shook her head and scampered down the steps.

"I'm coming. What is it?" She swung through the door to the back room and saw Peggy, Georgie, and Joshua standing around the bar. Cloth-wrapped pies were on top of the bars, and Georgie hadn't waited to start eating his.

"It's Archie," Joshua said, unwrapping a pie and handing it to her.

Violet took the pie, but her stomach fluttered, and she suddenly had no appetite. "What happened?"

"He's awake!"

"What?"

"It's true. After I sold the coat, I stopped in to see Mrs. Archie. The physician King procured was just leaving, and Mrs. Archie was crying. I thought the worst, but then I heard Archie's voice. I went inside, and he was sitting up with the two little girls by his side on the bed."

Violet set the pie on the bar. "He's awake?"

"Thank the Lord," Peggy said, smiling.

"The physician said he should rest a few more days, but he should make a full recovery. He said he had a—Oh, I forgot the word he used. But whatever it is, he's getting better."

"I'll go see him."

Joshua grasped her wrist. "The physician said he needs quiet and rest. No visitors for a few days."

"Oh, I see." She lifted the pie again, but now she was too excited to eat. "Georgie, will you take this pie to King? He must be starving. Just leave it by the bed if he's sleeping."

"Sure, Vi." Georgie scampered away, and Violet asked Joshua how much he'd sold the coat for, collected the money, and counted out what she owed to Ferryman.

"He wants me to deliver the payment to him personally," she said, then told Joshua what had happened after they visited Mrs. Greene.

"You can't go by yourself," he said. "I'll go too. I can stay back and out of sight."

Violet narrowed her eyes. "Just as long as you don't go looking for Lizzie."

"I won't. King promised he'd help her."

Violet pressed her lips together and forced herself to keep quiet. She would not point out that King was leaving in the morning. And even if he wasn't, he couldn't help Lizzie. No one could.

"Finish eating. We need to open the tavern. It's already past noon."

HE HAD TO stop Violet.

King woke from a nap to the sound of men's voices and the clink of glasses. The room was dark, but then, it was windowless, and doubtless always dark. He was hungry, though he'd eaten the pie Georgie brought him. That had been hours ago.

At least, he thought it was hours. It might have been minutes.

He sat and almost groaned. He felt as though he'd been dragged behind a horse then run over by a cart. He wouldn't feel any better lying around. That much he knew from experience. He'd been in plenty of fights, and the more he moved about, the better he would feel. He prodded at the particularly tender spots, decided nothing was broken, and forced himself to dress.

In the flat, he looked through the windows and saw it was not quite dark. It was four or five, by his reckoning. Good. He had enough time to stop Violet. That had been his one thought upon waking. It was as though while he'd slept, his mind had worked out a plan to deal with Ferryman. He had no idea if it would work, but he wanted to try.

He washed his face and hands, gingerly tugged on his coat, and resigned himself to a lopsided cravat. His fingers were too swollen to manage a decent knot. Then he pulled on his boots and clomped down to the tavern.

Georgie was in the back room and was the first to see him. The boy's brown eyes widened, and King realized he had no idea how he looked. "That bad, eh?"

Georgie nodded. He handed King a copper pot, and King turned it over and looked at the distorted reflection. His eye was black and swollen, and the cut on his forehead had started bleeding again. He stanched the blood with his handkerchief and took one last look. His lip was split. No wonder it hurt when he spoke.

"Does it hurt?" Georgie asked, handing him a mug of beer from the jug on the counter.

"It looks worse than it feels," King said, though it was a near thing, because it felt *bad*. He drank the beer and then another mug, and that helped slake his thirst. "Where's Violet?"

"Her and Joshua are behind the bar. Did you hear about Archie?"

King had been about to enter the tavern, but he paused and turned back to the lad. "Tell me."

Georgie told him, and King smiled before remembering—with some pain—that his lip was split. "Good lad." He nodded at the sink full of dirty glasses and mugs. "Better get back to work."

"I will, Pa!"

King opened his mouth to tell the boy he was not his pa and then decided he didn't mind it. He'd always known he would have to sire children one day. He was the heir to a dukedom. But that obligation was gone now, and he found he rather liked the idea of being more of a father and less of a duke. Good thing, as he wouldn't ever be a duke now.

King pushed open the door to the tavern and spotted Violet right away. Holy hell, but she took his breath away. She was behind the bar, acting as publican, and clearly in command. She filled a mug while tossing a rejoinder then giving a saucy wink. She was a petite woman, only a couple inches over five feet, but she seemed taller when she was behind the bar and in her element.

Her confidence was enough to make him want her, but when his eyes lowered to the swish of her skirts, his throat went dry. He liked the way her hips swayed as she moved, and her round bottom stuck out when she bent over. Her dark hair had come loose, and tumbled down her back in a tangle. She constantly pushed it off her shoulders, which meant it probably bothered her, but he liked seeing it in disarray. Whenever he'd been in Society, every woman he met had perfectly coiffed hair that didn't seem to move. King had even taken to bed women whose coiffure looked perfect before and after, despite his best efforts.

But Violet Baker wasn't a well-bred young lady. She didn't care about all the rules and dictates he'd spent his youth breaking. She would be neither impressed nor appalled at his bad antics at school. She didn't care if he had a title or what that title might be. She wasn't after him for his fortune or his name. She wasn't after him at all. In fact, she wanted him gone.

She swung toward him and spotted him standing in the doorway. Her blue eyes flashed concern before she set a drink before a patron and spoke to the next in line.

Those eyes would be his undoing. Such lovely eyes. There was an intelligence and a depth behind them that he hadn't known he'd wanted in a woman. She could certainly tell him to leave all she wanted, but he wasn't going anywhere. At least not until Ferryman was dealt with.

King stepped forward and into place beside Violet. She gave him a concerned look, and he winked at her with his good eye. Smiling still hurt just a little too much. It felt natural to work beside her, and after a few minutes they fell into a rhythm that was both efficient and satisfying. Joshua cleared tables and carried trays of drinks to seated patrons, but after a half-hour, King and Violet had taken care of the rush.

She leaned on the bar and let out a sigh. "I appreciate the help, but you should be resting. You look awful."

"Just the sweet words every man wants to hear."

She grinned. "It's surprising you didn't scare the patrons."

"Most of them look worse than me. They probably like me better like this."

"If you think a few bruises will make you fit in here, think again. Anyone with eyes can see you were born much higher than this place."

"You know what they say—it's not where you were born but

where you end up that matters."

She narrowed her eyes. "Who says that?"

"I did. Just now." He smiled and hissed in a breath. "Don't make me smile. Hurts too much."

"You really should be in bed, but if you can manage, I need someone to stay behind the bar for an hour while I go to the Black Bear and pay Ferryman."

"No."

"You can lie down when I return."

King grasped her arm, and she immediately pulled free. He knew she didn't like being controlled, but his panic was such that he couldn't think of another approach. "You're not going to see Ferryman."

"Not that you have anything to say about it, but he said I had to go alone. So off I go." She started away, and this time King was smart enough to let her pass.

"Joshua!"

The boy looked over, and King motioned to the bar before following Violet into the back room. She gave an exasperated sigh when he stepped in. "Now what? Georgie, go help Joshua behind the bar."

Georgie jumped down from the stool and happily left the dirty dishes behind.

King waited until the door shut. "Violet—Miss Baker, I'm asking you not to go."

Her brows rose. "You can ask or you can demand. My response is the same. I have to pay him. I've seen what he does when he's crossed."

King folded his arms over his chest. "And what's that?"

"Rape. Murder. Torching of shops."

"He won't torch your tavern. He can't collect from you then. And I won't let him touch you."

"It's not only about the blunt, King. It's about respect and setting an example for the rest of the neighborhood. If I cross him, I will be sorry."

"If you go tonight, you'll be sorry. He has more on his mind than taxes, I promise you."

She tossed her hair. "I can take care of myself." She pulled on her coat and stuffed her bag of money in the pocket.

"I don't doubt it for a moment, but I'm saying that you don't have to. Violet."

She looked at him, her eyes wary.

"You don't know me well, but I'm asking you to trust me. I'm asking you to let me keep my promises to Joshua and to you."

"To Joshua—you mean about Lizzie?"

"Yes. I told Joshua I'd help her, and I told you I'd protect you. I'll do both."

Her eyes softened, and she stepped toward him, taking his hands. "King, it's not that I don't trust you, but you don't know what you're talking about. Look at you. Ferryman could have killed you today. Next time he will."

"He may try, but he won't succeed. And if you keep giving in to him, he'll take more and more and more. He's a bully, and I know bullies. I was one. The only way to stop him is to stand up to him."

"And lose everything!"

"You think he won't take everything anyway? Tell me his demands haven't increased. Tell me he won't keep demanding until you can't meet his price. Then he'll take Georgie and Joshua and you as well. That's what he really wants."

Tears sprang to her eyes, but she swiped angrily at them. "And you want me to just give up and give it all to him now?"

"No! I want you to fight before it's too late."

"It's already too late."

He took her by the arms. "No, it's not. There's still time if you let me help you. Violet, don't let him control you any longer."

Her gaze flicked to his and held. There it was—what she really feared or hated. No matter. Fear and hate were two sides of the same coin.

"I know what it is to be controlled," he said. "My father tried it for years. He tried to break me. Why do you think I was in the wilds of Scotland tormenting witches? To show him I couldn't be broken or forgotten."

"And look where that has gotten you."

He pressed his forehead to hers. "Yes, look. Right now, there's nowhere I'd rather be."

She cocked her head dubiously.

"Very well," he acknowledged her. "I would rather you had a servant and a cook and a feather mattress, but otherwise, there's nowhere else."

"Uh huh."

"Perhaps a valet. And more blunt so I might see a tailor."

"Yes, you certainly seem content."

"Violet, don't go. Let him come to us, and we'll take him on. Better yet, we won't wait for his retaliation. We'll strike first. That was always my favorite ploy when I was younger. I had to study a lot of military tactics in school. Strike first and strike hard always works." Almost always, anyway.

Violet closed her eyes. "You are asking a lot, King. I could lose everything."

"Speaking from experience, sometimes that isn't the worst that can happen."

She opened her eyes and looked directly into his. King looked back at her. He was as surprised as she looked that he actually meant what he said. Somehow, over the past couple of days, he'd realized losing everything wasn't the end of the world. It was *almost* the end of the world, but he could imagine worse fates. Like losing Violet and the boys to this Ferryman.

King swallowed his fear. "Maybe God or providence or whatever you want to call it—magic, I suppose—brought me to you for this reason. Maybe something good can come of this curse."

"Or maybe you'll just bring me down with you."

"There's my Miss Sunshine." He stepped back. "I don't want you to go, Violet, but I'm not here to control you."

She turned to stare at the door to the tavern. King knew she was thinking about her brothers. She was probably thinking about Peggy and Archie and the tavern, too. Was she willing to risk it all to get it back? She had to know, as well as he, that right now, none of this was hers. Ferryman owned it and her, and the gang leader was taking over little by little, day by day.

"Fine. We'll do it your way. What *is* your way?"

Shit. She wanted a plan.

Her lips thinned and her gaze turned deadly. "Tell me you have a plan, King."

"I'm good with plans. Very good. Just give me a little time to refine it."

She shook her head. "What have I gotten myself into?"

He took her wrist, and she met his gaze before allowing herself to be drawn against his chest. "Give me some time, and I'll show you." He brushed her hair off her forehead. "You won't regret this." He was speaking of more than her decision to trust him with Ferryman, because he could sense that she wanted him as much as he wanted her. He felt her catch her breath when he touched her, saw her cheeks turn pink, and her eyes darken. For his part, he could hardly resist touching her whenever she was near. Her scent—simple ale and yeast—was intoxicating. His gaze dipped to her lips, and she wet them with her tongue in anticipation.

"Better not," she said before he could take her mouth. "Your lip is cut."

"I don't care," he murmured. "I've been thinking about nothing else but kissing you for hours."

"Just kissing me?" she teased.

"If I say more, you'll probably punch me."

"I'll definitely punch you." She stepped away. "Now, back to work. If you can manage?"

"I'll manage," he said, though without her body pressed to his, all the aches and pains from earlier came back in a rush. And she turned and strode through the door to the tavern, leaving him wanting her more than he had ever wanted any woman.

# CHAPTER FOURTEEN

V IOLET KNEW WHAT King wanted. It was what every man
wanted, only the look in his eyes when he gazed at her
wasn't like any she'd seen before. There was a tenderness there.
She wouldn't have thought it possible when she met him just a
few days ago, but there was more to him than she'd thought.

She wiped the counter as Joshua barred the tavern door and
Georgie put chairs on top of tables. King swept the floor—
listlessly and ineffectively, but he certainly looked good doing it.

Was she a fool for trusting him about Ferryman? Probably.
But he was also right that Ferryman would take more and more
until he got what he really wanted. And the arch rogue wouldn't
settle until he had full control of the Silver Unicorn, as well as all
three of them under his thumb.

Because Violet saw the same look in Ferryman's eyes that
she'd seen in King's—only Ferryman's was full of possession and
violence, whereas King promised pleasure and passion. That
choice was easy, and really King wasn't telling her anything she
didn't already know about Ferryman's intentions. She just wished
she had more time before having to confront him.

By the time Violet finished counting the money and putting it
aside for safekeeping, the boys were half-asleep and King was
groaning when he bent over. "Off to bed with all three of you,"
she said, herding them into the back room. "King, sleep in my

bed. You probably shouldn't even be up."

"Where will you sleep, Vi?" Georgie asked.

"I'll sleep down here." Not that she would sleep. She'd lie awake worrying what Ferryman had planned and listening for any untoward sounds that might herald his attack.

"I can't let you do that," King said. "A gentleman doesn't allow a lady to sleep on the floor."

"You're not a gentleman anymore," she retorted. "And I'll be fine."

"I must insist that you—"

"We'll sleep on the floor here," Georgie said. "Joshua and me, we're gentlemen."

"No, boys. That's not necessary."

"He's right, Vi," Joshua said. "You take our bed. We'll be fine down here." Joshua looked at King. "Right, King?"

"That's right. Very noble of you."

"Joshua—" Violet began to protest.

"Vi, we're *noble!*" Georgie whined, and she closed her mouth and nodded. Who was she to deprive them of their chance to be noble, even if it meant an uncomfortable night on the floor?

"Very well. Let me check the door one more time."

"It's bolted and the bar is in place," King said, taking her arm and steering her toward the stairs. "I did it myself."

"The lamps."

"I blew them out," Joshua said. He pushed the door to the tavern open to show her it was completely dark.

"What about the door to the back?" she asked.

Georgie ran over and bolted it then put the wood beam in place to prevent anyone opening it.

"Fine." She allowed King to lead her to the stairs then paused again. "You'll be cold."

"King has coal," Joshua said, and proceeded to pull the coal bin out and put two pieces in the stove.

"Use it all, if you want," King said. "We'll see you in the morning."

"I'll leave the door to the flat unlocked. If you need me, I'll be right inside."

King dragged her the rest of the way up the stairs, through the door to the flat, and then closed it behind her. "I know you like to do everything yourself, but you have to allow others to help you sometimes."

"I wanted to stay downstairs to listen for Ferryman. Only I couldn't say that in front of them," she hissed.

King shook his head and loosened his neckcloth. "He won't come tonight. He'll come when you're not expecting him. But don't worry. We'll be ready."

"What are you talking about?"

"I'm still working out the details. We can discuss it in the morning. Better yet, let Joshua and me take care of it."

He started for her closet, and she grabbed his arm and pulled him back. "Oh, no. You will not treat me like one of your Society ladies who sits home doing needlepoint while her man is away. I'm part of this. It's my tavern. If you go after Ferryman, I go too."

"I'd rather you not get anywhere near him. I'm trying to protect you."

"I don't need protection."

King seemed to consider this a moment. "Then what do you need?"

Violet swallowed, suddenly realizing how close he stood and how alone they were. Her eyes darted to the bed where the boys usually slept, and she had a sudden image of her naked body tangled with King's—all those lovely muscles bunched and tensing as he bent over her.

"I think I can manage that," he murmured, reaching out and tugging her waist until she was pressed against him. Violet drew in a breath, inhaling the scents of his brushed wool coat and bergamot tea. Underneath those scents were more familiar ones of her own soap, yeasty beer, and something that she could only describe as him.

She met his gaze then winced at his black eye and the swelling near his lip.

"Do I look that bad?" he asked.

"You never look bad," she murmured.

"Neither do you. I don't know how I managed to work next to you all night without doing this."

He bent toward her and kissed her gently. She had the urge to kiss him back, hard, but was conscious of his split lip. His kiss was teasing, and his tongue darted out to taste her lips and trace them lightly. She opened up, and he licked his way inside, igniting a fire in her belly and making her squirm to move closer to him, though she was already pressed fast and hard against him.

No one but King had ever kissed her like this. No man had ever treated her so tenderly or like she was something of value, something to be cherished and protected. She didn't need his protection, but it was nice to know she had it.

His hands moved up her back, bringing warmth and a tingling pleasure. They slid into the tangle of her hair, freeing the last of it from its confines. "I love your hair," he said, pulling back to look at her as he spread the dark tresses over her shoulders.

"It's a mess."

"That's what I love about it. It's wild, like you."

"I'm not wild."

"We'll see." He tugged her hair lightly, pulling her head back so he could nuzzle her neck. Flames of heat licked their way from her toes to her sex, making her breath come fast and her hands clench in his coat. His hands slid from her back to her bodice, and he cupped one heavy breast, making her nipples harden with an aching need.

"King," she said as he moved to her throat and unfastened a button just below his lips.

"Hmm?" he asked, sounding as though he had all the time in the world when she was on fire to be touched.

"Don't bother with that. Just toss my skirts up and—"

He pulled back. "Don't rush me. I want to see you naked."

"Later."

He shook his head. "I've been imagining it for days, imagining kissing you, licking you, touching you...everywhere." He opened another button.

Violet could hardly breathe now. His words were making her imagine things too, mostly his lips in all the places aching for his touch. She moved closer to him, pressing her body against him until she felt his hard length.

He chuckled, low and velvety. "And you said you were not wild."

He dipped his lips into the V of her bodice, and she let her head fall back, closing her eyes and enjoying the moment, not allowing herself to think about whether she should do this and what a mistake it might feel like in the morning. For a few minutes she could forget about the tavern and Ferryman and her brothers—

"Vi!"

She jerked. "Did you hear that?"

"It's Georgie," he said, kissing her throat. "Ignore him."

"Vi!"

"I can't ignore him." She pushed King back, and he moved away with a sigh.

Violet went to the door and pulled it open. "What is it, Georgie? Did you hear something?"

"No," Joshua answered. "He just realized you didn't read him a story or kiss him goodnight."

"I might have known it would be something important," King said.

"It *is* important."

But King had already crossed to the bed where Georgie slept and lifted the one book she possessed. It was a worn copy *of Gulliver's Travels*. "Should I wait up for you?" he asked.

Violet bit her lip.

"Never mind. I can already see you thinking. In five minutes you'll have a dozen reasons why this"—he gestured between them—"was a mistake."

"It *is* a mistake. We'll regret it in the morning. We—"

"Vi!"

"Goodnight, Violet Baker," King said, leaning forward and kissing her cheek. "Thank you for the bed."

He moved away, shedding his coat with a groan as he headed for her closet. Part of her wanted to go after him, but she turned and started down the stairs.

Half an hour later, she'd read a chapter, kissed both boys—even though Joshua pretended to hate it—checked all the doors again, and finally trudged back upstairs. The flat was cold, but she didn't want to waste coal, so she undressed quickly, washed, and climbed under the covers on the boys' bed. The room to her closet was closed, and she imagined King was asleep by now. She could hear his soft, regular breathing. For her part, sleep eluded her. She stared at the ceiling and thought about how Ferryman might punish her for not going to the Black Bear tonight, not paying her taxes, daring to challenge him.

She rose, went to the window of the flat, and looked out. The night was as foggy as the day had been, but she didn't see anyone loitering about. No sign of lamps moving through the gray mist. All was silent, but she knew somewhere out there Ferryman was fuming and plotting.

She should have never listened to King. If she went now, would Ferryman forgive her?

She snorted. He'd most likely take his payment, beat her bloody, and demand more. He would never be satisfied, and he would only torment her until he destroyed her. She had to fight back. Now that King was here, she had a chance.

Violet went back to bed and closed her eyes, then was promptly assailed by the image of King's scraped knuckles on the buttons of her bodice, his mouth on her throat, his bruised hand cupping her breast.

She rolled over and remembered the feel of his warm breath on her skin and the hard muscles of his body against her own.

Then there was the thick bulge of his cock against her belly. The heat she'd felt earlier rushed back, and she squeezed her legs together to quell the desire pooling there. Under the covers, she slid her hands to her breasts, which were tender to her touch. The hard buds of her nipples ached when she pushed down her shift and fondled them. She wanted King's mouth on them. Her other hand slid down to her sex, which was wet with need.

"You'll regret this," she muttered to herself as she slid a finger over the swollen bud between her legs. "You'll look at him tomorrow and everything will be awkward." She let out a low moan as she circled one finger over that yearning, sensitive part of her.

Violet pushed the covers of the bed back and padded to the closet where King slept. She opened the door quietly. If he didn't wake, she'd go back to bed. But as soon as the door opened, he said, "Violet?"

"It's me."

"What's wrong?"

She heard the covers move and could just make out the shape of him turning toward her.

"Nothing. Everything is fine. I just—" What was she supposed to do? Tell him she'd come to ravish him?

The silence hung between them for a moment, and Violet considered ending her embarrassment and just going back to bed. But she stood there, trying to work up the courage to say the words. Finally, she swallowed. "I want you," she said, so quietly she wasn't certain he heard.

"Thank God." He reached out and took her hand, pulling her inside the room. "Close the door behind you."

She pushed it closed, and then he tugged her onto the bed. Her hands came down on his chest—his bare chest—and she inhaled sharply. "You're half-naked."

"Not half," he said. "But let's get you naked." His hands were on her waist, fumbling with her shift. He'd never get it off that way. "Damn, but I wanted to see you naked."

SHANA GALEN

"I know a way," she said.

"A lamp?"

"No." She slid the shift off her shoulders, then took his hands in hers and guided them over her skin.

"God, you're soft," he said.

She moved to straddle him, and wriggled her hips. "You're not." She slid his palms, large and cool, over the swell of her breasts and then down until he cupped her.

"Beautiful," he murmured.

Together, her hands on his, they slid her shift down to her waist, and he glided his fingertips over her skin, making her shiver and bite her lip with need. The shift went to her hips, and King pulled her up, lifted the material, and tugged it over her head. The cool air brushed her skin, but it was a pleasant coolness in contrast to the heat that was King. She pulled the bedclothes back and settled down again, feeling the bare skin of his legs on the inside of her thighs. The coarse hair on his legs tickled the sensitive flesh of her inner thighs in the most tantalizing way.

His hands were on her waist, but he groped for her hands, and linked his own with hers. Pulling her close, he kissed her gently. At least, the kiss began gently. Lips brushed together, parted, then came together with more passion. Violet's fingers tightened on his, and he pulled her lower, until her breasts pushed against the hardness of his chest. She wiggled against him, liking the feel of his skin against hers.

She heard him groan, low in his throat, and his tongue swept into her mouth, tangling with hers in a slow seduction. He tasted of peppermint and promised pleasure. Violet released his hands and threaded her fingers through his thick hair. She felt his hands land on her bottom and squeeze gently before he slid a hand between them and cupped her sex.

She inhaled sharply as she felt his fingers slide over her most sensitive parts. Now she was the one moaning as his explorations brought her desire into sharper focus. One finger slipped into her channel, and she felt her muscles pulse with expectation. She

166

thought he might drive that finger deeper, but he slid it back out and swirled it over the small, swollen bud that ached the most. For a moment, Violet swayed, and she couldn't help but break off the kiss.

King nuzzled her neck as he teased her. "You like that?"

"Don't stop," she said.

"Oh, I don't intend to. In fact…"

Suddenly, her world shifted as he moved beneath her, reversing positions so that she was on the bed and he over her. Before she could protest, his hands were on her. Everywhere. One hand cupped her breast while another slid over her belly. His mouth soon followed, leaving a trail of heat that made every other part of her feel ice cold. She gasped when his hot mouth closed on her tight nipple. He suckled and pulled until she was panting for breath. Meanwhile, his hands were at work, exploring her body, and then that one magic finger found the place she wanted him again. She arched up to meet it and spread her legs to give him better access.

For a man who seemed to think of little but himself, he certainly knew something about pleasing her. She had thought their encounter would be quick, and she half expected to come away unsatisfied. She no longer thought she would leave this bed unsated. She just wished he would hurry up about it.

"King," she said, her tone insistent.

"Don't rush me, sweetheart."

Two fingers slid over her, then inside her, filling her and making her cry out with need.

"I want you inside me," she said. She heard his breath catch, knew her words had aroused him, but he didn't thrust his cock inside her as she'd hoped. Instead, he lowered his mouth to her belly and licked a warm trail to her navel. Violet wriggled, feeling ticklish and on fire all at the same time.

She wiggled her hips, pushing his fingers deeper, but he slid them out, resting them lightly at her entrance and circling it with tantalizing strokes.

"*King.*" In case he didn't understand what she wanted, she reached down, groping until she found his cock standing stiff and hard just above her leg. She slid her hand around it and was rewarded with a choked sound from the back of his throat.

With his free hand, he circled her wrist, not removing her hand but preventing her from moving it in the way that would have given him the most pleasure. Violet might have fought him if he hadn't slid his mouth lower then, nibbling at her skin and then blowing warm air on the soft hair at the juncture of her thighs.

"Open wider," he said, nudging her open with an elbow even as he spoke.

"You can't mean to—"

"Oh, yes, I can."

He moved lower, and her legs fell open. His mouth slid down to brush against the skin between her legs, and she jerked in response. Her hand opened, releasing him, and he moved lower, settling between her legs. His hand felt heavy against her inner thigh, while the fingers of his other hand were still light and teasing at her center. She felt suddenly vulnerable and exposed in a way she hadn't expected. She'd thought she'd come here and take him, but somehow he'd turned everything around. She was the one being seduced. She was the one being taken.

And then his mouth closed on her, and she let out the last whoosh of air, fisting her hands at the surge of pleasure. He was kissing her and suckling, and then his tongue darted out and stroked that small, swelling nub, and she couldn't stop a squeal. She put a hand to her mouth, trying to keep quiet as his tongue savaged her in the best possible way. She bit her thumb when he sucked at her again but couldn't stifle the cry of pleasure when his fingers entered her, driving deep and filling her.

Her hips bucked and her back bowed, her body reaching for the pleasure that still lay tantalizingly out of reach. She knew King was teasing her, pleasuring her with a skill she had not known was possible. He would bring her just to the peak of pleasure, but before she could slide over the edge, he'd pull back and bring her down again. Then, a few moments later, she was straining and panting again, her body tense and covered with perspiration.

"King, please."

She felt the rumble of laughter against her skin. "Ah, so you can be nice."

"I'll be very nice. *Please.*"

His tongue flicked at her, but he was still teasing her. "What do you want, sweetheart?"

She wasn't sure what she answered, something that certainly no lady would say, but his response was to let out a low growl. His hand tightened on her thigh, and his mouth went to work in earnest. Pleasure rose in her, and she half feared he would retreat, but this time he brought her to the brink and kept her there. Violet heard cries, panting, moans, and realized the noises were coming from her. Her hands had slid to her breasts and the hard nipples, so she had no thumb to bite to stifle the noises.

And then, suddenly, she was falling. She didn't know if it was his tongue or his fingers or what he had done, but white light exploded behind her eyes and her entire body contracted and then released in the sweetest crest. The waves crashed over her, subsiding slowly until she was spent and her throat raw with the cries of pleasure. She went limp, her hands falling to the side, feeling the wetness of tears on her cheeks.

She'd never felt anything like that before. She'd felt pleasure, but this was beyond what she had imagined possible.

And then King rose up and levered himself over her. "Do you have the energy for more?"

"No more," she said. But he chuckled and bent to kiss her as his cock teased the swollen flesh between her legs. To Violet's surprise, her body reacted to the feel of him. Her legs closed on his slim hips, and her own rose to meet him.

He slid inside her, filling her and stretching her sensitive body, until she was crying out again. The fading tingles of pleasure rushed back as he moved inside her, his thrusts deep and slow and unhurried. She'd wanted him inside her, and she wouldn't have ever believed he would feel so good there. She told him so, and he kissed her and told her she was the one who felt good.

"You're driving me mad with the moans you make," he said. But he didn't seem to be driven mad. He was so controlled, so attentive. When she made a particularly sharp sound, he repeated what he'd done until she made it again.

And then her entire body was tensing again as he nudged her higher and closer to climax yet again.

"King, I can't," she said, breathless with need. But even as she protested, her legs tightened on him, and she pulled his mouth down to hers. She heard his breath catch, felt him swell inside her, and knew he was close. And yet his control never wavered as he brought her, once again, over the edge in a climax that shattered her.

And then he was pulling out of her and groaning as he found his own pleasure. Violet reached for him, wanting the closeness of him again, and a moment later, he was beside her, pulling her into his arms.

She closed her eyes, warm and limp. For the first time in as long as she could remember, she slept deep and untroubled.

# CHAPTER FIFTEEN

K ING WOKE FIRST, the weight of Violet in his arms pleasant enough that he ignored the numbness of the arm she lay on for as long as he could. Finally, he worked it out from beneath her.

He needn't have worried he would wake her. She was sleeping heavily, her breaths even and deep. He pulled the covers over them and lay awake, listening for any sounds of trouble. He wasn't certain what had wakened him, but as he heard nothing unusual, he closed his eyes again.

The image of a catapult danced in his mind, and he realized that was why he'd awakened. He'd had an idea for how to deal with Ferryman, and it was one of his best plans yet. Of course, he needed to get Lizzie out first. Violet wouldn't like that, but King had given his word, and he never broke his word.

The room was dark as midnight, but he could feel it was close to dawn. Once the boys were awake, they would begin on the preparations for his plan.

King closed his eyes to sleep again, and Violet rolled over and snuggled closer.

He liked the feel of her against him, the softness of her hair on his arm, her light floral scent surrounding him. He'd never shared a bed before, never slept close to a woman or held her all night. He'd never wanted to, but he wanted Violet to stay where she was as long as possible. If morning never came, King didn't think he would mind.

She'd surprised him again last night. First, by coming to him. Of course, he'd known she wanted him. He wanted her even more, but he hadn't held out any hope he'd ever have her. When she opened the door, he'd thought he was dreaming. And then she was on top of him, and he prayed he was not dreaming. But her body had been warm and alive, and she was no coquette. She would have taken him inside her as soon as they were naked. It made him hard just to think how quickly he might have had her.

Except he hadn't wanted her like that. He wanted to take his time, learn her body, find out what she liked. He'd wanted to see her tough exterior crack. And he liked to think he'd shattered it. He thought he would have been content just to give her pleasure. The sounds she made and the taste and smell of her intoxicated him. He loved every shiver, every moan, every tensing of her muscles. He might have wished for a candle or lantern so he could see her body, see her face when she climaxed, but there was always next time.

At least, he hoped there was a next time.

Because when he slid inside her, his entire life had seemed to change. She'd felt as good as he'd expected—tight and wet—but something was different. Not the act itself—that was not so very different—but when he was with her, he didn't want only the physical pleasure. He'd wanted more. He couldn't quite pinpoint what it was he sought, but he'd wanted to be closer to her, give her more pleasure, give her... He didn't know. But there had been a tightness in his chest that hadn't eased until she wrapped her arms about him and came apart. His own climax had seemed less important—not that he hadn't enjoyed it. More than anything else, he'd wanted her in his arms.

He'd never felt this way, and wondered, idly, if it was some effect of the curse on him. More likely, it was just the effect of Violet Baker. He liked her more every day. He respected her more than he'd ever respected any woman—any man he could think of as well. And he cared for her. He didn't like to admit how much he cared for her, but surely he could admit it to himself.

He knew he was putting all of them in danger by not paying Ferryman what he demanded, but King would rather be beaten bloody again than have Violet risk herself by going to Ferryman's lair.

The memory of the fight the day before made his bruises twinge with pain. He'd forgotten them completely when he was with Violet, but now his eye throbbed and his lip stung. It might not have been the wisest course of action to kiss her so thoroughly.

And yet…he'd do it again. He *wanted* to do it again. He wanted to start all over and kiss every inch of her. King restrained himself, knowing that waking her would mean depriving her of sleep she would need that day in her work at the tavern. Before he'd wished his title and wealth back because he missed the privileges they afforded him. Now he wished them back so he might have given Violet the means to forgo her labors for a day or a week, or longer. He rather liked the thought of lounging about with her all day in his enormous bed. He'd feed her delicacies and make her drunk on the best wines.

And then he imagined taking her to Almack's or one of Prinny's garden parties, and he chuckled. She would hate it and probably cause a scene, and King imagined it would be the best event of any Season he'd ever had to endure.

"What are you laughing about?" she asked, her voice croaky with sleep.

"Garden parties," he said, squeezing her. "Go back to sleep. It's still early."

"How can I sleep with you crowding me out of the bed?" She elbowed him. "You're taking up all the space."

"You were sleeping just fine until now. You seemed quite comfortable."

"I was holding on to avoid falling off the edge." She sat. "I had better go sleep in the other room. I don't want Joshua or Georgie to find us together." She stood and began to feel around for her shift.

"Why not?"

"I don't want them to think you might stay."

King didn't think the idea of his staying was so far-fetched, but Violet certainly seemed against it. "Certainly, they don't form that opinion every time you take a man to bed." He couldn't see her, but somehow, he could sense that he'd said the wrong thing. "I don't mean to imply—"

"I've never brought a man to our flat. Not that there have been many men, but none has ever been inside my home or met the boys."

"I'm the exception, then."

"You're the mistake. I don't want the boys to become attached to you." She opened the door to the flat, and King could see the light outside was gray, verging on morning.

He rose. "Would that be so awful? I haven't run off yet, and I haven't any plans to."

"You're telling me if your friend arrives with a hundred pounds and an offer to stay at his country estate, you will refuse?"

King considered. As slim as he thought the chances for regaining his title and property were, he would try if given the opportunity. A hundred pounds would go a long way to paying legal fees.

"That's what I thought," she said. Her gaze dropped, and he realized he was still naked.

"I'd take you and the boys with me. What better way to keep you safe from Ferryman?"

She snorted. "I'd come back to find my tavern burned to the ground and Ferryman waiting to abduct us all. I can't run from my problems. Get dressed before Joshua finds us like this."

King raised his brows. "I thought you might want to take advantage of me. Again."

She gave him the ghost of a smile. He'd take it, considering her foul mood this morning.

"Maybe later," she said, and disappeared behind the screen with the washbasin.

King closed the door to the closet and dressed, trying not to think about what Violet had said. With each passing day, he was less and less inclined to believe Henry would come to his rescue, but surely his friend wouldn't abandon him altogether. There was also Rory. The letter King had written would reach him eventually. One of his friends would aid him, and when they did offer King an escape, would he really choose to stay?

He didn't like to think of leaving Violet, but neither did he like to think of himself mopping floors the rest of his life.

Nights with Violet might make up for the drudgery of the daily cleaning, though. And he didn't mind acting as publican. He rather liked bantering with the tavern's patrons, who seemed unimpressed by his breeding after the first night of gawking at him.

But escaping Seven Dials wouldn't help him escape from his problems. They'd just follow him wherever he went. He'd learned that lesson in school. It seemed no matter what he did to force his father's attention, no matter how many schools expelled him, the Duke of Avebury didn't love him. King had never made a formal decision to cease trying to force his father to notice him. He supposed, as he'd grown older, he'd just realized the effort wasn't worth the trouble.

But Violet was worth the trouble, and if he were to be a disgraced marquess without property and exiled from Society, wouldn't he rather be so with the lovely Violet Baker?

He heard the door open and Joshua call, "Hello." Violet answered him and asked if he'd seen any signs Ferryman had been about. Ferryman was King's immediate problem. His lost legacy would have to wait.

So he opened the door and told Joshua to fetch Georgie. The men had a task to complete.

VIOLET HAD NO idea what King was up to with her brothers. He'd shooed her out of the flat and the tavern's back room, and though she'd protested, she had enough to do in the front that she didn't argue too strenuously. Truth be told, she was rather glad he was keeping the boys occupied. It meant she didn't have to constantly think of jobs to keep them busy and out of trouble.

With the relative quiet in the tavern, she sat and studied her ledgers. Not paying Ferryman meant she had enough to replenish her supplies of beer and spirits. She might even be able to afford another table, and could send more money to Archie and his wife. She should go visit them, but she didn't want to be out and about alone, with Ferryman presumably unhappy with her.

What was she to do about the arch rogue? King said to trust him and that he had a plan. She couldn't think of a reason he wouldn't tell her that plan unless he didn't think she'd like it, but she'd deal with that when the time came. Right now she had him here to protect her, and she trusted that he wouldn't leave until she and the boys were safe.

Strange to have a man in her life she could trust and rely on. She'd always relied on her father, but he'd been gone three years now, and she was used to relying on herself. She shouldn't allow herself to get too used to not relying on herself, but she had slipped a little last night. She'd wanted the comfort of another person and—she could admit it—had wanted King. She was flesh and blood, after all. How long could she really resist that pretty face and that lovely body?

The experience had been more than she could have expected. She should have known that he would be skilled in bed. What else did he have to do with his time but seduce women and practice bed sport? But she hadn't expected him to be so...generous. No man she'd been with before—and there had only been a handful—ever cared so much for her pleasure. King had put her first and made her feel...

Well, she'd never felt like that before.

And then, at the end, she hadn't even had to ask him not to spill his seed inside her. He'd pulled out at the last moment, protecting her from pregnancy. She hadn't thought a man like him would care about something like that, but King was constantly surprising her.

So, yes, she did trust him. More than she trusted most men, and that was saying something.

Upstairs, something metal clanged and she heard Georgie call out that he was sorry, and King's deep voice give some answer. Violet looked back at her ledgers and began tallying another column. It seemed that Peggy should have been here by now. If the maid did not arrive soon, Violet would start readying the tavern to open.

A faint knock on the door made her glance up. Then she jumped down and went to the Judas hole, opening it and looking out. No one was there. Violet would have closed it again, except she heard a sound and caught the flash of something on the ground, leaning against the door.

"Oh, no!" Fingers fumbling, she lifted the heavy crossbar, let it drop, and pulled the door open. Peggy fell inside, her body lifeless. "King!" Violet called. "Joshua!" She turned Peggy onto her back and gasped as she glimpsed the girl's battered face. Blood ran down her nose, and both eyes were swollen shut. Her dress was torn at the throat, and Violet made out a letter W. She could hear the sounds of footsteps racing toward her as she parted the torn fabric, exposing Peggy's chest.

Written in mud were the words YOU BEEN WARNED

"What happened?" King demanded as he burst into the room.

Violet covered Peggy again quickly. "She's been beaten." She forced her voice to sound calm. "King, help me move her. Joshua, you close the door and bar it again."

King bent over Peggy's body and moved her feet. Together they lifted her and brought her to the back room. Violet looked over her shoulder to be certain they were alone, then uncovered Peggy's chest again.

"A message from Ferryman?" King said, voice low.

"Who else would have done this?"

"Vi?" It was Georgie calling down from the top of the stairs.

Violet covered Peggy again. She didn't want the boys to see the writing. "Fetch me water and some linen," she told Georgie. "Be quick, but don't spill it."

"Yes, Vi!"

"I knew he'd retaliate," she said, "but I didn't think he'd go after Peggy. This isn't her fault."

"No, it's not."

She looked up at King and saw his hands were clenched. Was it possible he was as upset as she? No, he was not upset. He was angry. Violet just hoped he was not so angry that he did something rash.

"I must go pay him. If I go now, maybe this will be the end of it."

"No!" Joshua said. He'd just come into the back room. "You know it won't end here, Vi. It will never end."

She rounded on him. "Then what do you want me to do? Allow Ferryman to beat us all bloody? What if this was you or Georgie?" She pointed to Peggy. "How could I ever forgive myself?" To her shock, her voice trembled, and a tear slid out from her eye. She swiped at it angrily. She was not about to cry. She was no weakling.

But then King took her shoulders and pulled her against him. Violet tried to fight, but once her cheek rested against his chest, and she felt the warmth of him and smelled the wool and bergamot tea scent trapped in his clothing, she couldn't stop the tears. And then she felt so ashamed, she buried her face in his chest.

"Ferryman won't touch another member of this family," he said. Violet knew it was the sort of promise he couldn't ever keep, but his words calmed her nonetheless. "Georgie, you know what we need to be ready. I need you to keep working on that while I have a talk with Joshua."

"Yes, Pa. Is Vi all right?"

"She's fine. She just needs a hug."

"Oh. Should I clean Peggy's face?"

"I'll do it," Violet said, voice muffled. She sniffed and quashed her tears. She had to get a hold of herself. She pulled back and wiped her cheeks. "I'm fine. See?" She gave Georgie then Joshua a watery smile. Neither boy looked convinced. "What is it you need to discuss with Joshua?"

King hesitated then seemed to come to a decision. He reached over and pushed a piece of hair behind her ear. "The boys and I are preparing for battle here."

"Battle?"

"That's right, Vi!" Joshua said. "We have piles of rocks ready to throw down on the street and water at the ready in case Ferryman tries to smoke us out."

"And I'm collecting bottles of gin," Georgie said. "We stuff rags in them and light them on fire then throw them on top of the invaders!"

Violet's mouth dropped open, and she gave King a disbelieving look. "Was this your plan?"

"Of course. Might as well do something with all those books I read on military strategy."

"King, I hardly think this will work." But truth be told, in the short term, it was a good counterattack. Ferryman and his men wouldn't be prepared for that sort of assault. Not at first, anyway.

"I'm fashioning some weapons as well," King said. "I'll be ready if it comes to hand-to-hand combat."

"Can I have armor?" Georgie asked.

"I think you could do with a shield," King said. "Maybe a pot would work for that."

Violet shook her head. This plan was so absurd, and yet she couldn't help but believe it might just have a chance.

"I know what you're thinking," King said. "What about when

Ferryman returns with a counteroffensive?"

"You mean when he comes back with enough men to storm the tavern or just burn it down?"

"We can't let it get to that," he said. "We have to strike first."

"What does that involve?"

"I don't know yet. I need to go to his headquarters, which, as I understand it, are the Black Bear. I need to get a sense of the place. Joshua and I will plan our reconnaissance mission."

"Your what?"

"It means we sneak around and take a look at everything," Joshua told her.

She shook her head. "I don't think that's wise. He knows both of you."

"That's why we sneak around, Vi," Joshua said as though this should be obvious.

"There's one more part to the plan," King said. "And this is the part you won't like."

"Don't tell her," Joshua said.

"Yes, tell me. I don't like any of the plan, so I can only imagine what you have in mind." She crossed her arms over her chest.

"I told Joshua we would rescue Lizzie. And that's what we'll do."

"No!" Violet shook her head. "That's too dangerous."

"We can't leave her there when we attack Ferryman," Joshua argued.

"You can't bring her here! Absolutely not."

"I'm getting that girl out, Violet," King said. "I gave my word, but more than that, *I* couldn't live with *myself* if I left her."

"Then go and get yourself killed. But I forbid you from taking Joshua."

"I'm going, Vi," Joshua said. "You can't make me stay."

"King!" She glared at him, but he shook his head. "I need him with me, Violet. I can't do it without him."

Violet looked at Joshua and back to King again. She knew those stubborn looks. The men's minds had been made up. Little as she liked to admit it, she could see Joshua was more and more a man every day. Even if she forbade him, he wouldn't obey.

She grasped King's lapels and yanked him aside. "If anything happens to him," she said, "I will blame you."

"Nothing will happen," he said.

"You'd better hope not, because if you come back without him, I swear to God, I'll make you sorry you were ever born."

"Violet—" He tried to pull her into his arms, but she shoved him back.

"Don't touch me. Don't ever touch me again."

# CHAPTER SIXTEEN

JOSHUA PAUSED ON the roof of the building overlooking the Black Bear. "That's it," he told King, who had paused beside him.

"Thank God." King slumped down and took a breath. "Give me a moment. I haven't done this sort of thing in years."

Joshua turned back to study Ferryman's lair. He wasn't worried about King. The man might complain, but he'd kept up with Joshua just fine. That earned him a measure of respect. Joshua's respect for King had been growing daily. Finally, they saw a way out of the trap in which Ferryman had caught them. King would help Vi stand up to the arch rogue. Just like he was helping rescue Lizzie. Joshua hadn't really thought King would keep his word. Most adults made promises they had no intention of keeping. King seemed different, and Joshua hoped he *was* different.

"Tell me how we get inside again," King said, sounding less winded now.

"See that window?" Joshua pointed to the first floor. "We go in that way. It leads to a room where none of the whores sleep."

"How do you know it won't be locked?"

"The latch is broken."

King glanced at him. "Convenient."

"That's why I broke it."

King laughed. "Very well. How do we get to that window? And don't say jump across to the roof."

"I won't say it, then."

"Holy hell. Can't we climb up from the alley?"

Joshua pointed to the ground floor below the window in question. "There's another window there. One of Ferryman's men might see us."

"For once, I should have listened to your sister." King sighed. "I'll follow you, then."

Joshua rose. "Ready?"

"As I'll ever be."

Joshua moved back a few paces then jogged to the edge of the flat roof and leapt over. The roof of the Black Bear was a bit lower, but the space between the buildings was only about five feet. He made it easily. With a grin, he turned back to King and waved at him.

King followed his example, stepping back and running for the roof. But he hesitated at the last moment, and his jump wasn't as powerful. Joshua watched in horror as he fell just short of the Black Bear's roof, his hands grasping the edge. Joshua ran to the edge, put his hands over King's wrists, and held on.

"What'd you do that for?" he demanded.

"Just trying to keep things interesting," King said, his voice full of sarcasm. "Pull me up."

Joshua tried, but he didn't have the strength. Fortunately, King got one arm over the edge of the roof and shimmied the rest of the way. He rolled onto his back and lay looking up at the gray sky. It was midmorning in London, though the overcast skies and persistent fog made it difficult to tell what time of day it might be.

"Come on. We're almost there."

King rolled his eyes toward Joshua, but he rose to his knees and watched him edge back over the roof, using a drainpipe to reach the window, slide it open, and jump inside. Joshua poked his head out and waved at King. Then he turned back to the room and jumped.

"Wot are ye doing 'ere?" Lizzie asked in a whisper. She held a blanket and seemed to be in the middle of straightening the pallets and clothing items lying about. She looked as pretty as she ever had, though she was just as thin, and her face was streaked with dust. But she had those big brown eyes that made Joshua feel warm inside.

"I've come to rescue you," he said, puffing out his chest so he'd look a bit bigger.

"Come to get me killed, more like. Joshua Baker, go 'ome before Ferryman finds ye 'ere and kills ye. 'E'd like nothing better. All night and morning 'e's been raving about yer sister Vi and the vile things 'e'll do to 'er when 'e 'as 'er."

"He won't have her," Joshua said, "and he won't have you either. King and I are taking you away."

"King?" Joshua pointed to the window, and Lizzie dropped the blanket and crossed the room to peer out. She ducked back in quickly. "That man is King?"

"He's our new publican. He used to be a nob—maybe he still is a nob—and he has a safe place for you to go."

But Lizzie shook her head, her limp brown hair rising and falling with the force of her movements. "There's nowhere Ferryman won't find me, and when 'e does, 'e'll kill me."

"Ferryman won't find you in Mayfair. You'll be safe, Lizzie. I promise. I told you I'd get you out of here, and I will."

A pair of feet came into view, and King said, "A little help, please."

Lizzie stepped back as Joshua helped guide King's legs into the window. He landed inside with a thud that made Lizzie look over her shoulder at the door then rose to his feet a bit unsteadily. "You must be Miss, er—" He looked at Joshua.

"Lizzie," Joshua supplied.

"I was hoping you'd provide a surname."

"What's that?"

"Never mind. It's a pleasure to meet you, Miss Lizzie. Ready to go?"

Lizzie gaped at him. "Ye've come for me?"

"None other. Master Joshua says you are in danger from

Ferryman. I know a safe place you can go."

"She doesn't think anywhere is safe," Joshua said. "But tell her what you told me."

King nodded. "I have a distant cousin in Mayfair. He has a big house and lots of servants to clean it. He will take you in as a maid. You can hide there, and Ferryman will never find you."

"Why would 'e do that, sir?" Lizzie asked. "Take me in, that is."

"Because if he doesn't, I'll threaten to show up on his doorstep, and right now I am *persona non grata*."

"Wot?"

"It means he'll be happy to have you as a maid, but we should go now. Before anyone discovers we're here."

Even as he said the words, the door to the room began to open. Joshua rushed toward it and pushed it closed again. "Lizzie, wot's this?" the woman on the other side demanded.

Lizzie's eyes were wide with fear, but Joshua gestured for her to speak. "I'm changing clothes. Give me a moment," she said.

"Like I care to see yer skinny arse. Open up."

"Just a minute!"

King strode across the room and reached above Joshua's head, closing the door completely. "Give me something heavy to brace it," he said to Lizzie.

"Lizzie?" said the woman on the other side of the door. "Who's in there with ye?"

"Oh, no!" Lizzie wasn't moving, so Joshua grabbed an old, broken stove and heaved it to the door.

King slid it against the door and dusted his hands off. "It's now or never, Miss Lizzie."

"Lizzie!" the woman yelled. Joshua stared at the door with dawning horror that, any moment, half of Ferryman's gang would be upon them. "Open this door or I'll get Ferryman, I will."

"That is our cue to exit," King said, striding to the window. "Lizzie, are you coming or not?"

Lizzie looked at the door then back at King. Joshua reached out and took her hand. "Lizzie, come with me. I want to help you."

"Lizzie! Open the door!"

"Joshua, I'm scared."

"Don't be scared. I promise I'll make sure you're safe."

"Ferryman!" the woman screamed. "Ferryman, Lizzie has a man in the room."

Lizzie went pale and groaned, but Joshua gripped her hand tighter and forced her to look at him. "Trust me, Lizzie."

"Joshua, we have to go. Now." King grabbed his shoulder and pulled him away from Lizzie. "We can't make her come if she doesn't want to."

Lizzie looked at the door then at the window. Reluctantly, Joshua released her hand and went to the window, where King waited. "Go up. I'll follow you."

Joshua put a foot out of the window. "Lizzie, *please*," he said. He gave her one last look, hoping it wasn't his last sight of her, and climbed up the side of the building, using the drainpipe and the ledges of the windows above.

He didn't look down until he reached the top, and when he did, he grinned broadly. Lizzie was climbing up, King right behind her.

Unfortunately, Ferryman stuck his head out of the window right then.

"King!" Joshua called. "Watch out!"

AND THIS WAS the part of the story where he fell to his death, King thought as a hand clamped on his ankle. Joshua called a warning—too late—and King looked down to see Ferryman himself leaning out of the window. He'd removed his hat, and his greasy brown hair fell in his eyes. "Stealing my dell?" he roared. "I'll gut you for this."

"Not today," King said. He'd worn his riding boots, which were not so easy to dislodge from his foot. In fact, Danby had always complained about them. Now King kicked out and dislodged Ferryman's hand, narrowly missing kicking the gang leader in the chin. But the man let go, and King climbed higher and out of Ferryman's reach. Lizzie was moving slowly, too slowly for his liking, but she had to make the climb in skirts, so King would forgive her. "Lizzie, I need you to hurry!" he called, looking over his shoulder at the window.

As he'd feared, Ferryman dispatched two of his gang to go after them, and they were climbing out and grabbing on to the drainpipe below him. That made four of them, three of the four grown men, holding on to one drainpipe. This would not end well.

Even as King thought it, the drainpipe seemed to shudder in his hand and pull back from its braces slightly. Lizzie felt it too and gasped.

"A little bit faster, Miss Lizzie," King called, unable to crawl faster with her blocking his path. One of the men below him reached for his foot, and King kicked at him. "Joshua!"

"I almost have her," Joshua called back. "Lizzie, hurry! Give me your hand."

Her foot caught on her skirt, and she slipped. King held his breath for the long moment when she dangled precariously by only her hands. The drainpipe creaked and jolted, making his heart lurch.

Lizzie found her footing again and climbed higher. King followed, still kicking as the men behind him tugged at his feet and legs. Finally, Joshua got a hold of Lizzie and pulled her onto the roof. King tried to move faster, but Ferryman's men were holding him back and slowing him down. In another moment, his hands would come loose, and he'd slide down to them. He looked over his shoulder at the long drop below. He'd rather not try his luck at flying today.

The drainpipe creaked again, and King judged the distance to the roof of the Black Bear. He was almost there, could see Joshua peering over the edge, eyes wide with fear. "Shake the pipe loose," he called.

"What?" Joshua called, sounding as though he thought King mad.

"Shake it loose of the bracings!" King ordered him. "Do it."

Joshua gave him a terrified look but went to work shaking the pipe. King held on, grateful the men below him had to do the same and were prevented from grasping at him. The pipe made an awful screech and began to bend backward at the weight of the three men.

"Give me your hand!" King called to Joshua.

Joshua reached down, and King took his hands, releasing the drainpipe as it bent and dipped. But he wasn't out of the fire yet. Joshua was thin and wiry, stronger than he looked, but it took a lot of strength to pull a man of thirteen stone up and over a ledge when gravity was working against him. King prayed Joshua's grip would hold as he tried to grasp the ledge of the roof. And then Lizzie's face came into view, and she grabbed one of King's arms with both of her hands and pulled as well.

Below him, the pipe made another loud screech, and the men echoed it as the loud pops of the braces breaking echoed through the alley. Then there was a horrible crack, an ear-splitting cry, and a *thud-thud*.

Holy hell, but that would be him in a moment if he didn't get hold of this roof. Lizzie's face was red with effort as she pulled, and King's fingers touched the ledge, groping for it. Joshua pulled harder too, a last burst of energy, and King had the ledge with one hand. Lizzie and Joshua pulled the other, and King took hold of the stone.

He tried to lever himself up, but his muscles were fatigued, and he slipped back down, leaving his body dangling over the edge of the roof precariously.

"King!" Joshua said. "They're coming onto the roof."

"What? How?" King hadn't seen a door when he landed on it earlier. He'd checked, thinking they could get inside the building that way.

"The chimney!" Lizzie said. "They're coming up through the chimney on the top floor."

Chimneys were small and narrow. That was one reason children were employed as chimney sweeps. King supposed it was too much to hope that Ferryman or his gang became stuck in there. If the brick was old enough, they could simply break through it.

King closed his eyes and gritted his teeth, pulling up with all his strength. If he didn't make it, Violet would never trust him again. Well, he'd be dead and probably wouldn't care that she didn't trust him, but he desperately wanted to prove to her that his plan would work.

And he desperately didn't want to die.

Sweat poured down his temple as he finally managed to get one elbow onto the ledge. His bruises ached, and the muscles of his arms were on fire. But he exerted one last burst of energy. With a roar and some help from Joshua, King rolled onto the roof. He would have liked to lie there for ten seconds and catch his breath, but there was no time. A glance at the chimney showed him Ferryman was doing exactly as Lizzie had claimed, breaking through the bricks of the chimney to access the roof. King struggled to his knees. "Go!" he ordered Joshua and Lizzie, though his voice was little more than a whisper.

"Follow me," Joshua told Lizzie. He moved back, standing almost beside the crumbling chimney, then sprinted forward and leapt across the roof to the building across the alley. He landed neatly, rose, and waved at Lizzie.

But she was shaking her head. "I can't jump that far."

"Yes, you can," King croaked. He didn't add that she had to. At that moment, Ferryman dislodged several bricks from the chimney, and his face appeared.

"I'll kill you for this," he hissed, pale skin streaked with soot and blood.

Lizzie gave King a terrified look. He rose to his feet. "Lizzie, you can do this. Do exactly what Joshua did."

On the other roof, Joshua was calling encouragement. Lizzie looked at King, then Joshua, then Ferryman, who was breaking through the lower bricks of the chimney now. If she didn't jump soon, Ferryman would kill them both. King couldn't jump until she did.

"Lizzie, come on. I'll catch you!" Joshua called. King might have argued that catching her was rather unlikely, but the words—and possibly the threat of imminent and violent death at the hands of Ferryman—finally convinced her. She took a step back, tucked her skirts into her belt, and hunched low. King wanted to close his eyes as she ran. If she second-guessed herself, if she faltered, it would be a long, deadly drop to the alley below. But she leapt across with all the skill of an alley cat. Her landing was not graceful, but Joshua was there to pick her up.

"King! Hurry!" he called.

Beside King, the last of the bricks holding Ferryman crumbled, and he pushed through. His rich purple coat was coated with soot and ashes, and as he moved, they fell from his hair. The effect was to make the arch rogue look ghostly. "I should have had my men kill you yesterday." He swung at King, who had been swung at enough times to duck out of instinct.

And then, following his instincts, he bent low and drove his shoulder into Ferryman's abdomen. As soon as he hit the man, more soot and ashes were dislodged from his clothing, making King's throat close up. He choked off a coughing fit and straightened, preparing to make his jump while Ferryman was off balance. But the gang leader grabbed King's coat and tugged him back. King swung wildly but missed. He might have swung again, but one of Ferryman's men emerged from the ruins of the chimney. And there were more behind him.

Joshua called frantically, and King knew he had one last chance. He had to go now, or he'd never escape. Ferryman groped for his shoulder again, and this time, King turned, planted his feet, and hit Ferryman squarely in the nose. The impact made his already bruised knuckles cry out in pain, but he ignored it. He shoved one of the gang members out of the way and ran for it.

The distance between the Black Bear and the roof of the other building seemed much farther than it had the first time he jumped. As his body entered the space between the buildings, he didn't look down. Instead, his mind conjured an image of Violet Baker. He didn't know why he should think of her in that moment, except to acknowledge that if he didn't make it, she would dig up his body and kill him all over again.

Or maybe he thought of her because he knew she was back at the Silver Unicorn worrying about him. He wanted to see her again. He wanted to hold her again. He wanted to tell her thank you for coming to collect her seven pounds, fifteen shillings the morning of his birthday. He couldn't think where he would be without her.

Possibly not flying through the air and landing with a bone-rattling thud on a rooftop in Seven Dials.

Lizzie looked down at him. "Are ye 'urt?"

"Probably," he said. At least, King *thought* he spoke. He couldn't hear anything over the ringing in his ears. Then the children pulled him to his feet and dragged him away.

VIOLET CLEANED THE last of the blood from Peggy's hair and rose to dump out the pink water in the basin. Georgie had helped her to settle Peggy on a pile of King's clothing. She would have rather moved the girl to the flat upstairs, but Peggy was too weak to walk, and Violet and Georgie couldn't carry her up the stairs on their own.

Violet poured a cool glass of water from a pitcher on the counter and helped Peggy drink. Once she'd swallowed a bit,

Peggy laid her head back on what looked like a waistcoat.

"Better?" Violet asked.

"Thank you, Vi."

"Peggy." Violet felt her throat close as she fought back tears. This was her fault. She'd known people would be hurt if she challenged Ferryman. She just didn't realize it would be innocents like Peggy. "I'm so sorry," she managed to say.

"What are you sorry for?" Peggy asked, showing a little spirit. "You aren't the one who did this."

"It's my fault. If I had paid Ferryman—"

Peggy put her hand on Violet's arm. "Then he would have come at you another way. I'll be fine. This was just a warning. I worry what he has in mind for you and the boys." She cut her eyes at Georgie, who sat close to her, patting her other arm.

Violet worried about that too. King and Joshua had been gone hours now, and it took all her strength not to give in to panic at the thoughts that crossed her mind. She pictured Joshua dead, King bruised and bloody, the two of them dumped into the river by Ferryman's gang. Why had she ever let them leave? She should have never allowed Joshua to go. King could do as he liked. If he got himself killed, that was his fault.

But she was only lying to herself. She was as scared for King as she was for Joshua. This was why she should never have allowed him to stay. It was bad enough she worried for Georgie and Joshua. Now she had another male to worry about, care about, fear losing.

Violet didn't think she could handle losing another person she loved.

Not that she loved King—not yet. But give him a few more days and he would wheedle himself into her heart. He'd inserted himself into every other part of her life.

"Vi, when will Joshua and Pa be back?" Georgie asked.

"I don't know," she answered for what felt like the thousandth time. "Soon, I hope."

*Never,* she thought, but she couldn't say that to Georgie. She had to be hopeful until she had a reason to despair.

Suddenly there was a crash at the back door, and she jumped. Peggy shrank into her bedding. "It's Ferryman," she said in a small voice.

"Violet! Open the door."

"No, it's King!" Violet said, and ran to the back door. She lifted the wooden bar and pushed the door open. Joshua, Lizzie, and then King spilled inside. Violet hugged Joshua hard. When he stepped back, King pulled her into his arms. Violet thought about hitting him. She was sorely tempted to punch him in the gut for making her worry so much, but his warmth and scent enveloped her, and her resolve weakened. He picked her up off her feet, hugging her hard.

"Is everything all right here?" he asked, setting her down.

"Fine. We've been worried sick about you."

"Peggy!" Joshua cried.

"I'm fine," Peggy said weakly. "Vi has me all fixed up."

"We need to bring her back to her mother," Violet said. "Mrs. Greene will have herbs and salves that will help her heal."

"Now might not be the best time for that." King released Violet, and she was appalled that she had the urge to go right back into his arms. What was wrong with her? "Ferryman and his goons are right behind us," King said. "Georgie and Joshua, positions."

Georgie jumped up, and Joshua saluted. "Yes, sir!" they said in unison.

Violet would have laughed if she hadn't been terrified. She pushed past King and closed the back door, lowering the bar over it. Meanwhile, Georgie and Joshua, followed by King, raced up the stairs to the flat. Lizzie followed. After checking on Peggy one last time, Violet went after them.

The men were scrambling about the flat. Georgie moved buckets to the windows. Joshua put two pots on the stove as King stoked it and loaded the last of their coal inside.

"Are you planning to cook him a meal?" Violet asked.

"Something like that," King said with a wink. "See anything yet, Lizzie?" he asked the girl, who was looking out the window.

"Not yet. But I know 'e's coming for ye. I 'eard 'im talking about 'is plans last night."

"What did he say?" Violet demanded.

"'E was goin' to wait until ye were all abed tonight then set the place on fire. Once 'e smoked ye out, 'e'd kill the man"—she pointed at King—"and take ye three."

"Might have worked if he'd tried it last night," King said. "But now he's angry and not thinking straight. He doesn't have the patience to wait and strike when we're not expecting it. Idiot plans to attack us in broad daylight."

"You sound as though you're happy about that," Violet said, moving behind Lizzie to search the street below.

"I am. We're ready for him, but he doesn't know that. How's that oil coming, Joshua?"

"Almost ready, King."

"Buckets in place, Georgie?"

"Yes, sir, Pa!"

Violet closed her eyes and tried not to scream. King was acting like this was some sort of game, but Ferryman and his gang weren't toy soldiers. They had real weapons and could kill.

"There he is!" Lizzie said, ducking back and out of view.

Violet moved forward and saw what Lizzie had just pointed out. Ferryman and a dozen members of his gang were marching down the street, scattering people, dogs, and anything in their way.

# CHAPTER SEVENTEEN

K ING MOVED TO Violet's side to gauge the enemy's progress. Sure enough, Ferryman was coming. It gave him an odd burst of pleasure to see the man still covered in soot and ash. "Don't look so dapper now, do you?" he muttered.

"They have planks with them." Violet grabbed his arm. "They'll break the door down."

"Let them try. Georgie. Joshua." King's two lieutenants turned to him, ready for orders. "Don't strike until I give the signal. We need to wait until the enemy is in position."

"Yes, sir!" Georgie said. "What's the signal?"

"When I say, *Go*. Not until then."

"What can I do?" Violet asked. King wanted to tell her to go into her room and hide, but as much as he wanted to protect her, he needed her help.

"Can you and Lizzie carry up a couple of those casks of wine? Not the biggest ones. The quarter cask."

Violet gave him a suspicious look, and it was deserved. She wouldn't like what he planned to do with those casks. But she didn't argue. Instead, she motioned to Lizzie, and the two women went out of the flat.

"Now that the ladies are gone," King said, voice low. "Listen up, men." He wiggled his fingers, and the boys moved in close. "We're going to fight like hell, but if things don't go our way—"

"They will," Joshua said, sounding more confident than King felt.

"They will, but every soldier needs a backup plan. And our backup plan is for the two of you to take Violet and run."

"I'm not running," Joshua said.

King took him by the shoulders. "If I say *retreat* then you need to go. We can fight another day, but only if you get away. Besides, Violet needs you. You have to protect her."

"What about Lizzie?"

King should have known the boy would ask about her. "Leave Lizzie and Peggy to me. But I need you two with Violet. You know a safe place to hide?"

"I do!" Georgie volunteered.

"Good. When it's safe, meet me back here." King glanced out the window again. Ferryman was below now, and the rest of his men were gathering around him. "Ready, men?"

"Ready!"

King could hear the thuds and grunts as Lizzie and Violet pushed and tugged the heavy cask up the stairway. He pushed the window open further and leaned out. "Good day to you, Mr. Ferryman," he called in his most upper-class accent. "How do you do, sir?"

Ferryman called out an expletive and frowned up at him.

"What can I do for you, sir? I'm afraid we're closed. You and your companions will have to return later."

Ferryman put his hands on his hips. "You'll be dead later."

"Well, now. That's not very neighborly." King was buying time, and he knew it.

"Want me to be neighborly? Come out now—you and those boys and Violet Baker. Bring me my dell back, too. Come out now, and I'll kill you quickly."

"And if I don't come out?"

Ferryman smiled. "Then I kill you slowly and painfully."

*Only if you can catch me,* King thought. But he said, "Might I have a day to consider your offer? I'll have my answer for you in the morning."

Even beneath the layer of soot, King could see Ferryman's face turning red with anger. Without moving his lips, he said loud enough for the boys to hear, "Get ready."

"Maybe I can talk to him," Violet said, panting. King glanced at her and saw she and Lizzie had managed to move one cask into the flat.

"No. Go get another." She gave him a look that said if she'd had a knife at hand, she would have flayed him. He smiled. "Please?"

She grudgingly turned and went back out the door, followed by Lizzie.

"Get in position, men," King said.

"Come out now or we come in," Ferryman said his two men with the wooden plank moved into position in front of the tavern. The door was barred and the heavy wooden shutters over the windows closed, but a few good blows with that plank, and Ferryman would be inside. King had to stop him from having that chance. His main concern had been that some of Ferryman's men would go to the back entrance and break down the door leading to the back room. King had no way to defend that position, as the flat overlooked the front of the tavern, not the back. But he had counted the men with Ferryman and watched closely. None of them had broken off to go around back.

"I'll give you to the count of ten," Ferryman said. "One!"

"Bring me those coals," King ordered Joshua.

"Two! Three!"

"One rock in each hand, Georgie," King said as he moved himself to get one of the pots of hot oil from the stove. He took the smaller one, seeing it was already bubbling.

"Four!"

King moved into position with Joshua at his side and Georgie kneeling at the base of the window.

"Five!"

"Joshua, you aim for the one holding the back of the plank."

"Six!"

"Georgie, you aim for the one in the front."

"Seven!"

"Who will you aim for?" Joshua asked.

"Eight!"

"I have my eye on Ferryman," King said.

"Nine!"

"And *go!*" King bellowed loud enough that Ferryman's men looked up. Joshua held a glowing piece of coal on the end of the small metal coal shovel, and he flung it at the gang member holding the rear end of the plank. A second later, Georgie hurled a rock at the one in front. He missed, but he had another ready, and that one hit its mark. Joshua's missile hit the mark too, striking the man in the head and causing him to howl and bat at the hot coal burning him. King held the pot of boiling oil in one hand, waiting to use it. Ferryman was too far away for a direct hit, and he didn't want to waste it. Instead, he lifted one of Georgie's rocks and hurled it at another gang member. Joshua released the other coal, and it glanced off the sleeve of one of Ferryman's thugs.

In the meantime, Ferryman was yelling at his men to ram the door. The two who had been hit first were replaced by two others, and Georgie and King pelted them hard enough that their first hit against the door was only a glancing blow.

"More coals, Joshua!"

Joshua ran to open the stove and fetch more as King and Georgie pelted the men below. "Move just a little closer," King muttered, his eye on Ferryman.

The door flung open, and Violet rolled the second cask inside the flat. "They're attacking," she said between breaths.

"And we're defending. That one, Georgie! Holy hell, duck!"

A man had lifted one of the rocks and hurled it back. Georgie hunched down, and King stepped aside, so the rock landed in the flat, knocking over a chair. Joshua jumped over it and moved into position, flinging another coal. One of the men mistook one of the pieces of coal for a rock and picked it up, then dropped it and howled in pain as he clutched his burned hand.

In the meantime, another two men had moved into position with the plank and rammed the door to the tavern. "Violet, stay back," King ordered her. "Joshua, help me with this cask."

He and Joshua rolled the first cask to the window, heaved it up, and pushed it out. The men saw it coming and raced out of the way, shielding their faces with their hands when the wood broke and wine and splinters flew everywhere.

King took the pause to race back to the stove, replace his unused and cooling pot of oil, and lift the larger one, now boiling. He went back to the window and looked down at Ferryman, who still stood tantalizingly out of reach. Georgie threw a rock at him, but he caught it and tossed it back, breaking the glass above them. Georgie jumped back, covering his face, and Violet raced forward and took him by the shoulders. "Are you hurt?"

"I'm fine, Vi!" Georgie pushed her back. But below, Ferryman had seen her.

"You'll pay for this, Violet Baker. When I get my hands on you—" He'd moved closer, and King saw his opportunity.

"Violet, come to the window. Just here." He shoved Joshua out of the way. "Yell down at him."

"You want me to *taunt* him?"

"Exactly. Taunt away. You're good at that."

She glared at King then stood at the window and called down, "I'd like to see you try even one of those acts, Ferryman. I heard you're so infected with the pox, your cock won't stand up!"

"Really, Vi?" Joshua asked.

She waved a hand as though to say she was just saying whatever fabrications came to mind. But Ferryman howled and screamed epithets at the window.

"Just a little closer," King muttered.

Violet seemed to hear him and leaned forward to stick her tongue out at Ferryman, who lunged toward the tavern, raising his fists in anger and calling on his men to destroy the place. King took his chance, shouldering Violet aside, thrusting the pot out the window, and turning it over. The hot oil poured out. Ferryman saw it and tried to move, but too late. It scalded one side of his face, and the chest and shoulder of the man beside him. Ferryman howled, his arms over his burned skin.

"More rocks, Georgie!" King called. Joshua was already pulling Violet aside to fling hot coals at the men gawking at Ferryman. Georgie hit another of them, and King hurled the pot, hitting another.

"Not my pot!" Violet protested.

Finally, the tight circle of the gang broke apart and two men grabbed the still-wailing Ferryman and pulled him away as the entire gang retreated. Presumably back to the Black Bear.

"Ye did it!" Lizzie said, looking out. "I can't believe ye did it."

"Vi, look at this," Joshua said, pointing out the window.

Violet and King looked down at the street below, where a half-dozen neighbors and shop owners had emerged. Mrs. Littman had her hands on her hips, surveying the debris on the street. Then she looked up at the window and began to clap. The other neighbors clapped too, and then began to cheer and chant, "Long live the King!"

Violet put a hand to her temple. "I don't know how his head will fit through the door after this," she muttered. "What about Lizzie and Peggy? I need to get Peggy home to her mother."

"Right." King hadn't been able to think about anything but the coming battle, but now he considered that if things didn't go well, it would be best if Lizzie and Peggy were far away. "Joshua and Violet, you take Peggy home. Do you think you can manage her alone?"

"We can do it," Joshua said.

"Good. Take Georgie with you and leave him with Archie."

"But Pa—!"

King knelt in front of Georgie and took him by the shoulders. "You acquitted yourself well today, soldier, but the next battle is too dangerous for a new recruit like you. Violet needs you safe if she's to concentrate on what we must do tonight." He needed the boy tucked safely away, too.

"But Pa, I can help!"

"I know you can, but a soldier has to follow orders." He gave Georgie a stern look. "Even when he doesn't like them."

The boy stamped his foot and folded his arms over his chest, but he didn't argue.

"What about Lizzie?" Violet asked, ruffling Georgie's hair.

"I'll take her and see her safely in a house in Mayfair," King replied. "I'll need a few coins to pass to the housekeeper in lieu of references and prior experience."

Violet waved toward the tavern below. "You know where I keep the lockbox."

King raised his brows, surprised she was trusting him with the blunt. She didn't seem to trust anyone but herself and Joshua with the money they took in, and she kept a tight control over that. He'd never met anyone so tight-fisted.

"Pack what Georgie needs and whatever you don't want to lose—just in case," he added. "And meet me at the back door in a quarter hour."

VIOLET RETURNED TO the tavern first, unlocked the back door, lifted the latch, and peered into the darkness, listening. She heard nothing, but she didn't relax until she stepped inside and stood quietly in the dark for a moment. She was alone. She would have felt it if anyone else had been here. It was almost six in the evening, and it felt strange to have the tavern dark and closed. King had been nothing but bad for business. Still, if all went well, maybe she wouldn't ever have to close the tavern again.

Either that or she'd lose everything.

Peggy had been delivered safely to her mother, who had put her to bed and begun to mix herbs and a draught for pain. She'd seen a burn on Joshua's arm—one he'd obviously been hiding from Violet—and insisted he stay and be treated. She'd send him home as soon as she was able to make him a poultice.

Violet had taken Georgie to Archie, and though Georgie's mouth had stayed fixed in a tight, angry line, he hadn't argued or whined or wheedled as he usually did when he did not like something. She had to give King credit for his way with her brothers. They obviously respected him. And why shouldn't they? Look what he had accomplished in just a few hours. She had woefully underestimated him. He was no weak, effete nob. He was smart and brave and resourceful.

She had just lit a lantern when she heard someone at the back door. Violet grabbed the first thing at hand, a porcelain mug, and held it aloft.

A moment later, King stepped inside the back room. He put both hands up as soon as he saw her. "Not a bad weapon. I considered using them on Ferryman but thought you'd kill me if I broke all your mugs."

Violet lowered the vessel. "I would have. Is Lizzie safe?"

"Yes. She's at a house in Mayfair, and I'm certain the staff is scrubbing and dressing her in clean clothing now. The house-keeper looked happy to have a young girl to take under her wing." He turned to lock the door then looked about. "What about Joshua?"

"Mrs. Greene is treating a burn on his arm. He'll be here shortly. Go ahead and lock it. He has a key. Just leave the bar off."

She took the mug and another to a jug of beer and poured two cups. She handed one to King and kept the other for herself. He murmured his thanks and drank deeply. She refilled both mugs and drank herself. She was still hungry, but her stomach was fluttering with nerves. She didn't think she would keep anything she ate down. "Do you want me to see if we have anything to eat?" she asked.

King gave her a sheepish look that was so unlike him, Violet stared.

"What's that look?"

"The housekeeper fed me when I brought Lizzie in. I'm not hungry."

"Well, don't feel guilty about it. You'll need your strength for tonight. Tell me the plan."

"Let's go upstairs. I want to keep an eye out the window. I don't think Ferryman is in any condition to come back tonight, but I'd like to keep watch anyway."

Violet let the way up the stairs, and the two of them settled in at the table, King facing the window overlooking the dark, empty street.

"The streets are never this quiet," Violet said.

"I imagine all of Seven Dials is giving the Silver Unicorn a wide berth tonight. They're waiting to see what will happen."

"So am I. King—"

At her tone, he turned from the window and looked at her.

"I wanted to ap—" She swallowed. "I wanted to say—" Violet tried again. "I mean to apol—"

"Why, Miss Baker." King grinned. "Are you trying to apologize to me?"

"Shut up."

"By all means. I'll sit here quietly and allow you to speak."

Violet gritted her teeth. "I didn't think you could do it—take on Ferryman, that is."

"To be fair, I wasn't sure I could do it either. We haven't won yet."

"Maybe I should wait for my apology."

King reached over and took her hand. "Maybe you could show me how sorry you are."

"Nice try." She pulled her hand away then straightened. "And I won't apologize for worrying about the boys. I still don't think you should have involved them. They're children, not soldiers. You had them thinking you were some sort of general."

"Who's to say I'm not?"

Violet cocked her head. "If you were in the army, I'll do a jig standing on my head."

"As much as I'd like to see that"—he winked with his good eye—"I'm afraid you are correct. I didn't serve in the army. But I did study a lot of military strategy in school. Had to read books and books about it—everything from the Romans to George Washington. So I know something about it. I hope you know I would never put either of the young masters in danger. You're not the only one who cares about them."

There was little King could have said that would have touched her more than those words. Violet felt her heart seize and then speed up. She was in trouble, and she knew it. She was beginning to care for King. Worse, he felt the same—at least about her brothers. She had not wanted to become attached to him, to need him or care for him. She had told herself from the beginning that he was not staying.

But what if he was?

No. She couldn't allow herself to consider that possibility. She couldn't allow herself to even imagine a time when she would not be alone and bearing the weight of responsibility for the tavern and her brothers on her own.

She might not even have a tavern to run after all was said and done with Ferryman. The situation was so volatile, she couldn't even risk opening tonight.

"What is your plan?" she asked. "Do we sit here and wait for Ferryman to attack again? He might have been overconfident tonight, but he won't make the same mistake again."

"I don't plan to wait for him to come to us. I think we go to him."

Violet stared at him, waiting for him to smile, to joke, but he was obviously serious. "Need I remind you there is no army, and you are not really a general? Attacking Ferryman is a quick way to end your life. You barely made it out with Lizzie."

King sat back and crossed his arms. "I wouldn't characterize the rescue that way."

"Joshua said—"

"Let's talk about the future, not the past." He leaned forward. "If we don't want Ferryman to come here, we need to give him something else to focus on. We need to give him a problem bigger than you or the Silver Unicorn."

"What's that?"

"The Black Bear. It's not only a source of income for him, it's his headquarters. I say we burn it down."

Violet laughed. "You cannot be serious. King, tell me you are not serious. Innocent people could be hurt."

"I've thought about that. First, we get everyone out with a raid by the Bow Street Runners. Then we sneak inside and start the fire. By the time Ferryman realizes what's happening, it will be too late."

"And exactly how will we convince the Bow Street Runners to come to Seven Dials and take on one of the most powerful crime lords in the city? Ferryman pays off local magistrates, and those he doesn't pay are afraid of him."

"Leave that to me. I still have a few friends in Town, though they're dwindling fast. We have to act quickly, not only to stop Ferryman but to take advantage of my name before it loses any and all clout."

Violet opened her mouth to ask how he could fall further, then remembered that his father was in the Tower, accused of treason. He would surely be executed, and then King's name would be sullied even more.

She rose and went to him, moving behind him and wrapping her arms about him so she too could see the street below. "King, Ferryman is my problem, not yours. You shouldn't wait to see your father. You may not have much time to say goodbye."

He stood. "I told you not to pay Ferryman, and I promised to protect you. There's nothing more important to me than you. I care more about you and the boys than I ever have for my father." He took a step back. "You'll think me some kind of callous monster for saying that."

"No." She moved closer to him, her heart in her throat. "I

don't think that of you at all." She swallowed and forced the next words out. "Despite my better judgment, I care about you too."

King smiled. "Miss Sunshine, did you just admit you care for me?"

She knew she shouldn't have said anything. Leave it to King to ruin the moment.

He took a step forward, and Violet realized she had nowhere to escape. The window was behind her, and she was out of options for running.

"You're in trouble now. Not only am I a fallen marquess, I'm a cursed one with a reckless plan to take on a notorious crime lord." He put one hand on the wall by her head. "Are you certain you want to throw your lot in with the likes of me?"

"I didn't say I want to throw my lot in with you."

"Then what are you saying?" He bent down and looked her directly in the eyes. "That you have feelings for me? That you *care* about me?" He slid a hand under her chin and held her gently. "You can admit it, you know."

Violet glared at him, hating how much she enjoyed his closeness and the feel of his skin on hers. She would swallow hot coals before she admitted she cared for him. "I do want to say something," she said, whispering so King leaned closer. "Shut up and kiss me."

# CHAPTER EIGHTEEN

KING DIDN'T HAVE to be asked twice. Violet put her arms about him, and he sank into the lushness of her lips. He'd been wanting to kiss her since they came up to the flat. The fog had finally cleared, and the sun was setting—the orange light flickered over her dark hair, making it look fiery. She was always beautiful, but the warm glow on her skin made her look more alive than he'd ever seen her.

She sank her fingers into his hair, pulling him closer to her heat and her life. She was strong and feisty and made of steel and velvet.

"I've never met anyone like you," he said, pulling back to tug her toward the closet with her small bed. It would be another hour before Joshua returned, but King didn't relish taking Violet on the floor. He pushed the door open and sat on the bed, settling her between his legs. "You're so alive. I think a part of me was dead inside before I met you."

"Stop talking." She took his mouth again as though to force him to comply. But even as she stripped him of his coat and his shirt, she couldn't strip away his thoughts. She was scared of what she was feeling, scared that he was putting it into words. King understood that very well. She'd lost the people she loved, the people she'd counted on to protect her. She was afraid to believe she might ever find someone who might love and protect her again.

King was shocked to realize that he was strongly considering the role. He wanted to be part of Violet's life. He couldn't imagine how he'd survived thirty years without her frowns and glares and narrow looks. He'd take them all for one of her smiles or the sound she made when he put his hands on her.

And that was exactly what he had in mind.

She rid him of his shirt and dropped it on the floor, and King began to undress her. She pushed his hands away and lifted her skirts, prepared to take him that way, but he shook his head. "Oh, no. I have been imagining you naked since—er, for some time now."

She gave him one of those famous narrow looks. "Some time? Such as since the first time you met me?"

King shrugged. He couldn't deny it. "I'm a scoundrel, but I'm not beyond reform. Before I finalize my reformation, let me see you." He rose and kissed her. "I promise I'll make it worth the effort."

Violet lowered her hands and allowed him to continue his work. He unfastened tapes and pulled out pins. Since she had to be able to dress and undress herself, her bodice and skirt were relatively easy to remove.

"You are far too good at that," she said when he had her stripped down to her shift. "I don't even want to know where you acquired those skills."

King's mouth was dry as his gaze roved over her bare shoulders and arms. Her shift dipped low, exposing her cleavage, and her rosy nipples tented the fabric. Then he looked lower. Her shift fell to just above her knees, and he licked his lips at her rounded calves and trim ankles. "I can't remember any other woman but you."

She made a sound of disbelief, but it turned to a gasp when he went to his knees and leaned forward to kiss her belly.

"We should close the door," she said as he ruched up her shift.

"We'll hear Joshua if he comes back. And I need the light to see you." The shift moved higher, exposing her thighs. And then his hand landed on her arse, and he licked his lips. "Now this is my favorite part of you," he said.

"King!"

He turned her around and put both hands on her plump bottom. She had a narrow waist, and he loved the way it flared out at her hips and rounded into perfect spheres that gave him more than a handful to enjoy. He kissed her there, and she laughed. "What are you doing?"

"I'd have thought you would have enjoyed seeing me on my knees, kissing your arse."

"How the mighty have fallen," she said.

"Oh, I don't know about that." He slid one hand down and between her legs, feeling her jump when he brushed over her sex. "We'll see just who falls first."

He slid his fingers over her and into her, and she inhaled sharply as he gave her a light nip on her rump. Then he stood and divested her of the shift altogether, turning her so her full breasts brushed against his chest.

"Better than I imagined," he said.

"And don't I get to have a look at you?" she asked. Her hands went to the waistband of his trousers.

"All in time."

"We don't have that much time," she said, unfastening the fall of his trousers. He grasped her wrists.

"You'll have your turn, Miss Baker." He put his hands on her waist and slid them up to cup her breasts. "You know, I think there is one part of you I like even more than your bum."

"What's that?" she asked, and he was pleased to hear she sounded breathless.

"Lie down, and I'll show you." He lowered her to the bed and used one knee to open her legs. She was pink and wet and open to him. "Yes, definitely my favorite part." He lowered himself to kiss the inside of her thigh and felt the way her muscles tensed as she anticipated his lips sliding higher. "Did you like when I kissed you here last night?" He allowed his mouth to linger at the juncture of her thighs.

"King," she said, her voice petulant, pleading.

"It's a simple question. Did you like when I kissed you?"

"Yes."

King rewarded her with a kiss that lasted long enough to make her moan. "What about when I licked you? Did you like that?"

"You know I did. Come here." She held her arms open. If there was a more inviting sight, he couldn't think what it might be.

"I like where I am right now. In fact, I could stay here for hours." As though to prove his point, he licked her. The sounds she made only encouraged him, and he spread her wide and began to pleasure her in earnest. Hearing her moan and pant was absurdly gratifying to him. He relished hearing her call his name and beg him to...

Well, he'd never heard a lady use language like that. It made him hard and hot.

King took her to the brink of climax twice before shedding his trousers and settling between her legs. By then, she was pink-faced and breathing heavily. He wanted to enter her slowly, but she wrapped her legs around him and thrust her hips up, taking him to the hilt. Now it was his turn to moan. He tried to move slowly to let the pleasure build, but she was having none of it. A moment later, they had rolled over so that she was on top, taking him the way she wanted.

King thanked God there was still some light filtering into the chamber so he could see her face and her body. Her dark hair swung over her shoulders, falling to the sides of her breasts, which jutted proudly as she rode him. King put his hands on her hips then slid them to her bottom, sliding his palms over the silky skin. But what he enjoyed the most was seeing her face. Her lips were swollen and red from his kisses, her eyes slightly unfocused, and a thin sheen of perspiration covered her brow. She was the most beautiful creature he had ever seen, and he fought giving in to his own pleasure so he could watch as she found hers.

Her head fell back, her lips opened, and her entire body tensed. He felt her inner muscles contract as she climaxed, and when her face fell forward, their eyes met. King's breath whooshed out at the blueness of her eyes and the beauty of her face. She was entrancing. But his own climax was coming, and he had to roll her over and take control. He thrust into her, making her cry out with the last ounces of pleasure before he withdrew and spilled his seed onto a towel at the side of the bed.

"Violet," he breathed, lying back beside her. He was generally pretty good with words, but they failed him now. He didn't know how to describe what had just happened, how he was feeling.

"I know," she said. She moved over and put her head on his shoulder. "I thought the first time... But it wasn't."

He knew what she meant. He too had thought the first time might be some sort of fluke. King didn't think their lovemaking could be any better than it had been. But this time had been even better. "Violet—"

"Shh."

He was glad she silenced him, because he had no idea what he was about to say. King was half afraid he might tell her he loved her. *Did* he love her, or was it merely the aftereffects of pleasure? King couldn't be sure, but he knew that even when he wasn't in bed with her, his feelings for her were more than just friendship. More than just lust.

The room grew darker, and Violet's breathing became deep and even. King rose, careful not to wake her, dressed, and went back to the window. The streets were still empty, but the little slivers of light that spilled out from the various buildings showed him a lone figure moving slowly and carefully closer to the Silver Unicorn. The boy stayed to the shadows, but King recognized him as Joshua. He went downstairs and opened the back door.

"You're here," Joshua said, coming inside and waiting for

King to close the door and lower the bar. "Did Vi make it back?"

"Yes. She's sleeping upstairs."

"Sleeping?" Joshua gave him an incredulous look. "It's barely past dark."

"I don't think she's slept much the past few days. Too worried. How are you? Violet said you'd been treated for a burn."

The boy waved a hand. "I'm fine. I didn't need any treatment. Vi tries to coddle me like I'm still Georgie's age."

King put a hand on his shoulder. "She loves you, and as far as I can tell, she loves only a handful of people in this world. Consider yourself fortunate."

King wondered what it might feel like to have someone love him. He supposed at one point, when his mother had been alive, she had probably loved him. But she'd died when he was very young, giving birth to her second child. That sibling had not survived more than a day or two at most. Then it was just King and his father, and King didn't think the Duke of Avebury loved anything or anyone but himself and his hunting dogs.

He certainly hadn't loved King.

Violet didn't love him either. He told himself she probably never would. She would most likely always see him as the spoiled and inept marquess—albeit a marquess who was diverting in bed. Pleasing her there wouldn't make her fall in love with him, and taking her to bed certainly wasn't making it easier for him to stop falling in love with her.

Joshua, like most boys his age, didn't like talking about feelings. He shrugged off King's comment. "Is there anything to eat?"

"No time to eat. You and I have a mission."

He made a face. "You said we'd have to wait until after midnight to fire the Black Bear."

"That's still the plan, but we need to go see a friend of mine first."

"Who?"

"The head of the Bow Street Runners."

"What?" Joshua took a step back. "You want to go *to* the

Runners?"

King smiled. He understood the boy's resistance. In his world, the Runners and the constables were the enemy as much as men like Ferryman. "We need them. Burning Ferryman's headquarters won't rid us of him. The only way to do that is to have him charged with a crime and put in prison or transported."

"You think the Runners don't know he's a criminal? They're as afraid of him as anyone in Seven Dials."

"At the height of his power and with his gang behind him, the Runners wouldn't risk taking him. But if we could put a chink in his armor, give them an opportunity to step in when he's at his weakest, then I think they might act."

"You think? Ferryman already wants us dead. If we send the Runners after him and they fail, he'll not only kill us, he'll feed our dead bodies to the dogs."

"That's a lovely image." King put it out of his mind. "I suppose I'd better make a convincing case, then." He went to his pile of clothing and tried to pick the cleaner and less wrinkled of his coats to change into. One had blood on it now, which he supposed had come from Peggy. He chose the other and changed into a clean shirt and the coat.

"Write your sister a note so she won't worry if she wakes up and we're not here."

"Aww!" Joshua stomped off, and King tied his neckcloth. When he was ready, he found Joshua at the bar, slumped over an ink-stained sheet of parchment, pen in hand. He peered over the boy's shoulder.

*Deer Vi*

*King mayd me go to the Runerz with him*

*Yu keep slipping.*

"Slipping?" King asked.

"No, that's *sleeping*."

"After we deal with Ferryman, we'd better deal with your

education," he said, taking the pen. It badly needed sharpening and a new nib, but he made do and added a line that they would return soon, and to be ready to go at midnight. He signed his name and gave the pen back to Joshua, so the lad might sign his. But after the boy took the pen awkwardly in his hand, King told him to just put a J and to run up and slide the parchment under the door to the flat.

Then the two of them crept out the back door to the tavern, locking it behind them. King insisted they sweep the area, but they didn't find any of Ferryman's gang creeping in the shadows.

Still feeling uneasy, King motioned for the boy to follow him. The Runners' headquarters was far enough away that they'd need to flag a hackney. King just hoped he still had enough influence to make the trip worth it.

⟫⟫⟫⟪⟪⟪

VIOLET WOKE ALONE. The flat was dark and cold. She was still naked, but the bedclothes had been thrown over her. She figured she could thank King for that. She might have called out to him or Joshua, but the door to her closet was open, and she could see the flat was empty.

She rose, pulled on her shift, and went to the door of the flat, thinking to yell down to the back room. Instead, she stepped on the piece of paper, lifted it, and then had to light a candle to read it.

She wasn't certain what time it was at the moment, but she washed quickly and dressed in a pair of trousers she had found for Joshua, but which had been just a little too big on him. They fit over her hips and bottom perfectly. She'd only worn them a handful of times—when she'd wanted to move heavy casks without the encumbrance of her skirts. She'd always felt immodest and exposed in them, but she'd been inside her own tavern and alone. Now she was preparing to wear them out. But how was she to run and climb—if it came to that—in skirts? She put on an old shirt of her father's—too big, but that was easily remedied with a waistcoat cinched tight. Thus, in boots, trousers, shirt, and waistcoat, she blew out the candle and stood at the dark window, looking out.

She heard the church bells toll half past eleven when she spotted Joshua and King coming down the street. Joshua was looking from side to side, and King had a hand on his shoulder and kept glancing behind them. They were being careful, and King was clearly keeping Joshua close. Violet stared at them and put a hand to her belly. It felt as though it were full of fluttering moths. She was afraid if she allowed them to escape, they would migrate to her chest, and then her heart would beat fast for King.

Who was she fooling? It was already beating fast for him. For the first time, she allowed herself to believe he really might protect them from Ferryman.

At that moment, King looked up and saw her in the window. He tipped his hat and made a gesture indicating he would go around to the back.

She met them at the door, not even waiting for them to come fully inside before she asked, "How did it go with the Runners?"

"My friend—his name is Perkins—said he'd gather some Runners and wait for our signal. Once Joshua and I lure some of the gang away, they'll raid the Black Bear. They have a dozen warrants for Ferryman's arrest. Perkins is all but salivating to be the one to take him. They can't get close enough."

"They've arrested him before," Joshua chimed in, "but then the Runners got threats, and one ended up dead."

"I assured Perkins that if they took Ferryman now, his gang would be in no position to strike back. It will take them time to regroup, and Perkins and the magistrate can use that time to try to sentence Ferryman. Once he's gone, the gang falls apart."

Violet sniffed. "There are a dozen rogues waiting to take his place."

"No doubt. But it takes time to deal with challengers and

quell infighting. In that time, we get stronger too. Maybe band together with the other businesses on this street. Fight back against any gang that comes in and demands taxes."

"We?" she asked, brow raised. Was King really thinking of staying?

"Er—you, that is," he said.

Of course he wouldn't stay. How could she expect him to? He was a nob, not a publican. But she'd have Archie back, and perhaps she could hire some other strong backs to keep order and tell off any upstart rogues.

"It's almost midnight," King said. "Let's gather what we need and finish...this..."

Violet glanced at him and noticed he was giving her an odd look. She raised her brows.

"Er—what is it you are wearing?" he asked.

Violet had forgotten she'd dressed in trousers and a waistcoat.

"Oh, she wears that to clean," Joshua said. "Doesn't she look ridiculous?"

"Not the word I would use," King answered.

"Should I go upstairs and fetch the materials we set aside?"

"Go ahead, Joshua."

Her brother scampered up the stairs. "What is it you've set aside?" Violet asked.

King waved an arm as though that was of no consequence. "You are wearing trousers," he said, his eyes roving over her. "I don't know how I didn't see that right away."

"I thought they would make movement easier. I may need to run or climb." As he was still staring, she snapped her fingers. "What should I gather? Knives for each of us? Surely we need some sort of weapon."

"I think you saunter into the tavern wearing those trousers and that is weapon enough." He put his arms about her waist and pulled her close. "Why didn't you wear these earlier?" He slid his hand over her bottom, making heat flood through her limbs.

"I didn't know the effect they'd have on you. If we survive

tonight, maybe I'll wear them again. When we're alone." She gave a pointed look at the stairs, where Joshua could be heard moving about.

"Right." King released her and stepped back. "Have to focus." His gaze strayed to her again, and he seemed to struggle to pull it away. "Weapons. Right. Grab three knives, small enough to tuck in a pocket or boot."

Joshua was coming down the stairs and tapped his pocket. "Already have my dagger."

Violet nodded approval. She'd bought him the small but wickedly sharp dagger at a pawn shop the year before. She told him to keep it with him whenever he was out and about. "Just remember that the first defense is to run." She hadn't bought herself a dagger, so she grabbed two sharp knives and handed one to King.

"Here's the plan," he said before outlining it for them. Half a dozen times, Violet wanted to say it would never work, but she didn't have a better idea, and they had no time to debate. They were out of time.

They had to act. Tonight.

# CHAPTER NINETEEN

JOSHUA CROUCHED BEHIND the Black Bear with Vi on one side and King on the other. He'd never admit it, but he was nervous. Whenever he'd come here before, he'd been scared that he'd be caught and get Lizzie in trouble. But now King assured him she was safe in one of those big houses in Mayfair. Joshua wished he'd had more time with her, maybe stolen a kiss before he'd said goodbye. But she was safe, and that was what mattered.

And now King would make sure everyone else was safe from Ferryman.

Joshua watched as King helped Vi stuff the materials she'd need in the pockets of the large coat she wore. Neither of them looked nervous. Vi had her mouth set in a line that meant she was determined to do whatever it was she'd set her mind to. Joshua had seen that look many times.

King looked—well, Joshua didn't think it was his imagination that King couldn't seem to stop staring at Vi. He obviously thought she was pretty. Joshua watched and tried to see if Vi looked back at King at all. He thought he caught one or two looks. He definitely saw their fingers touch and linger. Georgie would be thrilled. He wanted King to fall in love with Vi and marry her so he would stay with them. He had to admit, he liked the idea too. But as he was the man of the family, he should probably have a word with King and see just what his intentions were toward Vi.

King gave Vi the last of her directions and turned to Joshua. "Ready?"

Joshua nodded and started to follow King, giving Vi a quick wave.

"Not so fast." She grabbed his shoulder, turned him around, and gave him a hug.

Joshua pulled back. "Vi, I'm not a baby."

"You're never too old for hugs," she said, cupping his face. "Be careful."

"I will." He shrugged her off, feeling mildly embarrassed as he jogged to catch up with King. "Sorry about that," he said.

King moved into the shadows and crept along the side of the tavern, keeping out of sight. "She's right. You're never too old for hugs."

"She treats me like a baby sometimes."

King paused in the shadows near the front of the tavern and watched the men going in and out. "Wanting to keep you safe isn't treating you like a baby. It's a way to show she cares." He glanced at Joshua. "Count yourself lucky. Not everyone grows up having someone to care about them."

Joshua knew that was true. He knew dozens of orphans and whores who eked out meager livings on the street. Most of them had no one who cared if they lived or died. But Joshua hadn't considered that King might not have someone who cared for him. "Didn't your parents care about you?"

King sniffed, settling onto his haunches and watching the tavern. "My mother died when I was very young. Younger than you were when you lost your mother." He squeezed Joshua's shoulder. "And my father sent me away as soon as I was old enough. Even before I went away to school, he had no time or patience for me. He didn't even allow me to come home from school on breaks."

Joshua wished he knew what to say to that, how to make King feel better. So he said the first thing that came to mind.

"Violet cares about you."

King seemed to go still, then turned his head slowly to peer at Joshua. "What makes you say that?"

Joshua shrugged. "I don't know. Just the way she acts." He furrowed his brow, thinking hard. "She looks at you when you're turned away, and her expression is kind of soft. Sometimes she looks at me that way and Georgie. The same kind of look, but different too."

King made a sound that indicated he'd heard and looked back at the tavern.

"Do you—" Joshua cleared his throat. "Do you care about her too?"

King didn't answer for a long moment, and Joshua wondered if maybe he hadn't heard. Then he said, "I do care about her. I care about her more than I've ever cared for anyone."

Joshua stared. "Do you *love* her?"

King took a breath. "I don't know. I might." He looked back at the tavern entrance. "If I did, would that be acceptable to you?"

Joshua pretended to think this over. In reality, his heart was pounding—and not just because he was about to risk his life in Ferryman's tavern, but because he wanted so badly for King and Violet to fall in love and for King to never leave. "It might be," he answered, trying to keep his tone unconcerned. "I should probably ask your intentions."

King laughed, surprising Joshua.

"What's so funny?"

"I've never been asked that before."

Joshua didn't know what that should make the question funny.

"You're a good brother, Joshua. As for my intentions, I don't have an answer for you. I think it's up to Violet, but I can promise you one thing."

"Go on," Joshua said. His chest felt tight when adults made promises. Very few of them ever kept them.

"I promise I won't ever hurt her. Or you. Or Georgie." King

took a breath. "Good enough for now?"

"Yes."

He stood. "Then let's go."

WALKING INTO FERRYMAN'S lair through the front door—after refusing to pay him, stealing his dell, and scalding him with hot oil—was probably the most idiotic thing King had ever done. Which was precisely why he was doing it. No one would expect this—least of all Ferryman.

King spotted the arch rogue as soon as he entered. The gang leader sat in a large armchair near the fire facing the door. Several of his men sat near him, hunched over tankards of ale and looking somewhat worse for wear after this afternoon.

Ferryman didn't see him immediately, but one of his men near the door did. "What are you doing here?" the large man bellowed. King looked up at him. The man was most likely chosen to stand at the door because he was large and imposing.

"I told you we shouldn't have come," Joshua said loudly.

King flicked a look at Ferryman. One side of his face was red and shiny with some sort of salve. The gang leader had come to attention, though, his ice-blue eyes fixed on King.

"And I told you to stubble it," King said, cuffing Joshua on the side of the head. It was a light cuff, but Joshua reacted with a yip, as though he'd been struck hard. The lad might have a future on the stage. King looked at Ferryman. "You're the last person I want to see tonight, but we have a problem."

Ferryman rose. "You are my problem, Lord Kingston. Or is it Mr. Kingston now?" It was Mr. Oxley, but Ferryman didn't wait for a correction. "Now that you're here, I can squash my problem." He made a sign, and the thug at the door grabbed King and pulled his hands behind his back. King had been expecting this and didn't resist. Another man grabbed Joshua, who made a show of struggling, but not with enough vehemence to warrant retaliation.

"I told you this would happen," Joshua said. "We should let Resurrection Man take over."

Ferryman had been about to issue another order—probably something about tossing Joshua and King in a dank room and throwing away the key—but now he froze. "What did you say, boy?" He hobbled across the room. Up close, the oil burn looked even worse. King could see where the skin had bubbled up and swelled in angry protest.

"It's nothing," Joshua said, defiant. "Ask *him* if you want to know. It was his idea to come here." He jerked his head at King.

Now Ferryman turned those pale eyes on King. "What did the boy say? Spit it out, or I'll have you spitting out teeth before I ask again."

"It's Resurrection Man," King said, watching as Ferryman's nostrils flared. Joshua had told King that Resurrection Man was Ferryman's arch nemesis. Apparently, he hadn't exaggerated. "Resurrection Man and his gang are on Clover Lane, breaking windows and demanding security payments."

Ferryman reared back as though struck. "That's my territory!"

"Not anymore," King said.

"You couldn't hold it, so Ferryman is taking over," Joshua added. "Some people say they're glad."

"Why, you little brat." Ferryman raised a hand to strike Joshua.

King tried to lunge in front of Joshua but was yanked back by the man holding him. "Wait! We're here for your help."

Ferryman stilled then looked slowly at King. "Why would you want my help? You've been doing everything you can to rise up against me."

"Vi is scared," Joshua said with a roll of his eyes. "Resurrection Man wants more coin and use of the tavern. She told us to come and apologize."

"We don't like you, but we like Resurrection Man even less."
King pretended to swallow a bad taste in his mouth. "We're here
to ask for help."

"Oh, I'll help you, I will," Ferryman said. "I'll have both of
you beaten bloody." He signaled, and a man stepped forward and
slammed King in the belly with a fist. King doubled over and
coughed.

"Tell him, Joshua," he wheezed. Holy hell, but that punch
had hurt.

Joshua shook his head.

"Tell him!"

Ferryman looked from King to Joshua then grabbed the boy's
chin. "What are you hiding, brat? Tell me." Joshua shook his
head, and Ferryman grabbed his cheeks with one hand until his
mouth opened. He grasped the boy's tongue and held out a hand
for a dagger, which he then put to Joshua's face. "Use your
tongue, brat, or lose it."

"Fine," Joshua said, the word almost unintelligible. Ferryman
released him. "Resurrection Man is coming here. We heard him
say once he finished on Clover Lane, he was coming to the Black
Bear to finish the job."

"He's daft!" one of Ferryman's men called.

"Oh, he's been spoiling for a fight," Ferryman said.

"If 'e wants a fight, we'll give it 'im!" another gang member
said, and the sentiment was echoed by loud calls and cheers. King
and Joshua were thrust aside as Ferryman directed half his men to
go cut off Resurrection Man and the other half to prepare to
defend the Black Bear.

"I can't believe it worked," Joshua said under his breath to
King.

"Neither can I."

Joshua gave King a sharp look, but then both of them had to
move aside or risk being trampled. The patrons of the Black Bear
were not waiting for Resurrection Man to make his appearance.
They were making their way out of the tavern.

This was exactly what King wanted. The fewer innocents here, the less likely anyone would be hurt when Violet started the fire. Speaking of which, he hoped she saw the people pouring out of the tavern. That was the signal.

King moved aside as Ferryman's gang thundered through the door, headed toward Clover Lane. He hoped the Bow Street Runners were in position. With half his men gone, Ferryman was weaker than he'd ever been. Now to see if King could stir up some chaos.

"Do you smell that?" he asked a tavern wench rushing past him, trying to hold on to her tray of mugs.

"Smell wot?" she asked.

"I smell it," Joshua added. "It smells like smoke."

"Smoke?" the tavern wench said.

"Smoke?" A man trying to flee looked over his shoulder in search of the nonexistent smoke.

"Do *you* smell smoke?" King asked another man.

"Fire!" a woman cried.

As far as King could see, if Violet had started the fire, it hadn't spread to the public room yet, but he wasn't about to contradict the woman.

"Fire!" a man echoed, and everyone who hadn't been scared away at the mention of Resurrection Man rose and began pushing to get out.

"Sit down!" Ferryman bellowed. "There's no fire."

In that moment, a maid rushed in through the door to the kitchen. "Fire!" she cried. Behind her, King clearly saw black plumes of smoke.

"Good girl, Violet," he muttered. "Joshua, I believe our work here is done." He put a hand on the lad's shoulder, and the two of them joined the crowds pushing out of the tavern. King really could smell smoke now. The fires Violet set in the back must have caught quickly and spread easily.

"Not so fast!"

King felt himself pulled back. He caught Joshua's eyes and

indicated he should run. Then he was swung around to face Ferryman and his swollen face.

"What is this?" Ferryman demanded. "You show up, and suddenly Resurrection Man is starting a war and then my place goes up in flames."

"Bad luck." King shrugged. "I've had it myself lately."

"This isn't bad luck. This was some sort of plan. But I'm not stupid." Ferryman pulled out a dagger, and King, who had been expecting this, countered with the knife Violet had given him. Ferryman saw it and let out a derisive snort. He made a lunge at King, who tried to deflect and lost his knife. It went skittering across the floor toward the back. King followed it with his eyes then looked up and saw the flames licking at the ceiling. Violet had not held back when she'd set the fire.

He glanced back at Ferryman just in time to jump back before the dagger could graze him.

"I'll enjoy killing you," Ferryman said, baring his large yellow teeth in something between a smile and a grimace.

"Speaking of bad luck," King said, backing up and beginning to feel the heat of the fire. "You know it always comes in threes."

"What are you talking about?" Ferryman stalked forward.

"Your bad luck. First, Resurrection Man comes for you." King held up a finger. "Then a fire starts." He jerked his head toward the growing flames and held up another finger.

"That's only two."

"I don't want to ruin the third surprise for you." King feinted to the side as Ferryman lunged at him again and missed.

"You're bluffing. There is no third thing."

"Tell that to Bow Street."

Ferryman paused just long enough for King to dart around a table and out of the corner Ferryman had been forcing him into. Now he had a path to the exit. The tavern was all but empty save for a few of Ferryman's men, waiting for orders—and blocking the door.

"You're bluffing," Ferryman said again.

"Then come outside and see for yourself," King said.

Ferryman looked at King then gestured to one of his men, who ducked out the door. That was one gone, but there were still too many to allow King to escape. Sweat began running down his brow as the fire made things hotter. He'd thought Ferryman and his men would try to organize a team to fetch water and extinguish the fire, but they seemed strangely unconcerned. It appeared King would have to lead them outside, as he doubted the Runner would enter a burning building—even if Ferryman was the prize.

He waited another few heartbeats then said, "Your man isn't coming back. Bow Street has him."

Ferryman shook his head.

"They're out there," King said. "If you didn't believe it, you'd go see yourself. You're scared."

"Bow Street can't take me."

"Not if you had your whole gang, but you sent half of them away, and others fled from the fire. Now you have a handful and Bow Street waiting on the other side of the door. There's no escaping that way." King pointed to the back of the tavern, where the flames continued to grow and smoke poured in. His throat and eyes had begun to burn, making him want to cover his nose with his sleeve. They couldn't stay in here much longer. The fire was growing in size. "Perkins!" King called, coughing. "I have him, Perkins!"

Ferryman seemed to come to some sort of decision. "Take him outside," he ordered one of his men. "I'll fillet him on the street right after I call his bluff."

Two men grabbed King and dragged him through the door. King didn't resist. He wanted out of the burning tavern. As soon as he was through the door, he gulped in the cool night air. He scanned the few people still milling about but didn't see Joshua.

He did see Perkins and about a dozen Runners, all armed and standing ready. As soon as Ferryman's men saw the Runners, they released King and ran. Perkins raised a hand, indicating his men should remain in position. He wasn't chasing any of the minnows when the big catch was coming through the door.

King moved aside and glanced at the tavern. Flames were coming out of the back windows now, and smoke poured into the dark night. A few men had arrived with buckets, prepared to start a brigade, but the Runners were holding them back. Now Ferryman sauntered out of the tavern, dagger still in his hand.

King thought he would remember the look of shock on Ferryman's face for the rest of his days. The crime lord's eyes widened, and his jaw dropped. The expression was so perfect as to be almost comical. He had quick reflexes, though, and only paused a moment before turning to run. But the Runners had anticipated this. They closed in and cut off his escape, sweeping him up as well as some of his men. They were armed with clubs and various other blunt objects, which they used liberally to persuade Ferryman to go with them.

King decided that was a good time to make his exit. He stepped back and into the crowd of people gawking, then slipped into the alley and raced down to the rear of the Black Bear. Fire leapt from the roof of the building and some of the upper windows. There would be no salvaging the tavern, nowhere for Ferryman's successor to gather his men. By the time the next arch rogue came to extort Violet, King would be ready with blunt and brutes to defend the place.

That was, if Violet allowed him to stay.

He lifted a hand to protect his face from a shower of sparks then spotted Violet cowering under a broken awning hanging from the building nearby. "What took so long?" she demanded. "I was about to come looking for you two."

"Two? Didn't Joshua meet you?"

Her eyes widened. "He's not with you?"

"No. He got out before me. I thought he'd find you straightaway. That was the plan."

Violet started for the front of the tavern. "Apparently, he didn't follow the plan. Children often don't follow plans."

King caught up to her. "I'm sure he's watching Bow Street take Ferryman away."

She glanced at him, her face red in the glowing light of the fire now eating up the tavern. King's heart began to pound, but he shook off the panic. Joshua was out of the tavern. King saw him leave.

⟫⟫⟩⟨⟨⟨

VIOLET CUT THROUGH the people gawking at the burning tavern or at the Runners loading gang members into the back of their wagon and called for Joshua. King echoed her. It seemed no one answered, but if they had, she wouldn't have been able to hear them. Neighbors were passing buckets of water in a line, attempting to put out the fire before it spread. Ferryman and his men were yelling. The Runners were shouting orders.

In short, the scene was one of pandemonium. That was exactly what they'd wanted—except Joshua was supposed to be with one of them at all times. That had been the plan.

King and his plans! She'd known this was too dangerous.

"Joshua! Joshua!" Violet grabbed a man. "Have you seen a boy with blond hair and brown eyes? He's about this tall." She held a hand to her shoulder.

"No. Excuse me. I need more water."

She grabbed another man and repeated her question. He shook his head and shook her off. Behind her, she heard King asking people too. No one had seen Joshua. Where was he? Had Ferryman taken him?

That wasn't possible. Ferryman was being led away by the Bow Street Runners.

Had Joshua gone back into the tavern? She glanced at the building, which was now completely engulfed in flames. Why would he go back? Fear and panic beat at her chest like the wings of a hawk. She had to find him. She was running out of time.

A hand grabbed her shoulder, and she shrugged it off and turned to see a boy about Joshua's age. "Are ye looking for Joshua?" he asked.

Violet grabbed the boy's thin shoulders. "Yes. Have you seen him?"

The boy nodded and pointed to the tavern.

"Are you sure?" It was King's voice, and he was right beside her.

"I saw 'im run back in," the boy said.

"Oh my God." Violet felt dizzy and grasped at King's arm to keep her balance. "I have to go in after him. I have to get him out."

"No." King took her arm and pulled her out of the crowd. "You're staying right here."

"He's my brother." She struggled to get out of King's hold. "I have to help him."

"I'll help him." That surprised her, and she ceased struggling. He released her and pulled off his coat. "But if I go in there, I need to know you are right here. Safe."

She nodded, too scared and shocked to find words.

"Good." He draped the coat over his head. "I'll be back in a few minutes. Stay right here." He started away, but Violet grabbed him back. She took his face in both hands and kissed him hard and fast.

"Come back," she said. "You still owe me two pounds—"

"And fifteen shillings." He gave her the ghost of a smile. "I know."

And then he was gone, striding through the crowds of people, coat over his head. Even this far away, in the shadows where only the glow of the fire reached her, she could feel the heat of it burning her face and the smoke making her throat scratchy. How could Joshua be alive in there? How could King survive?

Violet clenched her hands and forced the tears back. She couldn't lose Joshua. She was not one for prayer. God hadn't answered her in the past—or if He had, those answers seemed to indicate she was not His favorite person.

But she prayed now. She clasped her hands together and prayed as hard as she could.

Because not only couldn't she bear to lose Joshua, she couldn't lose King either.

# CHAPTER TWENTY

KING STUMBLED INTO the Black Bear, coughing and blinking the tears from his eyes. They were watering at the smoke, and his throat threatened to close. He couldn't breathe, couldn't see, struggled to move forward against the backlash of the heat.

This was why he hadn't ever wanted to fall in love. It made men do stupid things.

"Joshua!"

King doubted his voice could be heard over the roar of the fire. Where could the boy be?

He stumbled through the public room, seeing no one.

Why was it only now—when he was about to die—that he could admit to himself he was in love with Violet Baker? He'd been in love with her since the first time she demanded he pay her the ridiculous sum of seven pounds, fifteen shillings. It had been the worst day of his life, and she swept in and made it even more terrible.

And more wonderful.

But he didn't only love Violet. He loved Georgie and Joshua, though if King ever found the boy, he would kill the lad for this. Running back into a burning building. For what?

King stilled.

For whom was the better question. Joshua had a soft spot for Lizzie. She was safe in a townhouse in Mayfair, but might he know other children living here? Lizzie had been upstairs. Perhaps Joshua had run up to make sure the rest of the children escaped.

King glanced toward the stairway to the first floor. Flames licked at the ceiling, but they hadn't engulfed it yet. Pulling his coat tight over his head, he ducked down and ran for the stairs. Sparks and burning pieces of wood fell around him, but he made it to the stairs and climbed quickly, not wanting to linger on any unstable stairs. The smoke was worse on the first floor. The fire burned to his left, so he went right, stepping into the thickest cloud of smoke. Even if he'd wanted to call for Joshua, he couldn't have made his throat work.

King got down on his knees. The smoke rose, and on the floor, he could see marginally better. He crawled down the corridor, pushing doors open and peering inside. Holy hell, but he couldn't see anything. He had to go into the first room, feeling his way around.

No one here.

He turned to crawl back out and heard the pop and whoosh as something below exploded. Most likely a cask of beer or wine. King crouched lower as a wall of flame rose in the doorway. Ash and heat like none he'd ever felt emanated from those leaping flames. He was dead. This was the end.

Violet would be furious.

And then the room seemed to grow cold. King couldn't explain it. Perhaps this was what death felt like—like icy fingernails creeping down his back.

He'd only felt this sensation once before. King began to tremble as the shape of the old woman formed in the flames.

It was the Scottish witch.

Somehow, he'd always known he'd see her again.

Last time, in his bedchamber, he'd thought he was drunk. He wasn't drunk now. Perhaps he was hallucinating. But she looked pretty damn real.

"George Oxley, Marquess of Kingston." The witch stared

down at him. "Nae the marquess anymore, are ye?" She smiled, and he didn't want to look at that gaping mouth.

"You've had your revenge," he said, unsure whether he was speaking or only thinking the words. How could he speak? His throat was raw, and he kept coughing from the smoke.

But she nodded as though she'd heard him.

"Nae enough, George Oxley. Never enough."

She began to mumble, her words too low for him to make out. She was speaking some sort of chant and moving her hands in a circle, stirring up the fire. King stared at her, his eyes streaming, the skin of his hands, where he held the coat, beginning to blister.

And then he realized what she was saying.

She was repeating the spell.

*"Give me my revenge; ease my plight.*
*These three lads have taken what's mine.*
*At the age of thirty, repay them in kind."*

*My God,* he thought. It hadn't been a coincidence that he'd lost everything on his birthday. She'd cursed him. Made certain he would lose everything then. And not just him—Henry and Rory as well. Rory had always been the oldest. He'd already turned thirty, and his curse—

"No," he said to himself. "No." Because he knew what Rory had lost, and it had been worse—so much worse than what King had faced. And Henry—Henry's birthday was just a few days after King's. What had he lost? Was that why he hadn't come back to help King?

*"Pilfer, purloin, and pinch what it is they love best.*
*And then and only then will I find my eternal rest."*

King stared at the witch, her words echoing in his mind. *What they love best.* Was that what she had taken from him? What he loved best? His money, his title, his standing in Society.

That was all he'd had. All he'd ever had—few friends, almost no family. King had clung tightly to his name and his inheritance.

But the witch had taken that.

Why had she come back now? Her work was done…unless she meant to take more from him. Unless she was angry that her curse hadn't had the desired effect.

Yes, she'd taken everything from him, but she hadn't ruined his life. In fact, he'd found his life. He'd found Violet and the boys, and even the bloody Silver Unicorn, with all the mugs that needed washing and floors that needed mopping.

He'd found a life he hadn't even known he wanted.

Was the witch taking Joshua from him now?

She laughed and rose over him as he cowered on the floor. And then, slowly, King climbed to his feet.

"You've had your revenge," he said. At least, he thought he spoke. Holy hell, but he did not want to consider that he was communicating with the witch through his thoughts alone. "Now leave me and mine in peace."

She seemed to shrink in size—or perhaps it was his imagination.

"Begone!" he yelled, and this time he heard the words break free from his raw, blistering throat.

She seemed to flicker then rose up, brighter and stronger. "Ye will nae break the curse. Never!"

The flames surrounding her brightened, and King had to turn away and shield his face. The light was almost as bright as daylight, and he spotted a small form in the furthest corner of the room.

*Joshua!*

And then the flames went out and the fire was gone, and it was just King standing in a black, smoke-filled room.

HE WAS DEAD. She knew he was dead, and Joshua with him. No

one could survive that blaze. Even the fire brigade was having trouble withstanding the heat long enough to get close enough to throw water on the flames.

This entire night had turned into her worst imaginings made flesh. She'd wanted to be rid of Ferryman, wanted to burn his gang to the ground. But doing away with the arch rogue was not worth the life of Joshua. It wasn't worth King's life either.

Tears streamed down her face as she climbed to her feet and stared at the burning tavern. This was her fault. She had set the fire. She had agreed to the plan. She should have made Joshua and King stay home tonight. They'd be safe in the little flat, together.

"Miss, is everything all right?"

Violet turned to the man looking down at her. He had a kind face, clean and not stained with soot. He held out a handkerchief and mopped her wet face. She didn't know how to answer the man. No, she was not all right. She'd never be all right again.

Her gaze flicked back to the tavern, as though looking at the fire should be answer enough for him. She looked back at the man then gasped and turned to the tavern again.

But it hadn't been a mirage. She hadn't imagined the dark figure of a man carrying a small form through the flames and smoke.

"King!" she cried, stepping forward. He seemed to stumble. "King! Oh, no. King!"

His head turned, and he located her and began to move forward. Violet didn't wait. She ran to him, took Joshua from his arms, and sank to her knees. King crumpled beside her, his coat falling away. She took in his face—he was black from smoke and ash, but unhurt.

No. Not unhurt. She saw no physical injury, but there was something in his eyes she didn't like. Something that scared her. "What is it?" she asked.

King looked at her, then his gaze slid to Joshua. "Is he breathing? Tell me he's alive."

Violet looked down at the thin boy in her arms. Sudden terror gripped her. She lowered him and put her head to his chest. For a long moment, she didn't hear or feel anything. And then, very faintly, she heard his heart beating. Felt his chest rise as he took a breath.

She looked up at King. "You saved him. He's alive."

"Thank God."

And then he collapsed in a heap on the ground.

⟫⟫⟫⟫⟪⟪⟪⟪

HE DREAMED OF the witch. He saw her rising from the flames, chanting the curse, laughing as he stumbled about in the smoke and falling ash. He had to find Joshua. Violet would never recover if anything happened to Joshua, and she'd already faced so much loss.

In the dream, King groped about in the darkness, searching for Joshua's body. But there was nothing in that darkness. No matter how far or wide he stretched his hands, he felt nothing but the thick heat of the air. He fumbled in the darkness for what seemed an eternity before he finally felt something solid. King held on, running his hands over the object until his mind categorized it as a human form.

He'd found Joshua.

But then a burst of flames shot up behind him, and in the brightness of the blaze, he saw not Joshua but the face of his father. It was a face so much like his own that for a moment King thought he was looking at his reflection.

"George," his father said.

"What are you doing here?" King asked his dream father. "You're in the Tower."

"I came to say farewell."

King reached for him to shake his hand or embrace him—he wasn't sure which.

"King," his father said. Except his father never called him *King*. "Wake up."

King's eyes snapped open, and he stared unseeing into the darkness. Then a light appeared, and he turned his head to see Joshua standing in the doorway holding a candle.

"Is he hurt?" Joshua asked.

"Nightmare, I think."

King glanced in the direction of the voice and found Violet sitting on the edge of the bed. *Her* bed. He was lying on top of it, and he was safe. His father was far away, locked in the Tower of London. Ferryman was in the custody of the Bow Street Runners, and his headquarters were a steaming pile of smoke and ash.

He pushed up to a sitting position. "What happened?"

"You were moaning and groaning. It woke me and Vi," Joshua offered.

"Have some water," Violet said, holding a cup to his lips. King realized he was incredibly thirsty and drank the water as well as another after she poured it from a pitcher.

"How did I get to the flat?" he asked. King had almost no memory after finding Joshua. Everything was black and hazy.

"You collapsed in front of the Black Bear, but we managed to rouse you long enough to get back here," Violet said.

"And Ferryman?"

"The Runners took him," Joshua said. "And the Black Bear was still burning when we left."

"Good." King lay back down. He was so tired, his eyes and throat still stinging from the smoke.

Violet said something to Joshua, and he retreated, leaving the candle.

"I'm in your bed," King said, pushing up again.

"Lie down," she said, placing a hand on his chest. "Georgie is still with Archie, and I can sleep in his place, even if Joshua does hoard the blanket. More water?"

King shook his head. He realized he lay in his shirt sleeves and stockings. She must have removed his coat and boots. Now, she pulled a blanket over him and busied herself tucking it about him.

"Joshua and I washed the soot off your face and hands as best we could, but in the morning we can draw water from the well and you can have a proper bath. I'll need to launder all the clothing and bedding anyway. Everything smells like smoke." She paused and looked down at him. "For now, sleep. I'll need your help in the tavern tomorrow, so you'll want to rest while you can."

"In the morning, I have to go see my father."

Violet drew back, her expression going carefully neutral. "I thought you didn't want to see him."

He hadn't. But the dream had seemed so real. His father was his last living close relative. He needed to say goodbye, to put an end to the animosity between them. "I dreamed of him and the witch."

Violet sank down on the bed beside him. "The witch?" she whispered, obviously keeping her voice low so Joshua didn't hear.

"I saw her in the fire," King said. "It was like before. She rose from the flames, and she repeated the curse."

"King, it was hot and hard to breathe. You imagined it."

"Maybe so, but I remember the curse now. Do you want to hear it?" He watched as her throat worked, and then she nodded. "I don't remember all of it, but part of it, I'll never forget: *These three lads have taken what's mine. At the age of thirty, repay them in kind.*"

"Age of thirty. The day I met you was your birthday."

"Exactly. And that was the day my father was found guilty of treason. There's more to the curse. She said, *Pilfer, purloin, and pinch what it is they love best. And then and only then will I find my eternal rest.*"

"What does that mean? Pilfer and the other word?"

"They mean steal—steal or take what they love best. Once she's done that, she will be able to rest in peace."

"But you said you didn't love your father."

"But I did love my title, my name, my place in the world. That's what I had taken away."

"But the witch's sister gave me the counter-spell. There's still a way to reverse the curse."

"Maybe. If I believe the witch's curse was real. If I believe it can be reversed. How can one reverse my father betraying his country? That's why I have to see him. I have to speak with him and say"—he cleared his throat—"say goodbye."

"I understand. You should wash in the morning and go." She rose. "There are still a few hours before sunrise. Sleep, if you can."

King grabbed her hand. "Lie with me."

Violet glanced at the door. "I can't. Joshua—"

"Just lie here, Violet. Beside me. I want to hold you, nothing more."

She glanced at the door and the flat beyond again and then set the candle down and gestured for King to move over. He did so, and she lay down beside him, her back to his chest. The bed was tiny, and he had no choice but to put his arm about her, resting it on her waist. She blew the candle out and settled in against him.

She fit perfectly, almost as though she'd been carved to fit in the space between his knees and chin. He rested his chin on the top of her head, allowing the light scent of her hair to tease his nose. The smell of smoke was overwhelming, but beneath it lingered the unique scent of Violet.

# CHAPTER TWENTY-ONE

V IOLET WOKE A little while later. Her muscles were stiff and her leg numb. She tried to move and found King had thrown his leg over hers, and her own leg had fallen asleep. Gently, she pushed him onto his back, which only partially worked, as there wasn't room for him to lie fully like that. But it gave her enough time and room to squeeze out of the bed and move into the flat.

The pale curtains had been torn during the fight with Ferryman, and the window glass that had broken still glittered on the floor. With the broken window, the room was cold, and she pulled her wrapper around her and looked down on the street.

A man and a dog passed by, just visible in the gray light of early morning. The dog kept close to his master's heels as they set off for work that day. *A rat-catcher,* Violet thought. *He's headed to the better part of town, where people can afford not to live with rats.*

She glanced over her shoulder at the door to her bedchamber. King was from that part of town. The horror he must have felt when he'd been forced to sleep on the floor of the back room… She knew he'd seen a rat or two on those nights. He'd complained about them, complained about everything in that bland, dry way he had that made her laugh.

She'd never felt sorry for him, and she didn't think he wanted her pity. If he could find a way to avoid doing any labor, he would take it, of course, but when she needed him, he was always there.

She'd needed his help with Ferryman, and he had done more than she'd ever anticipated. In fact, it was hard to believe that she wouldn't have to worry about Ferryman knocking on the door of the tavern today, or any day, to demand payment. She wouldn't have to look over her shoulder out of fear that his thugs were following her. She could breathe for now, knowing Georgie was safe, she was safe, Peggy and Archie were safe. And, of course, thanks to King, Joshua was safe.

King knew it too. He'd felt some responsibility to her. She hadn't understood that at first, but as she came to know him, she began to understand that was the sort of man he was. He might have been spoiled and privileged, but he had a keen sense of honor and duty. For some reason, Violet and her brothers had become part of his duty—at least for a little while.

Now he spoke of the curse and seeing his father. She was safe, and he was moving on. The Silver Unicorn wasn't his life. He'd been born for greater things, and even if he'd had his title and wealth taken from him, he could do a lot better than a small tavern in Seven Dials, or Violet Baker and her two brothers.

She didn't know why the thought of his leaving should cause a pang in her chest. She'd always known he wouldn't stay for long. He'd stayed longer than she'd ever anticipated. He'd stayed *too* long. She'd become attached, despite telling herself not to.

She shouldn't have gone to bed with him. She'd never had trouble controlling her feelings before, but King's touch, his kisses, his whispered urgings, did something to her. And once her feelings had bubbled to the surface, she couldn't seem to push them down again. And now, not only would she miss having him near to help with whatever she needed and keep an eye on the boys, she'd miss stealing looks at him and the thrill of—what was the word he used?—pilfered kisses.

She'd miss much more than stolen kisses, but there was no point in thinking about that. She couldn't keep him here, and she was a fool for wishing he would stay. Everyone left her, in one way or another. Even Joshua and Georgie would leave one day. She was helpless to stop it, but she was in control of her feelings. She could decide to be strong. She could decide not to care.

There was enough light now that she washed and dressed then pinned her hair up. Then she gathered her broom and dustpan and began to sweep up the broken glass and set the flat to rights. Joshua tried to sleep longer by putting the blanket over his head, but finally he rose and offered to go fetch hot rolls for breakfast. She gave him a few coins and went downstairs to find a board to secure over the broken window.

When she came back upstairs, King was standing at the window, looking out. Violet entered and, in the moment before he turned to face her, caught her breath at his silhouette. She couldn't help but admire his long legs, lean hips, trim waist, and broad shoulders. Yes, he could do a lot better than her.

"Good morning," he said, his voice still raspy from sleep or the smoke.

"I thought you'd sleep another two or three hours," she teased.

"The bed is too uncomfortable," he said, and though his tone was light, and she knew he meant to tease her, she stiffened with offense.

"Joshua went to buy bread to break our fast. I'll go to the well and fetch water for a bath. You look…"

She wanted to say he looked like a chimney sweep after a day of work, and that was true, but even beneath the smeared soot and ash, his face was so handsome it made her chest tighten. He had those beautiful green eyes and that slow, seductive smile.

"I can fetch the water. While Joshua is gone, I want to talk to you."

This was goodbye, and she didn't want to hear it. Not yet. "We can talk later," she said. "I can't take you seriously looking like you just fell out of a chimney." And then, because he looked as though he might argue, she turned and fled back down the stairs, forgetting that she'd meant to nail the board over the broken window. Violet gathered her buckets and secured them on a long pole she could fit across her shoulders to carry the water back. She went out, feeling a sense of lightness at not having to fear Ferryman or his men as she walked along the road to the well.

She knew someone would try to take Ferryman's place. Perhaps it would be Resurrection Man. They'd made up the story about his trying to encroach on Ferryman's territory, but Ferryman had believed it because Resurrection Man had done it before. He'd almost certainly try it again. Or perhaps one of Ferryman's lieutenants would rise to the top and consolidate power. She'd be ready this time and would take the money she saved from Ferryman's taxes to hire her own thugs. Archie would be well enough to return soon, and he would know where to find such men and how to keep them in line.

Violet reached the well, pulled up the bucket, and poured the water in her first pail. The work did not require her to think, and as much as she tried to keep her mind occupied with formulating ideas for the tavern and her brothers, she couldn't stop it from wandering back to where it wanted to go: King.

He was leaving her. That was good, she told herself as she lowered the bucket again. She'd told him to go a half-dozen times. The only reason she'd allowed him to stay in the first place was because Archie was injured. And whose fault was that? King's!

Injuring Archie and wrecking her tavern wasn't all he'd done. He'd caused all this trouble with Ferryman, which had put Joshua and himself in danger. It had worked out in the end, but what if it hadn't? Violet should be glad to send King on his way.

She cursed as she hauled the heavy bucket up and poured the water into her pail, splashing some on her dress. In frustration, she pushed the bucket back into the well and then leaned her head on the well's wooden supports and blinked back tears. What was wrong with her?

She drew in a deep breath and swiped the tears away. No more of this. King was going, and she'd be fine without him. Just fine.

She hefted the heavy pails onto her shoulders and trudged back to the tavern. King had better appreciate this effort. After today, he would have to haul his own water, and she'd have one fewer person to take care of. Things could go back to the way they were. She could forget King had ever existed.

She came in view of the back door, and it opened, revealing King. "Let me help you with those," he said, coming out and taking the buckets from the pole. He lifted them easily. "If you'd given me a moment, I would have fetched them myself."

"I can do it," she said. "I managed without you for twenty-one years, and I'll manage when you're gone."

He stilled and looked at her.

She looked back at him and raised her brows. "What?"

"Nothing." He shook his head. "Joshua is back, and we've heated the stove. I'll warm the water."

"Good. I'll nail the board over the window." That would give her something to do so she wasn't tempted to peek at King washing.

"I already did that. Go eat the rolls Joshua bought."

"Fine. Do you know where the tub—"

"I have it, Miss Sunshine. Go."

He was back to the teasing name he'd given her. She should he happy for that. It was so much less personal than when he said her name. She hated the way it sounded in his upper-class accent. At least, that was what she would tell herself.

She clomped up the stairs, annoyed he'd covered the window and determined to find something wrong in the work so she'd have to do it over. But it was well done, and that just made her angrier.

"Saved two rolls for you, Vi," Joshua said, looking up from his plate at the table.

"Georgie will be home soon. I had better leave one for him.

We can't expect Archie to feed him *and* house him." Her tone was sharp, and Joshua looked up at her from under his brows.

"I bought two for him as well."

That was thoughtful. Clever Joshua. At least, that was what she meant to say. Instead, she said, "How much did you spend on rolls? Soon we'll have no blunt!"

"I'm sorry, Vi. I—"

Violet didn't let him finish. Instead, she went to him and hugged him. Hard. "I'm sorry. I'm tired and cranky and taking it out on you. You did everything perfectly, Joshua."

"The bread wasn't expensive," he said. "I made sure to haggle."

"Shh." She drew back and looked at his face. It was clean of soot, but he still smelled of smoke. She'd need to fetch more water so he could bathe. "I was so worried about you last night. I thought I'd lost you. And then what would I do?"

"You'd have to fetch your own breakfast," he said with a tentative smile.

"We can't have that. From now on, you be more careful. No chasing after girls or trying to save people in fires. I can't lose you, Joshua." She hugged him again, and he patted her back, as though she were the one who needed comforting.

"You won't lose me, Vi. I promise."

"Good." She drew back and kissed his forehead.

"But I can't promise not to chase after any girls."

She laughed. "I suppose not. Maybe wait another year or two, though, yes?"

"I'll think about it."

She sat in the other chair and began to eat the bread. A few minutes later, she heard the door and Georgie's voice. "Hi, Pa! Joshua? Vi? I'm back."

KING HAD JUST finished rinsing his hair with the water he'd held in reserve when Georgie stepped into the back room of the tavern. For a moment, the boy stared at him as though he didn't know who he was, and then he grinned. "Hi, Pa!"

King didn't know why being called *Pa* should make his heart feel as though it were one of Gunter's ices on an August afternoon, but it did. "Good to see you back, Master George."

Georgie called for Violet, and King hastily grabbed a towel and wrapped it about his hips. Just in time, it turned out, as Joshua and Violet came running down the steps. Violet had eyes for no one but Georgie, which gave King time to tuck the ends of the towel into place before Joshua grabbed hold of his little brother and Violet glanced at King.

And then she glanced again, her cheeks turning pink and her blue eyes widening. But that wasn't shock in her eyes. King knew desire when he saw it. He'd been about to put on a shirt. Now he held off. She wanted to pretend she was unmoved by him, but he knew differently. He still needed to talk to her, but now Georgie was back, and she'd be busy with him. He might hope to have a word with her this afternoon, but then she'd be opening the tavern. Once the business opened, it would be even harder to take a moment with her.

Violet looked away from him—but not until her gaze swept down his chest—and hurried Georgie upstairs. King dressed in his best, which were the clothes that weren't stained with soot or impossibly wrinkled. He attempted to tie a cravat without a looking glass, but gave up on the elaborate style he'd planned and tied a simple knot. His father was in prison. Certainly, he wouldn't care about King's appearance.

Except he probably would.

Joshua came down the stairs as King pulled his boots on. How he missed Danby in moments like these. The valet knew how to get the damn boots on without any fuss. He kept them polished, too. And after last night, King's boots were sorely in need of polishing.

"Is your brother well?" he asked.

"Yes. He says Archie is doing much better and wants to come back in a few days."

"Good." Then Violet really wouldn't need him.

"Are you going somewhere?" Joshua asked.

King glanced at him. The soot had been wiped from his face, but black streaks were still smeared along his neck and caked in the whorls of his ears.

"To the well, to fetch water for your bath."

"Aw! I took a bath last week."

King ruffled his hair. "After being trapped in a burning building, you must take another. Come with me."

Joshua called up to Violet to tell her where they were going, and the two lifted the buckets and carried them out. They walked in companionable silence, moving aside as people passed them. It was full morning now, and those who had work were off to start their day. A few gave King odd looks, which told him he'd either done a poor job dressing or looked too good and out of place in Seven Dials.

They waited in line at the well, and when it was their turn, King hauled up the water and filled both buckets. On the way back, he glanced at Joshua. "Should we talk about last night? You disobeyed a direct order."

Joshua's shoulders slumped, which was a feat considering he was already hunched from carrying the heavy pail. "I know. I should have listened to you and met Vi."

"Yes, you should have listened to me. You almost died. It was pure luck I found you when I did. You risked not only your own life, but mine as well. And what if your sister had decided to go in and look for you? I had to practically hold her back."

"I can explain why I did it."

"Oh, I know why you did it." King moved aside to allow an older woman to pass. "You were worried not all of Ferryman's girls got out."

"Just because they're whores, doesn't mean they should burn

up."

"I agree completely, but that's why we made every effort to clear the tavern before the fire spread. I watched the whores leave with the rest of the crowd."

Joshua stopped and lowered the pail, turning to face King. "You couldn't be sure they all got out. I just needed to check."

King paused and lowered his own pail. His wet hair was stuck to his forehead, and he slicked it back. "A word of advice, Master Joshua. Think more with this head." He tapped Joshua's temple. "And less with the other. Take it from someone who thought too much with the other on occasion and wants to save you the same grief."

"Did you have a sweetheart, King?" Joshua asked. King shook his head and lifted both pails to give Joshua a moment to breathe. "Was she pretty?"

"No, I didn't have a sweetheart." At least, he hadn't ever thought of the women who passed through his life for a night or two in that way.

"Is Vi your sweetheart?" Joshua asked. "I know you like her."

"I doubt she would appreciate being referred to as my *sweetheart*."

"Oh, she'd hate it. But you do like her, don't you?"

King jerked his head toward the tavern. "Here. Carry these inside. When I get back, you'd better be so clean you squeak."

"Where are you going? You aren't coming in with me?"

King shook his head. "I have something important to do. I'll be back before the tavern is busy."

"But King—"

He turned and began to walk away. "We'll talk about it later, Joshua. I'll be back."

But when he looked over his shoulder, Joshua was still watching him, his gaze fixed, as though he feared he'd never see King again.

# CHAPTER TWENTY-TWO

K ING HAD VISITED the Tower of London once as a child. He'd been seven or eight, and he remembered the visit for two reasons. Firstly, because he'd seen lions and other amazing creatures. He thought he might have seen an elephant. He'd told all his friends he did. But he'd probably just embellished the story with that detail, because now he didn't remember the elephant. But he did remember the lions. They'd been lying about in their den, sunning themselves. One, a large male, had yawned, and his teeth had been yellow and enormous.

The second reason he remembered the visit was because he'd gone with his father. For a period of a few months when King was seven or eight, his father had seemed to take an interest in him. He'd taken King to Astley's Amphitheater and a boat race on the Serpentine, and to the menagerie at the Tower.

Then King had been sent to Eton, and his father seemed to forget him. His life for the next ten years seemed to be one long effort to make his father remember him. It hadn't worked, and King had gradually stopped caring. Then *he'd* been the one to forget.

Except that was a lie. He'd never forgotten his father or stopped wanting his love. He had just learned to stop trying to earn it.

So it was fitting that the first time he returned to the Tower in over twenty years, it was to visit his father. He didn't remember how he had arrived for his first visit, but he was quite certain he hadn't come by barge through the Traitor's Gate, as he did now. It was a beautiful day for a ride on the Thames—if one didn't breathe too deeply. The sun was shining, and the spring air felt pleasantly mild. The barges sailed along at a good pace, passing under London Bridge, until the arched stone entrance of the gate came into view. They floated underneath as a guard swung the metal doors open. The interior of the entrance was dark and cool, the water below green from the moss growing on the stone.

The guard called out to King, who replied, "Visitor to see the Duke of Avebury."

"Former Duke of Avebury," the guard replied. "Who are you?"

King let out a breath. "His son."

The barge came alongside the stone steps, and King looked at them a long moment before ascending. He knew the history. He'd either accidentally learned it at school or been told when he visited the menagerie all those years ago. The Traitor's Gate was where the prisoners entered—Sir Thomas More, Queen Anne Boleyn, Lady Jane Grey. Had his own father been brought to the Tower this way?

King didn't know. At least, it was no longer the practice to display the heads of executed prisoners on the pikes beneath the bridge. His father wouldn't be put to death by beheading, at any rate. Hanging was the preferred method in these times.

"This way," the guard said as King climbed the stairs. He followed the guard into the Tower complex, a sprawling but organized walled fortification. He saw other soldiers moving about, all looking quite busy and important.

"Bell Tower," the guard announced, pointing to a tower on the edge of the inner wall, not far from Traitor's Gate. It was obviously an old structure, and Norman in style, though how King knew that, he couldn't have said. "This is the duke's son," the guard told the soldier standing at the Bell Tower.

"This way." The soldier opened the door and led King up a set of stairs to a room at the top of the tower. He paused outside the door. "Your name?"

"Ki—I mean, former Marquess of Kingston."

The soldier rapped on the door then lifted an enormous ring of old keys from his belt and unlocked a padlock. He pushed the door open. "Former Marquess of Kingston to see the former Duke of Avebury." He looked at King. "You have half an hour."

King didn't want even five minutes, but he forced himself to enter the chamber and not to shudder when the soldier closed the door with a clang. Like the rest of the structure, the room was made of stone, white stone that had been bricked at one point. The bricks still covered the upper part of the walls. Lower down, the brick had crumbled away, and the stone was raw and uneven, a mixture of red, white, and yellowed material.

His father stood at the window, a small, rectangular window cut into a deep recess with an arch above. He could have seen the Tower grounds if he'd stood inside the recess and looked down, but he stood just outside, hands clasped behind his back, face to the light, until he turned and gazed at King.

King stared back at him. It was impossible to look at his father and not feel as though he were looking at himself in twenty-five years. They had the same wavy brown hair, the same green eyes. They were even the same height and build. The only differences between them were the lines carved in the duke's face and the shrewdness in his eyes. King knew he could look skeptical and even jaded, but he'd never been shrewd or cunning. Perhaps that was why his father was confined to the cell and he was not.

"I didn't think I'd see you here," the duke said.

"I didn't think I'd come," King answered.

"Why have you come? To chastise me for ruining your life? To scold me for my crimes?"

King shook his head. "I imagine you've had enough time alone to revisit your choices and wish you'd made others.

Nothing I say will change what's been done." He looked about the chamber. "Not bad for a prison cell. Have they handed down the punishment yet?"

"Execution," the duke said. "I suppose they won't tell me until the night before. But"—he gestured to a chair as he moved to another and took a seat—"I am not the first person to await my execution within these walls."

King took the other seat, noting it was rather comfortable for a prisoner's chair. The room was sparsely furnished with only these chairs, a table, and a bed. But the furnishings were of good quality.

"Sir Thomas More was held here. Princess Elizabeth was held here as well. She wasn't executed, obviously, but she must have spent many a long night wondering if that would be her fate."

"What about her mother?"

The duke shook his head. "I'm told she was held in the Queen's House, which is the neighboring structure, just there." He folded his hands. "But you haven't come for a history lesson."

"No. I was never much of a student."

"You never made much of an effort. You were too busy try-ing to find ways to be expelled from every institution—trying to garner my attention, I suppose." King looked up sharply. The duke let out a breath. "Oh, I knew what you were about, even before you were old enough to realize why you did what you did."

King swallowed the question that rose in his mind and forced himself to sit silently.

"You don't have to ask it for me to know what you're think-ing." His father leaned back. "Why didn't I give you that attention then? Do you want the truth?"

King had come to say goodbye, but he supposed that he wanted to know why his father had done what he'd done before it was too late to ask. He made a gesture of affirmation.

"The truth is I thought you were better off away from me. Was I a traitor even then? Maybe not the first few years you were at school, but yes. I have been a traitor for a long time, George. It's lucrative, but even more than the money, I liked the power that having knowledge the French wanted and forcing them to pay me to attain it gave me. I liked the thrill of deception and the fear of discovery. You wanted a father. I didn't want to play that role." The duke waved an arm. "I could sit here and say that I kept you away to protect you from being implicated in my crimes."

King realized he was gripping the arms of the chair, and forced himself to release them.

"But I didn't think I'd ever be caught. I just hadn't any interest in children. That would have been your mother's realm, but she died. I suppose I might have remarried, but why when I had an heir to my title?" The duke shrugged. "And now I have no title."

"And I will have no father. But then, I suppose I never did."

"Now is when I am supposed to say I regret my actions. I wish I'd spent more time with you, loved you as a father should. Do you want me to say that?"

"No." King rose. "I've heard all I need to. I thought I should tell you goodbye before it was too late. I didn't want to regret not seeing you." He smiled ruefully. "Somehow you managed to make me regret making the effort."

He turned to go.

"George."

King knew he should keep walking. He didn't want to hear whatever else his father might say. But his legs ceased moving, and he stood, back to his father, waiting.

"I do have one piece of advice for you."

He let out a bitter laugh. "Fatherly advice? This ought to be good."

"It is. It is the one thought I've had consistently since I entered the Bell Tower."

King glanced over his shoulder, brows raised.

"Life is too short. Don't waste the time you have left."

He blew out a breath and shook his head. "The time I have

left? Because of you, all I have is time. I have no name, no fortune, no friends. Am I supposed to cherish this turn of events? Thank you that at least I'm not dead?"

"I expect no thanks from you, but I do believe, inadvertently, I have been kinder towards you than towards myself. All my life, I have been ruled by greed. It didn't matter how much money I had; I wanted more. It didn't matter how much power I had; I wanted more."

"Well, I have no money and no power. Well done."

"It is well done. Maybe you will find what I never did."

King started for the door. "And what's that?"

"Meaning? Love? Family? I wish I knew. I hope, whatever it is, you find it."

"And I hope you go to hell." King rapped on the door, summoning the guard.

"No doubt of that, George. Give it a few years, and perhaps you will see me there."

The door opened, and King stepped out, cursing under his breath. He followed the guard down the stone steps and pushed past him and out into the sunshine.

Why had he bothered to come? Had he really thought his father would give him what he wanted? And what *did* he want from his father? Love? King didn't think his father was capable of love, unless it was love of power and money.

The guard who had met him at the Traitor's Gate approached, and King walked to meet him. "I'm ready to go." He returned to the barge, and when he floated back under the gate and onto the Thames, King did not look back at the Tower or his father's cell.

He wanted nothing more than to return home and...

*Home.* Where was home? He had no home. The house had no doubt been leased to someone else, someone who could pay. His personal items had been sold to recompense his creditors. His family home, the country estate where he'd played as a child, had been returned to the Crown. So where was home? He'd been living at the Silver Unicorn, but Violet had made it clear she was allowing him to stay temporarily. He'd managed to extend that stay by working in the tavern and helping her to take on Ferryman.

But now Archie was recovering, and Ferryman was no longer a threat. King would be expected to move on. He would have to pack what little he had and leave. He could find another place. Perhaps he could go to the Continent. There were scores of former noblemen wandering about the Continent.

With a pang, King realized he did not want to leave. He cared about the boys, and he cared about Violet. It was more than that.

He loved her.

He'd known he loved her for days now, but he'd loved her since the day he'd met her. She didn't love him. He thought she felt something for him—lust, most likely—but not love. She'd been hurt before by the loss of others, and it was clear to King she didn't want to allow anyone else too close for fear of being hurt again.

He turned his head into the breeze coming off the water and tried not to laugh—or perhaps he was trying not to cry. How was it the one woman he'd fallen in love with wasn't capable of loving him back? It was his father all over again.

*Life is too short.*

King didn't need his father to tell him that. One day he was a wealthy marquess, and the next he was a poor publican. Who knew if the witch's curse held more repercussions for him in the future?

*Don't waste the time you have left.*

The echo of his father's voice as he'd spoken those words forced King to sit. The seat on the barge was wet from the spray of water, but he didn't care. The only thing that mattered was that he loved Violet. He might never find a woman like her again. No, he would definitely *not* find a woman like her again. She didn't love him, but then again, she didn't know he loved her.

He had to tell her. He couldn't guess at her feelings. He

might be wrong. What if she loved him too?

The barge had barely touched the dock before King was out and striding back to Seven Dials. It was late afternoon now. The tavern was certainly open, and he knew he'd find Violet there.

He was out of breath by the time he reached Clover Lane. As he'd guessed, the tavern was open and doing a brisk business. Violet was behind the bar, with Joshua running to and fro, delivering mugs of beer.

King stepped inside and paused to take in the scene. He didn't remember the first time he'd come inside the Silver Unicorn. He'd been too drunk. But he remembered coming there the morning after. The tavern had been in shambles, with broken furniture piled against the wall, shards of glass glittering on the floor, spilled spirits making the wood sticky.

Now it looked clean and cozy. It could use a few more tables and the mirror behind the bar Violet was always going on about, but all in all, it was a decent establishment. He was proud of what they'd rebuilt. He was proud of the effort the boys had put in. He admired Violet's determination.

He gave her an appreciative glance now. She was lovely as she moved purposefully behind the bar, giving this man a smile and that a sharp rejoinder. Her hands were never still as she wiped the counter, poured beer, or palmed the coins slapped down before her. Strands of her dark hair, which had been neatly pinned this morning, fell down about her shoulders and framed her face. She repeatedly tucked one recalcitrant lock behind her ear.

But of course, her best feature—well, second best—was her eyes. Her blue gaze was everywhere, alert and assessing and...glaring.

King realized she was glaring at him. But of course she was. He was standing in the middle of the tavern doing nothing but grinning like a child. He couldn't help but wink at her just because he knew it would make her cheeks turn pink, and she was so pretty when she blushed.

He watched the color rise in her cheeks then forced himself to join her behind the bar before she started throwing things at his head. He tugged his coat off, tossed it aside, and rolled up his sleeves. As though they'd worked together for years, he took one side of the bar and Violet took the other.

By the time evening fell, the crowds had thinned, and Violet stepped into the back room, presumably to relieve Georgie from washing duty.

King gestured to Joshua. "Take over for me a moment, will you?"

Joshua grinned. He loved working behind the bar, and he was good at it. He couldn't be left alone long in case of trouble, but King didn't think this would take long. And he couldn't wait another moment to tell her.

He left Joshua wiping the bar and stepped into the back room. As he'd guessed, Violet had her hands in soapy water. She looked up. "Who's behind the bar? Joshua?"

"Yes." He went to stand beside her, took the wet mug she offered, and began to dry it.

She washed another mug and handed it to him. "Joshua said you had something important to do today. Did you complete your errand?"

"I did." Telling her was harder than he'd thought. He couldn't seem to find the words.

"Good." She handed him another mug, her movement jerky. Clearly, she was annoyed he hadn't elaborated, but she wouldn't ask for more details.

"I went to see my father," he said, when she practically shoved the next mug at him.

Violet dropped the mug back into the water and turned to look at him. "You said you would, but I didn't think you would go so soon."

"I thought I'd better not waste any time. He's in the Tower awaiting execution." Of course, she knew this. It seemed not to matter how many times he'd looked into those blue eyes of hers—they still made him stupid.

"How is he?"

King snorted. "The same as ever. Proud and unrepentant and...cold. I don't think he cared a whit that I had gone to see him."

"I'm sure that's not true."

"Yes, it is. He's never cared about anyone or anything other than himself."

Violet reached out and put a wet hand on the bare skin of his forearm, where he'd rolled up his sleeves. "King, I'm sorry."

King had learned never to take it for granted when Violet offered him affection. He covered her hand with his. "He'll be executed in the next few days. A week at most. Hanged by the neck until dead. I imagine that's punishment enough for any man."

"Can you forgive him, do you think? For ruining your life?"

King stilled and tightened his grip on her hand. "I do need to forgive him, but that's for never being a father to me. He didn't ruin my life. He sent me away as a child and all but abandoned me, but because of him, I met Rory and Henry. The friendship we formed saved all of us." He looked her directly in the eyes. "And because of my father, I met you."

She tried to pull her hand away, but he held fast.

"The day I met you, I thought my life was over. I thought I was ruined. The truth was, my life was just beginning."

"Have you been drinking when I wasn't looking? This is no beginning." She gestured to the small, dark back room with her free hand.

"I don't mean this place." She tugged her hand away again, and he let her go. "When I spoke to my father, he did give me one piece of advice. It's trite. Nothing original. But for once, he said something I needed to hear. He said, *Don't waste the time you have left.*"

Violet lifted her brows, in tacit agreement that this was no great piece of wisdom.

"I don't want to wait another moment to tell you how I feel."

"King, don't—"

He stepped forward. "It makes you uncomfortable. Believe me, I'm not comfortable either. Look, I'm shaking." He held out a hand that was indeed trembling. "I've never said anything like this before."

She shook her head.

"I'm glad my father spied for France, or the witch cursed me, or whatever it was that led me to you and the boys. Meeting you has been no curse. I care for Joshua and Georgie...and you."

"You don't have to say this."

"I want to say it. I want to tell you I love you, Violet Baker. I think I've loved you since the second time I met you."

And just like that, his hands stopped shaking, his breathing steadied, and a sense of calm washed over him. This was right. Telling her was right.

Except the way she was looking at him now was very, very wrong.

# CHAPTER TWENTY-THREE

VIOLET COULD SEE King had stopped shaking. A sense of calm had washed over him, and he smiled at her now, seeming relieved to have shed his burden.

Only he'd placed it on her. Now she was the one shaking. She was the one feeling scared and sick. Why had he said it? Why couldn't he have kept quiet and allowed things to go on as they had been?

He was looking at her expectantly, waiting for her response. Did he expect her to say she loved him back? She didn't. She loved Joshua and Georgie and the Silver Unicorn. She couldn't help but love them, even though that love made her feel helpless because, at any moment, she might lose one of them. She'd almost lost Joshua the other night. As she'd sat outside the Black Bear praying and pleading with God to save him, she'd felt, once again, that horrible roiling in her belly that she remembered when her mother and then her stepmother and then her father had died. It was fear and grief and terror at her utter powerlessness to do anything to stop their deaths.

And now King stood here, looking at her, telling her he loved her. He wanted her to love him back. He wanted her to give him the same power Joshua and Georgie had over her. Violet couldn't do it. She didn't love King. She'd never love him or any other man. It was far too easy for a man to fall out of love, to walk away and leave those behind brokenhearted. She wouldn't risk that, and she wouldn't allow Georgie or Joshua to risk it either.

"I know this talk of emotions makes you uncomfortable," King said finally, breaking the silence. "But I thought you might say something in return."

Violet put her hands on her hips. "You want me to say I love you too?"

He actually took a physical step back. "Do I want that? Of course. But I don't expect it. Perhaps, given time—"

"I think you should leave."

King cocked his head and narrowed his eyes. "Say again?"

"You heard me. You need to leave. You were never supposed to stay here. You've been here too long as it is. Thank you for your help with Ferryman, but it's time you moved on."

"Violet, you're scared. I've surprised you."

He reached for her, but she shied away. She couldn't allow him to touch her. If he did, she would lose her resolve. And she was determined that he leave. Now. Tonight. If he stayed any longer, Georgie and Joshua would become more attached to him than they already had. *She* would become more attached to him.

"I'm not scared. But I need to protect the boys. They already care too much for you. You need to go now, before they begin to depend on you."

"I want them to depend on me. I want you to depend on me."

"No. That's impossible." He frowned and opened his mouth, ready to argue. Violet cut him off. "Get your things and go."

"What? Now?"

"Yes."

"Violet, let's talk about this."

"There's nothing to say. I should have made you leave sooner. It's better this way." She started for the door to the tavern. Joshua had been left alone too long already. She'd step away and give King time to gather his things and go. When she came back, he'd be gone.

"Better for whom? Violet, don't do this. Give me a chance. I know you feel something for me."

She whirled around. "No, I don't. I don't feel anything, King. This is why you need to go. I don't want to hurt you."

"Too late for that." He swept past her, entered the tavern, and returned with his coat. He shoved his arms through it and began to gather his other belongings. He lifted the odd assortment of clothing items then tossed them aside. "Keep them," he said. "Sell them." He strode for the back door, opening it to the dark night.

"I don't want your charity."

"Then throw them out," he said, stepping through the door. "It won't be the first thing you've thrown away."

The door closed behind him, and Violet's legs gave way. Her eyes stung with tears, and she had a lump in her throat. She had to choke back the tears for some reason. What was wrong with her? He was gone. This was what she'd wanted.

She'd simply need to keep reminding herself of that.

>>><<<

KING WALKED THROUGH the dark night, unsure where he was headed until he looked up and saw himself standing in front of the Town house of the Duke of Carlisle. Henry's house—not rented. The house had been in his family for years. It was after midnight now, but perhaps that was the perfect time for the disgraced former Marquess of Kingston to knock on his friend's door.

He trudged up the steps, took the knocker in hand, and rapped hard three times. He waited a moment then did it again, just in case the footman sleeping in the hall thought the knock a dream.

King heard a bit of shuffling, and then the door was opened by a footman who was about the same age as King and who, by

the redness of his eyes, had indeed been asleep in the chair by the door. He looked at King, his eyes taking him in from head to toe, and started to close the door again.

King stuck his foot in. "I'm here to see His Grace. Tell him King needs to speak with him."

Obviously, King's imperious manner, incongruous as it must be with his disheveled appearance, gave the servant pause. He seemed to consider then shook his head. "Come back in the morning."

"I'm not coming back in the morning. I'm here now. Carlisle is my oldest friend, and I need to see him."

"Carlisle?" The servant's brow wrinkled. "You have the wrong house."

King's head spun for a moment. He stepped back, looked at the façade of the house, then nodded, satisfied. He'd been here a thousand times. This was Henry's house. "No, I haven't. This is the house of the Duke of Carlisle. Go wake him—"

"This *was* the home of the Duke of Carlisle," the footman said, sounding almost smug. "Not any longer."

Carlisle had sold the house? That wasn't possible. But then, a short time ago, King wouldn't have thought it possible that he'd no longer have *his* title or his house.

And Henry's birthday was just after his own.

"Where is the duke?" he asked.

"Don't know. Don't care." The footman tried to close the door again.

King shoved his shoulder against it. "One more question, then I'll leave you in peace."

The footman glared at him.

"Who lives in the house now?"

"My master," the footman answered. "The Marquess of Shrewsbury."

And the door closed in King's face.

It was just as well, since he stood there feeling dumbfounded for a good ten seconds. Shrewsbury? He was Henry's arch nemesis. Henry would not have given Shrewsbury the house.

But he might have lost it.

King closed his eyes. How many times had he warned Henry that he gambled too much? Took risks too great? How could Henry wager his family's house? Then another thought occurred to King. What if that wasn't all Henry had wagered?

It was very late, but there was always someone at White's. King couldn't go in, of course. Not now. White's was the gentlemen's club where King and his friends were members, but his membership had surely been revoked. He found himself walking that way regardless. Henry didn't always gamble there, but if he'd been playing Shrewsbury, it had most certainly been at White's, as the marquess didn't frequent the seedier gambling establishments.

It was a short walk from Henry's to the club. King didn't bother to go to the door. He went around back and found a couple of grooms playing dice near the mews. They looked up at his approach then went back to their game, dismissing him as unimportant.

"Gentlemen," King said. The grooms both rose to attention, recognizing the authority in his voice. "I have a question for you."

"And who might ye be, guv?"

"I'll ask my question first. The Duke of Carlisle. What do you know of him?"

The two grooms looked at each other and shrugged. King fished in his waistcoat and found a couple of pennies—remnants of his former life. He tossed them to the grooms, who caught them deftly. "He left Town," one groom said, pocketing the coin.

"Why? Has it to do with the Marquess of Shrewsbury?"

"Lost everything to 'im, I 'eard," the shorter groom said. "Don't know if it's true."

"Everything?" King frowned. "What do you mean, *everything*? Surely not his title or his estates?"

The grooms shrugged again. Something this momentous would be in the papers. And there would be dozens of copies of every paper in London inside White's. Unfortunately, King couldn't go inside to read any of them.

The master of the house would toss the papers in the rubbish bin tomorrow when the new editions arrived. King could come back then and read one. If there was any hint as to where Henry might be, King could try to scrape together the funds to find him.

He turned his back on the grooms, who had returned to their game of dice, and walked away, avoiding St. James Street for fear of seeing someone he used to know. He didn't have anywhere to go or anyone to see. No reason to stay in London. It would only remind him of *her*.

Even now, Seven Dials called to him. Violet was there with her bluer-than-blue eyes and her long, dark hair and the scent of yeast and barley that seemed to cling to her. The pull of her was strong, but King had some pride left—not much, but enough to turn the other way. He'd told her how he felt, and she had made it clear she didn't share his sentiments. No matter that he saw the fear in her eyes. No matter that he knew—yes, he *knew*—she had feelings for him.

But he couldn't make her love him, and he wouldn't try. He'd spent the first twenty years of his life trying to make his father love him. He couldn't waste any more of his life trying to convince someone that he was worthy of their love. Maybe he wasn't. Maybe there was something fundamentally wrong with him that made him chronically unlovable. Maybe he'd spend the rest of his life alone.

He walked along streets and through parks until he was tired. He'd reached Hyde Park and spotted a bench, where he sat heavily. As soon as he stopped moving, the chill of the night air cut through him. King didn't care. He was numb. He was tired. He lay down on the bench and stared up at the sky. The witch had realized her revenge after all. He'd taken everything from her, and now everything and everyone King cared about had been ripped away from him.

JOSHUA KNEW IMMEDIATELY something was wrong. Vi came back into the tavern and took over the bar for him, telling him to go to bed. Her voice was hard and cold, and for once, Joshua didn't argue. He didn't like to leave her alone in the tavern, but then, she wasn't alone. King was there.

Except when Joshua went to the back room, King *wasn't* there. His clothes were still lying about, though that pile had dwindled. Joshua looked in the yard for him, and in the flat, but King was nowhere to be found.

An uneasy sensation settled in Joshua's belly, and he began to wash mugs and wait for King's return. He couldn't have gone far, and he wouldn't be gone long.

But that uneasy sensation grew as the minutes passed and King didn't return. Joshua heard the tone of Vi's voice through the door. She was not herself. Something was amiss, and Joshua was beginning to fear that it might be King. Had he left them? No. He wouldn't do that without a goodbye to himself and Georgie.

But then, why wasn't he returning?

The last of the patrons left, and Joshua heard Vi closing and locking the tavern for the night. When she came into the back room, she started at seeing him. "I told you to go to bed," she snapped.

"Where's King?" he asked, ignoring her tone.

"Go to bed." She swept past him and bolted the back door. Apparently, King wasn't returning tonight.

"Did he leave?" Joshua asked. "Is he coming back tomorrow?"

Vi sighed and turned to face him, her expression hard and determined. It reminded him of the way she'd looked when she told him his mother had passed away. He didn't like it. "He had to go, Joshua. You knew from the start that he was only here for a short time."

Joshua shook his head. "But that was before we knew him. He was my friend. He wouldn't just leave." He narrowed his eyes. "What did you do?"

Vi put her hands on her hips. "I didn't do anything. He's gone. Now go to bed, and don't mention him to me again."

Joshua didn't argue. He stormed upstairs, tore off his clothing, and tumbled into bed. Georgie was sleeping, curled in a ball, and Joshua was glad for the warmth of his little brother. And yet he couldn't fall asleep. There had been something comforting about knowing King was downstairs. He had felt safe. Now he felt angry and scared and confused. Why had King left them?

He was still lying awake when Vi came to bed. She went to her closet and closed the door, and he heard her lie down on the bed. Joshua closed his eyes and tried to sleep, but in the silence that fell, he heard something else.

Vi was crying.

JOSHUA WAS UP and out of bed with the sun in the morning. Georgie groaned and rolled over but went right back to sleep when Joshua crept out of the flat. Vi had fallen asleep at some point in the night, probably exhausted from her tears. She almost never cried, and Joshua realized that he'd had it all wrong. It wasn't her who had done something. It was King. And that rat-faced arse had promised Joshua that he'd never hurt Vi. Well, Joshua would make sure he was sorry.

He just had to find the man first.

It wouldn't be difficult. Joshua had a network of friends and contacts all over London. Someone had seen King and could point him in the right direction. That was how he'd found Lizzie. He hadn't gone to see her in the new, fancy house in Mayfair, but he'd found it and kept watch over it for a few hours. It seemed like a good place. He hoped she was safe and happy there.

SHANA GALEN

But King? Oh, Joshua hoped he was miserable.

An hour later, after going from street urchin to street urchin, he found King asleep on a bench in Hyde Park. The sun was just coming up and a few riders were out on Rotten Row, but otherwise, they had the place to themselves. Joshua stared down at King. His hair had fallen over his forehead, and he had a shadow of beard on his jaw. Joshua nudged him. King didn't wake, so Joshua nudged him harder.

King blew out a breath and an expletive as he came awake. "What the holy hell? Joshua?" He sat up, his eyes bleary and red. "How did you find me?"

"I'll always find you—you boil-brained gudgeon."

King squinted at him. "Boil... What?"

"Stand up and fight me like a man," Joshua said.

"Fight you?" King raked a hand through his already disordered hair. "What's happened?"

"I'll tell you what's happened," Joshua said, aiming a vicious kick at King's shin.

"Ow!" King jumped up, stepping aside before Joshua could kick him again. "What the devil is the matter with you? Did Violet send you?"

"No."

"No, she wouldn't. I suppose she didn't tell you what happened, and now you blame me."

"Yes, I blame you!" Joshua made to kick again, but King grabbed for him, swung him around, and wrapped an arm about his shoulders.

"Kick me again, and you'll be sorry. Now, without violence, tell me what's wrong."

Joshua took a breath, found the words caught in his throat, and tried again. "You made her cry," he said, his voice much smaller than he would have liked. "You promised you'd never hurt her."

The tight hold on Joshua's shoulders loosened, and he would have fallen forward if King hadn't caught him around the waist.

268

But this time the embrace was gentle. "Joshua," King said, his voice soft.

Joshua pulled away. "Don't coddle me. I'm not a baby."

King released him. "Fine. If you're a man, then act like a man. Stop striking out at me like a child having a tantrum and listen to what I have to say."

Joshua folded his arms. "I'm listening."

"If Violet is crying, it's not because of me. She sent me away. She's the one who doesn't want me."

Joshua didn't believe it. The words didn't make sense. Still, King hadn't ever lied to him before. "What do you mean, she doesn't want you?"

King took a breath and lifted his gaze to the dewy grass of the park beyond. "I told her I loved her last night. It was while you were tending the bar. I told her I loved her and you and Georgie, and I wanted us to be together. She sent me away."

"She didn't understand," Joshua argued, but it was a knee-jerk argument. He knew his sister, and she had understood very, very well. He hunched his shoulders. "Fine. She understood. But don't you know any better than to tell her things like that? She doesn't like talking about feelings. It makes her itchy."

"Itchy?"

"That's what Georgie and I call it. Whenever we used to talk about our mam and cry and say we missed her, Vi would scratch her head or her neck or her arms. She'd listen and she'd try to comfort us, but she was allergic to that sort of talk."

"Well, she wasn't scratching when I was talking to her. She was…" King's gaze strayed to the park again. "She was quite clear that she wanted me to leave. She doesn't want you or Georgie to become dependent on me."

"More like she's afraid *she'll* depend on you." Joshua sat on the bench. "She hates to depend on anyone else."

King sat beside him. "I've noticed."

"She's afraid if she depends on you, if she admits she *loves* you"—Joshua made a disgusted face—"then if you leave, she'll be really hurt."

"But I won't leave. I don't want to leave."

Joshua sighed. "Everyone leaves. Except me and Georgie. And one day, we'll leave too. Then she'll be all alone. She'd probably rather be alone than hurt. I was little, but I still remember how much she cried when her pa died. She cried every night for months and months. I thought she'd never stop."

King leaned back on the bench. "You're unusually wise for only thirteen."

"I'm almost fourteen," Joshua said, and grinned. "And I'm not wise—well, I am, but not about Vi. I just know her really well. You would too if you'd lived with her as long as I have."

"Very well, then, since you know her so well, what should I do?"

"You shouldn't have left," Joshua said, kicking at the dirt beneath the bench. "You should have stayed and fought. That was your first mistake."

"Noted. Can I fix it, or is it a lost cause?"

"Lost cause? You mean, is it too late to make things right?" He turned to King. "You can fix it."

King stared at him for a long moment. "Er—how?"

Joshua shrugged. "I don't know. Not by sitting here!"

King smiled. "So I should go back?"

"Yes."

"Even though she told me to leave."

"You left all your clothes. You can go back for those. Now that Vi's had a night to cry about losing you, maybe she'll want you again."

"I doubt it," King said.

"Me too," Joshua said.

King elbowed him, and Joshua smiled. Vi might not love King, though Joshua was pretty sure she did—but *he* sure loved King. Not that Joshua would tell him, but he sure wasn't about to let Vi send him away. Surely he and Georgie had a say in this too.

"So you'll come back."

"I'll think about it. I have some other business to tend to this morning. And you'd better get back before Violet wakes up and finds you gone."

Joshua rose. "I'll see you later, yes?"

King smiled. "Hurry up." He tossed Joshua a shilling. "And buy something for the three of you to eat for breakfast."

"I will!" Joshua ran off, his stomach beginning to growl at the thought of food. It was hungry work, solving all of the adult problems.

# Chapter Twenty-Four

V IOLET WOKE AND didn't need a mirror to feel how puffy and dry her eyes were. People said crying was supposed to make one feel better, but it only ever made her feel worse. And now she looked awful too. She supposed she couldn't blame King for that. She was the one who had sent him away. She was the one who had fallen in love with him.

She flopped down on her bed and pulled the lumpy piece of material that passed for a pillow over her head. Why had he insisted on telling her he'd fallen in love with her? She'd told him not to say it. But once the words were out, she couldn't allow him to stay. He would want her to reciprocate, and she had been fighting her feelings for him for days now. He could have stayed longer if he hadn't insisted on revealing his feelings. Given time, she might have been able to ignore how she felt about him, bury it under layers and layers of other concerns. But now it was out there, and she would think about it every time she looked at him. She wouldn't be able to forget how he felt and how she felt, and that feeling would only grow so that when he left her, the pain she felt now would be nothing comparatively.

It was better to end things now before it hurt too much to end them.

She heard the door to the flat open, lifted the pillow off her face, and listened. Joshua said something to Georgie, who replied with one syllable, indicating he'd been sleeping. Violet pulled the door open and peered out. "Joshua, where were you?"

He held up a wrapper. "I bought breakfast."

Georgie sat up. "Breakfast! What is it?"

"Currant rolls."

"My favorite!" Georgie jumped out of bed and grabbed the wrapper, running to the table and plopping himself on a chair, bare feet and legs hanging over the edge.

"Where did you get money for currant rolls?" Violet asked as Joshua pushed past the clothing hanging on the line and came into view before her closet door.

"King," he said, biting into a roll as though this answer was perfectly reasonable.

She went very still. "King? But I told him to—" She closed her mouth, realizing she hadn't yet concocted a story for King's disappearance.

"You told him to leave. Yes, he told me you kicked him out."

"What?" Georgie said, mouth full of roll. "You made Pa leave? Why?" He came to stand before Joshua.

Violet took a breath. "First of all, he's not your pa. Secondly, I told you he was only here for a little while. He has his own life, and he needs to sort that out. Why would he want to stay here and work in a tavern?"

"Because he's a markiss," Georgie said, his lower lip beginning to stick out and tremble.

Violet cut her gaze to Joshua, who raised a brow.

"I never thought you'd lie to us, Vi."

Her mouth dropped open.

"I found King. He was sleeping on a bench at Hyde Park. He didn't want to leave us."

"We'll talk about it later," she said, shooting a meaningful glance at Georgie.

"Why? Georgie loves King too. We all do. Even you, Vi."

"No, I don't, Joshua."

"You don't love King?" Georgie asked.

"No." She shook her head and hoped she sounded convincing. "Not like he wants me to love him. Trust me to understand men better than you do, boys. King thinks he loves me, and if I don't love him back, over time, he'll be angry. He'll leave, and then we'll all be hurt."

"I'm hurt now," Georgie said, starting to cry. Violet went to him and wrapped her arms around him. She felt like crying too.

"So am I," Joshua said. "So are you, Vi. You do love him, or you wouldn't have been crying."

Her head shot up. "I wasn't crying."

"I heard you, and your eyes are all red and swollen. If you love him, why did you send him away?"

"Why, Vi?" Georgie echoed.

"I don't have to explain everything," she said. "Sometimes you just have to trust that I know what I'm doing. Believe me, I'm saving you a lot of heartache later. He thinks he loves us now, but he'll leave one day."

"You can't know that," Joshua said. "You're just afraid he'll leave, so you sent him away so you don't have to wonder and worry about it."

"Everyone leaves, Joshua. You think a marquess will stay? No. He'll make us all fall in love with him, and then, once we depend on him, once we need him, he'll go."

"What if he stays?" Joshua asked. "What if he's the one exception? He loves you, Vi. I think he loves me and Georgie, too. We should give him a chance."

"No." She rose. "No," she said more forcefully. "He's gone, and that's the end of it."

"You won't even give him a chance?" Joshua said, hands on his hips.

"Please, Vi," Georgie said. "For us. Don't be scared. You always hold my hand when I'm scared. If you get scared, I'll hold your hand. Like this." He took her hand and squeezed it.

Violet felt like crying all over again. She must be incredibly transparent for six- and thirteen-year-olds to see right through her. She had been scared. She was *still* scared, and maybe, just maybe, she had let her fear control her. She, who hated being helpless more than anything, had been so afraid she'd be hurt, she'd ended up hurting everyone, including herself.

She swiped at her eyes, which were watering again. "Well, it's too late now. He's gone."

"He's coming back," Joshua said.

Violet went very still. "What?"

"He's coming back. I told him to give you another chance."

She reached for her hair, which was a tangle of snarls. "When?"

"He said he had some business and then he'd be back. Any moment, I assume."

"I have to get ready," she said. "Go eat your breakfast. Let me get ready."

An hour later, Violet was scrubbed and brushed and wearing her best dress, which was nothing King hadn't seen before, as she only owned two. The boys were clean too, the flat was tidy, and she was pacing with impatience. How long would his business take? What if he didn't return? What if she'd done all of this for nothing and looked like a fool? Why had she ever listened to Joshua—

She heard a knock on the back door and dropped the towel she'd been folding the last five minutes.

"I'll get it," Joshua said.

"No, I'll get it," Georgie said, and ran ahead of Joshua. Both boys flew down the steps, sounding like a procession of horses.

Violet held her breath. It might not be King. She shouldn't get her hopes up. But then she heard his voice, heard the boys greet him, and knew it was him. Her heart began to pound, and her hands began to shake.

"You're behaving like an idiot, Vi," she told herself. "He probably just came back for his clothing. He doesn't want you after the way you treated him last night."

But she heard his voice and then a heavy step on the stairs, and she knew he was coming up. She clenched her hands in her skirts and waited for the door to open. It did, and there he was, looking better than she remembered. His brown hair, which had grown a bit long, was swept back off his forehead. His green eyes settled on her right away, making her shiver with their intensity. His business this morning must have been to shave, because his jaw was clean of stubble, and she could see his full lips perfectly when he gave her that slow smile that always made a lump form in her throat.

He closed the door behind him.

"The boys," she said.

"They're busy downstairs." His voice was deep and low. She heard no hint of anger or resentment in it. "I wanted to talk to you alone." He had a paper under one arm, and he removed it and laid it on the table beside where she was standing, her back to the window.

"About last night," she began.

He moved closer, and her throat closed up again. "Go on."

"I shouldn't have sent you away."

He was standing close enough now that she could smell the familiar scent of him, the bergamot and wool and something that she couldn't define but which was definitely him.

"Not without giving you a chance to say goodbye to the boys."

King raised one brow in that infuriating way that she secretly loved. "True. But I don't think that's all you want to say. Is it?"

"You don't have to leave," she said. "You can stay if you want."

"Very generous of you. But I don't want to stay if you don't want me here." He reached out and took her hand. "Do you want me here, Violet?"

She swallowed. Why would that lump not go away? Why did his touch make her cheeks feel warm and her lungs refuse to fill with enough air? She fisted her hands and forced the words out. "I want you here. I want you, King."

His hand tightened on hers. And now that she'd started, she couldn't seem to close the dam again. Her words spilled forth.

"I want you to stay. I never wanted you to go. I was stupid. Scared I would lose you."

"There's my Miss Sunshine. Seems odd to send someone away if you don't want to lose them, but I'm sure no one has ever accused you of being conventional."

"If you're angry with me, I understand."

His free hand came up to cup her jaw, and she had the impulse to nestle her cheek in his warm palm. "I'm not angry. I don't think I could ever be angry with you, Violet. I love you. Still. Always."

She swallowed. He had to go and say that again. Why couldn't he just kiss her and not say all the things that made her feel as though she might have to run and keep running?

Violet closed her eyes. "King, I..." Her throat closed up, and she could barely force air through it, much less words. She cleared her throat. "King," she managed.

"You don't have to say it yet," he said, leaning down and kissing her lightly. "You don't have to say it ever. I can see that you love me when you look in my eyes." He met her gaze. "And when I kiss your lips." He kissed her again, this time with more passion. She almost forgot what they had been talking about when he pulled back. "And when I hold you in my arms." He pulled her against him, and her chest finally expanded with the air she'd been needing.

This was what she wanted. To be in his arms, be settled against him. When they were like this, there wasn't any need for words. He kissed her again, and before she knew what happened, he'd swept her into his arms and was carrying her back to her closet.

"King, put me down."

"As you command." He lowered her onto her bed, the bed she had just made, and then came down on top of her.

"King, the boys!"

"I told them we had a lot to talk about and not to come up until I came down to get them. But if you would rather we didn't..." He started to stand, and she pulled him back down again.

"I would rather you stay right where you are and start taking off clothes."

He loosened his neckcloth and tossed it aside. "Good enough for you?"

"It's a start."

He grinned at her, and they both jumped up and started taking clothing off as fast as possible. Violet was determined to be the fastest, but once he had his shirt off, she got distracted by the muscles of his shoulders. And his back. And that flat belly. And then he pushed his trousers down, and she caught sight of his thighs and his growing erection, and she forgot all about undressing. She stepped forward, bare-breasted but still in her skirts, and took his cock in her hands.

He made a sound of appreciation, and she stroked it until he was panting and pushing her back down on the bed.

"I think I won," he said, nuzzling her neck as she continued to stroke him.

"Let's see if you win again," she murmured.

"Oh, no. You need to win this one." And with a flick of his hand, he tossed her skirts up. His hand glided from her knee to the tender skin of her inner thighs and then to the flesh of her sex. She didn't realize how much she'd wanted his touch there until he stroked her. She couldn't stifle a moan. "Swollen." He kissed her lips. "And wet." He kissed her again. "What if I just touch you here?"

"King!" She bucked her hips and had to bite down to keep from crying out loudly enough that the boys might hear.

"I thought you'd like that." His hand moved away, replaced by his cock, and then he was sliding into her, filling her with a delicious thickness.

"I like this even more." She wrapped her legs around him,

pulling him deeper, sighing with the pleasure that grew each time he slid deeper into her, slowly withdrew, then entered her again.

"I need to ask you something," he said, his voice gravelly.

"Whatever it is, yes. Like that. Yes."

"Will you marry me?"

Violet stilled, her hips pushed tight against his. "You're not thinking straight."

"Oh, yes I am. I've wanted to ask you before."

"But you didn't think I'd say yes."

He pushed deeper into her. "You seem amenable at the moment." He pulled back, and then she felt his thumb against that sensitive part of her, sliding and stroking and swirling. "You don't have to answer now." His voice seemed very far away as she began to see white stars in her vision. "I can keep doing this until I finally convince you."

"Don't stop."

"Never." He kissed her, and as the stars went bright, she rose with them, her climax making her cry out and sob as he pushed into her again, making the pleasure that much sweeter. He moved against her, and when she felt him swell, he began to pull back, but she wrapped her legs around him. She didn't want him pulling away, didn't want him to spill his seed outside her.

He stilled. "Is this your way of saying yes?"

"Yes," she murmured. "*Oh, yes.*"

*Six months later*

KING LAY WITH Violet in his arms in their new bedchamber. Maybe *bedchamber* was too grand a word to describe the small room he'd built in the rear of the back room. He'd never built anything before, and it had taken him a few tries to wall it off. But the framing had not been the worst of it. Installing the door had been a challenge like no other.

It was worth it in the end, as they finally had a private space. Joshua had taken the closet upstairs in the flat, and Georgie now had the bed in the middle of the flat to himself. King said his next task would be to make a bedframe for Georgie, but Violet had begged him to hire someone to do it. The tavern had been doing well, and they had a little money. He'd even bought her a new mirror for behind the bar as a wedding present.

"What are you thinking?" she asked, sounding exactly the way he liked—satisfied. She ought to be, considering what he'd just done to her. He could still taste her on his lips. He wouldn't mind tasting her again. King didn't think he'd ever get enough of her.

His wife.

"I'm thinking I might like to settle between your legs again in a few minutes," he said, one hand roving over her bare breast.

"Again?"

He heard the hitch in her throat. She might pretend to be shocked, but he could hear that she wanted him.

She turned and kissed him then lay in his arms, her head on his chest. "What else have you been thinking about? You seemed distracted tonight."

That was her way of pointing out that he'd dropped two mugs of ale and gotten three orders wrong.

He swallowed, wondering if now was the time to bring it up. Well, no time like the present. "I was thinking we might go to Scotland. Not for good. For a week or two."

She propped herself on an elbow. "Is this about the curse?"

"Yes." He hadn't been able to find any trace of the witch's sister, despite having asked Perkins to search for him. The Runner owed him, as the capture of Ferryman had made him an instant hero. But Perkins had come up empty-handed when it came to the witch.

He *had* been able to confirm what the papers said about Henry. The duke had lost everything in a game of cards. The Marquess of Shrewsbury had it all now, and the last King had heard, Henry was living in the dower house on what had once been his family estate. Might he convince Henry to go to Scotland with them? What if they were able to reach Rory and convince him as well? King was not usually in favor of returning to the scene of the crime, but in this case, he thought it might be helpful. It couldn't hurt.

And if he could regain his title or some of his property or wealth, he could give Violet and the boys so much more. He could dress her in silks, and the boys could try every sort of delicacy. They could live in a house instead of above a tavern in Seven Dials.

He knew what Violet would say. She didn't care about any of that.

But King wanted to give her more. And he assumed Henry and Rory might like to recover what they'd lost as well.

"I haven't been able to find the witch's sister, and I know there's more to the counter-spell. Mrs. Greene said to seek the witch's sister in the place where it all started. If the three of us— Henry, Rory, and me—go back, maybe we could change things. Make amends."

"You don't need to change anything for me," she said.

King hadn't thought she would want to go. He couldn't say he wasn't a little disappointed.

"But I haven't ever been to Scotland," she added. "I might like it."

He took hold of her shoulders. "You'll go?"

"If we can take the boys."

"Of course." He pulled her into a hard embrace. "I want you to meet Henry and Rory."

"They'll think you married beneath your station."

"They'll love you as much as I do. And I do love you, Violet."

"I love you too."

King went very, very still. "What did you say?"

She laughed. "You heard me."

"I did, but you've never said that before. Maybe I want to

hear it again."

She took his face in her hands and kissed him. "I love you, George Oxley."

"I love you, Violet Baker Oxley."

And in that moment, he didn't care about anything but her—not the curse, not the counter-spell, not the leak in the roof that was dripping water into a pan just outside their bedchamber door.

King loved Violet, and if he had a curse to thank for her, then maybe he'd travel all the way to Scotland and say thank you.

But not tonight. Tonight he'd show Violet just how much he loved her.

Again.

# Author's Note

Dear Reader,

I hope you enjoyed reading Vi and King's story as much as I enjoyed writing it. This is a work of fiction, but there are elements in the novel which are true. Seven Dials is a real section of London. Of course, the Tower of London is a real structure, and it did once hold a menagerie. Now, you can visit it and see the Crown Jewels, among other things. The Bell Tower is the area where many famous people were jailed before execution. And many of those esteemed personages did enter through the Traitor's Gate.

A bill of attainder is not a fictional element. It was an act by a legislative body that declared a person or group of people guilty of a crime. It revoked a person's right to own property or possess a title, and it often meant a sentence of death. The first use of a bill of attainder was against Hugh le Despenser, the first Earl of Winchester, and his son. This bill was passed in 1321 in response to the men's support of King Edward II.

In England, the last bill of attainder was against Lord Edward Fitzgerald. Fitzgerald led a rebellion in Ireland in 1798, and for his role in the uprising, he was condemned to death. The House of Lords also attempted to attaint Queen Caroline, wife of George IV (who in this book is still the prince regent, or Prinny), but the House of Commons refused to consider the bill. This was the last bill of attainder passed in England.

The last British peer to be executed was the fourth Earl Ferrers, Laurence Shirley. He was hanged for the murder of his steward in 1760. Lord Edward Fitzgerald, though attainted in 1798, was not executed. He died of an infected wound while still in prison.

Now, dear reader, you may be noting that my novel is set in 1816, and as noted above, the last bill of attainder that passed both houses of Parliament was in 1798, and the last peer executed was in 1760. This is where I have taken creative license. King's father, the Duke of Avebury, is not a real figure, but if he had been and he had been a traitor, I imagine the Parliament would have passed another bill of attainder against him in 1816, which was still within the time frame that these bills were being considered. Also, as the punishment for treason is almost always execution, I imagine the duke would be hanged for his crimes.

Again, these elements of the book are fiction, not fact. I wanted no confusion, as I know many of you, like me, read historical romance because we enjoy history.

Happy reading!
Shana

# About the Author

Shana Galen is an award-winning writer and the bestselling author of passionate Regency romps. Kirkus said of her books: "The road to happily-ever-after is intense, conflicted, suspenseful and fun." *RT Bookreviews* described her writing as "lighthearted yet poignant, humorous yet touching." She taught English at the middle and high school level for eleven years. Most of those years were spent working in Houston's inner city. Now she writes full time, surrounded by four cats and one spoiled dog. She's happily married and has a daughter who is most definitely a romance heroine in the making.

Website: shanagalen.com
Facebook: Facebook.com/ShanaGalen
Goodreads: goodreads.com/author/show/93709.Shana_Galen
Bookbub: bookbub.com/authors/shana-galen
Instagram: instagram.com/shanagalen
TikTok: @shanagalen
Amazon Author Page: amazon.com/author/shanagalen
YouTube: youtube.com/@shanagalenauthor
Twitter: @shanagalen
Pinterest: pinterest.com/shanagalen

Printed in the USA
CPSIA information can be obtained
at www.ICGtesting.com
LVHW021258210124
769167LV00014B/522